SAVAGE CROSSING

Frank Sullivan

Whimsical Publications, LLC

Florida

Savage Crossing is a work of fiction. Names, characters, and incidents are the products of the author's imagination and are either fictitious or are used fictitiously. Any resemblance to actual events or persons, living or dead, is entirely coincidental.

To purchase the authorized electronic edition of *Savage Crossing*, visit www.whimsicalpublications.com

Cover art by Janet Durbin
Editing by Melissa Hosack

ISBN-13: 978-1-940707-56-3

Published by
Whimsical Publications, LLC
Florida

"You won't believe how fast he'll grow into it," she had advised knowingly. "Heck, Gina, before you can say *Humpty Dumpty*, the little guy will be tall enough to climb out."

"Really?"

"Sure."

"Wow, that is hard to picture."

"Yes, I know. But that, Gina, honey, is when the trouble *really* begins!"

Gina took heed of every bit of advice Sarah Jane gave her on the subject of motherhood and child rearing. She and Alexander had been of invaluable help to her and Richie. More help than her own family, she thought bitterly. That was for sure. The only one of them to pay a visit since she got home was her mom, and even then she had spent the whole time drinking wine, criticizing, and complaining. But Sarah Jane and Alexander, now, they really *were* there for her when it mattered. And of course, having two healthy kids of their own, Gina thought confidently, they really knew what they were talking about on the subject.

Joshua let out a little gurgling sound as Gina drew nearer. He was not crying or distressed. He had probably kicked off his blanket and was now cooing softly to himself in the darkness. He was not due a feeding yet. And besides, he had gotten his wind up just fine after his last bottle. She leaned over to look in. This was just a routine check, she told herself, yawning. That was all. No big deal. She simply wanted to make sure he was okay for her peace of mind before she went back to bed. She would make sure he was covered and still lying on his side. But things were not as she expected when her eyes adjusted to the dimness. Something caught her eye, causing Gina to raise her eyebrows in surprise.

"What on earth is *this* doing here?" she muttered in disbelief, eyeing a small four-by-six framed photograph lying before her at Joshua's feet, its thin picture glass reflecting the ray of meager light flickering in through the curtains.

The photo was the one Richie's sister had taken a few days earlier of them in the hospital. They were sitting side by side on the bed, holding their newborn son between them. Richie was beaming with pride, his left arm wrapped around her shoulders. And they were both smiling happily for the camera. It was the first snap ever taken of the three of them together as a family, and Gina had come to treasure it. But finding it here was strange, to say the least. She was certain it had been hanging on the wall beside the TV when she had gone to bed that night. Richie had only stayed up a couple of minutes later, keeping one eye on the ball game as he conducted his routine sweep of the house. She was sure he had switched everything off as usual, locking up until finally unplugging the TV before going to bed himself. Why on earth would he bring this upstairs? She shook her head in confusion at the unexpected discovery. And more importantly, she asked herself, just how on earth could he be so irresponsible as to leave it lying there in Joshua's cot?

Grumbling again, Gina lifted the photograph with one hand and tucked Joshua's baby blanket back in with the other. That was when the now-familiar sense of dread came upon her once more, an icy shiver running the length of her spine as she became aware that she was not alone with her child. There was a presence in the room. She could feel it now. She froze for a second, realizing that somebody or something was standing behind her.

Up until that moment, the figure in the shadows had remained silent and motionless. The instant Gina raised her head and tried to turn around, however, it sprang into action without the slightest hesitation. The intruder lunged forward and slapped a hand over her mouth from behind, stopping her turning and forcing her body violently against the edge of the cot. She kicked her legs out in retaliation but was slammed even harder against the wooden rail, knocking the wind from her lungs. And then she saw a shaft of moonlight reflecting off metal as the attacker raised a long, double-edged kitchen knife to her chin.

Gina tried desperately to scream for Richie, but it was no use. Her attacker's hand pressed firmer against her mouth, and she bit into her lip and tasted blood. She tried to struggle, to raise her arms and swing away. But she was helpless, gasping in shock as her attacker wedged her body harder against the cot and brought the razor-sharp blade sweeping violently across her throat.

ACKNOWLEDGEMENTS

"Ships are the nearest things to dreams
that hands have ever made,
for somewhere deep in their oaken hearts
the soul of a song is laid."

Robert N. Rose

CHAPTER ONE

SOMETHING BAD

She opened her eyes in the darkness, for a moment or two not knowing where or even who she was. But slowly, as the fog of tiredness receded, her mind focused, and she realized she was still at home in bed, having just been alerted by a strange rasping sound from the baby monitor. She raised herself onto one elbow, held her breath, and listened intently into the blackness. Silence. It was gone. All she could hear now was the sound of her son, Joshua, cooing softly to himself in the nursery next door.

Maybe the noise had just been in her head. Her imagination. Just her overtired mind playing tricks on her.

Gina Regazzoni sat up and rubbed her eyes. She had not really been asleep when she thought she had heard that sound, at least, not in the way that most people defined it. Ever since she brought her newborn son home from the Miami Valley Hospital a few days earlier, she had barely closed her eyes for more than a couple of hours. She did, of course, feel worn out all of the time. That, she supposed, was simply to be expected after the birth. She had become even more tired and listless since arriving home, devoid of energy. Yet somehow, unexplainably, despite this overwhelming fatigue, her mind and body just could not relax enough to drop off into any kind of proper, restful state.

Gina was an intelligent young woman and well aware of the contradiction. The absurdity of being so tired yet unable to sleep was not lost on her, especially in her state. But that did not really bother her so much. What did, more than anything else right then, was how it was causing tension between her and her husband, Richie. Gina was not usually bad tempered and did not mean to be nasty to the poor guy, but for the past few days, she found herself snapping at him for the silliest of things. It was so crazy and out of character, and yet, she just could not help herself. She was living on her own nerves—fiery and tetchy.

That very afternoon, she had almost taken Richie's head off for simply forgetting to put sugar in her coffee. There was screaming, and doors were slammed with such force that they almost came off their hinges. An hour had passed. There had been tears. Then, red-eyed and full of remorse, she had apologized, lowering her head and begging forgiveness. Richie was a kind and understanding husband. He had smiled compassionately, brushing off the outburst in his usual, loving manner. He had kissed her softly on the forehead, telling her it was okay and not to worry about it. But then, predictably, within only a couple of hours of them making up, that same, unstoppable wave of tiredness had returned and Gina had let fly her anger over something else.

In reality, however, that was not her biggest problem. At least, that was not the main thing troubling her now in the darkness as she opened her eyes to the real or imagined strange raspy sound on the baby monitor. The most overriding worry on Gina's mind, and probably the real reason for her lack of sleep, was her baby. Ever since bringing him home, she had found herself filled with an uncontrollable sense of unease. It was terrifying—an overpowering, all-consuming feeling of dread. She could not quite put her finger on the cause. It seemed silly, but somehow, something just did not feel right to her.

She could sense something off in her bones, a gut-feeling that would not go away. Gina felt as if there was some sort of dark, ominous cloud hanging over her and her newborn baby. In much the same way as birds flying low warned of an oncoming storm, she felt as if she could foresee dark signs for her future. Something bad was about to happen.

Richie offered reassurance when she told him about her fears. He explained she was just being an overprotective new mother. He argued how it was probably natural to have such feelings of insecurity. He also pointed out how it might have something to do with the fact that the delivery had been so hard on her. Gina could not argue with that. Twelve hours in labor had definitely taken its toll, not only on her body, but on her mind as well. And then, of course, there was the usual, obligatory advice from her family. Her mom had warned how postnatal hormones "can do the darnedest things to a woman's head," recounting for the hundredth time how Aunt Betty had "gone off the deep end" after giving birth to her cousin Alice.

"Gina, honey, you just need some time to adjust," she had advised over the phone. "Why not give it another few days and then...well look, honey, if there's still no change, maybe give the doctor a call and get some of those sleeping pills I take."

But while Gina listened to all of the advice and reluctantly accepted most of the facts, she still had that feeling. It just would not stop—that niggling, cautionary voice in the back of her mind that simply would not go away.

"Hey, Richie," she whispered into the darkness, nudging her sleeping husband who was snoring sporadically, lying on his side with his back to her. "Richie."

"Huh?" came a muffled response.

"Joshua's awake," she said quietly.

"Okay, honey."

Gina waited for a few seconds, still listening to the gentle cooing from the monitor. "He's awake, Richie. It's your turn to go check on him." Then, a bit louder after a short pause, she said, "Richie, did you hear what I just said?"

"Huh?"

Gina nudged him a little harder in the ribs but just got that same unintelligible grunt.

"Goddamnit!" she exclaimed, grumbling aloud as she sat up on the edge of the bed and pushed her feet into a pair of light blue slippers.

Richie's mom had picked them out when they went shopping in Wal-Mart the week before Joshua was born. She had bought them for her as a gift, along with some toiletries and a matching blue dressing gown. Gina stopped for a moment and considered putting it on, but then, realizing it was either hanging up in the closet or lying in a pile of clothes in the corner, decided against it. Either way, she was too tired and too fed up to go looking. So she pulled herself to her feet wearing nothing but a faded pink t-shirt and panties, and set off, trudging wearily out the door and off down the hall.

She continued to mutter beneath her breath as she walked, furious with Richie for not waking up to help. Why did she have to do everything herself? Things would definitely have to change or there would be trouble, she resolved. Richie would have to man up. He would have to start pulling his weight around the house or he could just pack up his stuff and move out.

The nursery was dark except for a thin shaft of moonlight peeping through a gap in the curtains. The window was open slightly and they fluttered gently on the warm night breeze. A faint strip of light flickered across the floor toward the other side of the room, reflecting off a large, wooden cot that stood in its center. Their best friends, Sarah Jane and Alexander, had bought it for them as a baby gift. Gina smiled a little, recalling how absolutely tiny Joshua had looked when they first put him in. At the time, she was just worried it might be too big for him, but Sarah Jane had assured her he would fill it out in no time.

"You won't believe how fast he'll grow into it," she had advised knowingly. "Heck, Gina, before you can say *Humpty Dumpty*, the little guy will be tall enough to climb out."

"Really?"

"Sure."

"Wow, that is hard to picture."

"Yes, I know. But that, Gina, honey, is when the trouble *really* begins!"

Gina took heed of every bit of advice Sarah Jane gave her on the subject of motherhood and child rearing. She and Alexander had been of invaluable help to her and Richie. More help than her own family, she thought bitterly. That was for sure. The only one of them to pay a visit since she got home was her mom, and even then she had spent the whole time drinking wine, criticizing, and complaining. But Sarah Jane and Alexander, now, they really *were* there for her when it mattered. And of course, having two healthy kids of their own, Gina thought confidently, they really knew what they were talking about on the subject.

Joshua let out a little gurgling sound as Gina drew nearer. He was not crying or distressed. He had probably kicked off his blanket and was now cooing softly to himself in the darkness. He was not due a feeding yet. And besides, he had gotten his wind up just fine after his last bottle. She leaned over to look in. This was just a routine check, she told herself, yawning. That was all. No big deal. She simply wanted to make sure he was okay for her peace of mind before she went back to bed. She would make sure he was covered and still lying on his side. But things were not as she expected when her eyes adjusted to the dimness. Something caught her eye, causing Gina to raise her eyebrows in surprise.

"What on earth is *this* doing here?" she muttered in disbelief, eyeing a small four-by-six framed photograph lying before her at Joshua's feet, its thin picture glass reflecting the ray of meager light flickering in through the curtains.

The photo was the one Richie's sister had taken a few days earlier of them in the hospital. They were sitting side by side on the bed, holding their newborn son between them. Richie was beaming with pride, his left arm wrapped around her shoulders. And they were both smiling happily for the camera. It was the first snap ever taken of the three of them together as a family, and Gina had come to treasure it. But finding it here was strange, to say the least. She was certain it had been hanging on the wall beside the TV when she had gone to bed that night. Richie had only stayed up a couple of minutes later, keeping one eye on the ball game as he conducted his routine sweep of the house. She was sure he had switched everything off as usual, locking up until finally unplugging the TV before going to bed himself. Why on earth would he bring this upstairs? She shook her head in confusion at the unexpected discovery. And more importantly, she asked herself, just how on earth could he be so irresponsible as to leave it lying there in Joshua's cot?

Grumbling again, Gina lifted the photograph with one hand and tucked Joshua's baby blanket back in with the other. That was when the now-familiar sense of dread came upon her once more, an icy shiver running the length of her spine as she became aware that she was not alone with her child. There was a presence in the room. She could feel it now. She froze for a second, realizing that somebody or something was standing behind her.

Up until that moment, the figure in the shadows had remained silent and motionless. The instant Gina raised her head and tried to turn around, however, it sprang into action without the slightest hesitation. The intruder lunged forward and slapped a hand over her mouth from behind, stopping her turning and forcing her body violently against the edge of the cot. She kicked her legs out in retaliation but was slammed even harder against the wooden rail, knocking the wind from her lungs. And then she saw a shaft of moonlight reflecting off metal as the attacker raised a long, double-edged kitchen knife to her chin.

Gina tried desperately to scream for Richie, but it was no use. Her attacker's hand pressed firmer against her mouth, and she bit into her lip and tasted blood. She tried to struggle, to raise her arms and swing away. But she was helpless, gasping in shock as her attacker wedged her body harder against the cot and brought the razor-sharp blade sweeping violently across her throat.

≈   ≈   ≈

Richie stirred. A strange gurgling rasp came over the baby monitor. It did not frighten him, but it registered enough to wake him. He sat up, rubbed his eyes, and slowly swung out of bed. He yawned repeatedly as he stood and shuffled toward the door, scratching an itch down the front of his shorts as he went.

Seconds later, he reached the nursery and stood in the doorway to allow his eyes to adjust to the darkness. Gina was leaning over the cot directly in front of him, her back hunched across the rail so all he could see was her ass in those tight pink panties. It aroused him a little, and he stepped into the room and immediately pushed himself up against her as he placed his hands gently around her waist.

"Sorry, babe," he whispered. "I was just so damn tired. It took me a while to wake up."

When he got no reply, he moved his hips against her to get a reaction, feeling the softness of her buttocks against his crotch. He half-expected some sort of response or rebuke, but none came. Richie was a healthy, friendly guy, an optimist by nature. In his heightening state of arousal, he misread this lack of response as an invitation. So he moved a little bit more, swaying in a circular motion against her. He squeezed his hands tighter around her waist and then moved them slowly up toward her breasts.

"Hey, do you forgive me?" he whispered mischievously.

Silence, except for the gentle cooing of little Joshua in the cot.

"You're teasing me now, babe, you know that?"

But even as he said these words, he felt something warm and moist beneath his hands. He rubbed his right fingers together. The moisture was sticky. Something was wrong. He could feel it now.

"Hey. What's this?" he whispered, suddenly concerned that his wife had not uttered a single word since he arrived.

Gina often applied the silent treatment when she was pissed with him. That was her way. Her weapon. But she would never let him take her from behind or move like that against her if she was mad. So he released his other hand from her breast and leaned across to switch on the nursery lamp nearby.

Richie emitted a loud shriek when the soft yellow light flickered on, staring in utter disbelief at the scene of horror that lay before him. As Joshua began crying at the top of his voice, his screams filling the room, Richie could only stand frozen in shock.

Gina's lifeless body was slumped over the edge of the wooden cot, her faded pink t-shirt now stained crimson red. Her eyes and mouth were open in a silent death scream, the gaping wound across her throat dripping furiously onto the blood-soaked blanket still wrapped around the crying infant below.

≈   ≈   ≈

Detective Isabella Garcia arrived at the Regazzoni's house on the outskirts of Hialeah around one a.m. She scanned the surrounding area before emerging from her silver Ford Marauder and stretching her tired limbs in the hot night air. The neighborhood was an affluent one with well-kept lawns and tall Cuban Petticoat palms lining the street on both sides. It reminded her of the one she used to live in ten years ago before the divorce, and for a split-second, her mind wandered until the passenger door swung open and jolted her back to the present. Her young partner, Detective Mike Ryan, stepped out of the vehicle a few seconds later with a coffee in one hand and a large folder and clipboard in the other.

"Hey, Mike, you might want to leave that here," Isabella advised him, motioning toward the coffee cup. "Once inside, you won't be able to put it down."

As he placed the cardboard cup on the hood of the car, she moved her eyes carefully around the scene. There were three patrol cars parked nearby, sirens off, lights flashing in the darkness, and dozens of concerned-looking neighbors gathered in small tightly-knit groups directly outside the house. Every light was on now, with a couple of uniformed officers coming and going from the building. While one was busy sealing off the crime scene with plastic yellow tape, two others were taking statements and particulars from those they could find who might have seen or heard anything relevant to the case.

"Ah, if it isn't the love of me life," an older officer exclaimed teasingly as they stepped up onto the porch. Sergeant McGregor was a genial, overweight man in his late fifties who was close to retirement. He had arrived in Miami from Scotland about twenty years earlier, immediately joining the police force, but never losing any of his heavy Scottish accent or humor.

"Hi, Sarge," Isabella said politely, returning a warm smile.

"Sweetheart." He continued with a courteous nod. "You never did call me last weekend like you promised. You do know you're breaking me wee heart, don't ye?"

Isabella smiled. "Like I've already told you, Sarge, if I ever start dating again, you will be the first one I call."

"Lord almighty, if only that were true," he said with a rueful grin. "And if only I were fifteen years younger too."

She smiled and patted his arm affectionately. In her late thirties, Isabella was Latina with olive skin, hazel brown eyes, and black shoulder-length hair tied back in a tight ponytail. She wore a simple gold chain with a tiny crucifix around her neck and was smartly dressed in dark gray trousers and a matching jacket above a white satin blouse.

"So then, what have we got?" she asked McGregor, changing her tone now to reflect the seriousness of the situation.

"*Och*, I'm afraid it's a bad one." He sighed. "Detective Brewster and the medical examiner are already here. You'll find them upstairs in the nursery." Then, as they walked through the open doorway and entered the house, he said, "Second door on the right, sweetheart. Prepare yourselves, though. It's not a pretty sight."

Isabella nodded her understanding as she led her young partner up the narrow staircase toward the nursery. Mike followed close behind her with his folder and clipboard held tightly under his right arm. He had just made detective only a few weeks earlier and seemed eager to gain as much practical field experience as he could. He may have scored high in his exams, but he still had a lot to learn. What Isabella liked about him, however, was that he acknowledged that fact without any pretense or bravado. That was what made a good detective. She knew from experience. He was wise enough to listen, content to simply hang back and take it all in.

Isabella knew Mike had been fortunate when he was assigned to her. Not because she was regarded as one of the best at what she did. Hell, that was for others to decide. But she took her role as a teacher very seriously, unlike some of her colleagues back at the station. She knew that the future of the force depended on new guys like Mike, and she set out to be the best mentor she could be. She tried to be patient, informative, and helpful to him from the very start. Some of the other detectives treated their younger partners like new kids in school, too busy to share their knowledge, looking down on them as a burden and waste of their valuable time. But she was not like that. She had more than twelve years of experience on the job. In that time, she had pretty much seen and done it all.

"So, guys, what have we got?" she asked the two men standing in conversation by the body when she and Mike entered the nursery.

"Single homicide," said Walker, the old, gray-haired medical examiner. He was busy making notes on his clipboard but glanced up matter-of-factly for a second or two over the top of his bifocal glasses. "Victim's larynx and carotid artery have been severed by what appears to have been a six to ten-inch blade."

"Have we got a name yet?"

"Her name is Gina Regazzoni," said Detective Byron Brewster, the tall black man standing with his arms folded beside the medical examiner. "Twenty-nine years old, married, and the mother of a ten-day-old baby."

"No shit?"

"Yeah, it's true. And get this, the poor little guy was in the cot beneath her when her throat was cut."

"Christ."

"Bled right out on top of him."

"So, where is he now?" she asked with concern. "Is he okay?"

"Don't worry. He's safe," said Brewster. "The paramedics are taking him to Miami General for tests. But, apart from the blood, it doesn't look like he was harmed."

"Jesus Christ!" Mike whispered disbelievingly as he stepped past Isabella to view the bloodstained corpse hanging over the wooden rail. He had not seen as many dead bodies as the others and still seemed to find it all a bit disturbing. Gina's face was pale now, like dull marble. With cheeks drained and gaunt, her eyes and mouth still open in a grotesque fashion. "What kind of sick bastard would do such a thing?"

"That is exactly what we are here to find out," Isabella muttered thoughtfully as she hunched down to get a better look at the wound on the woman's throat. She used the tip of a plastic pen to hold back Gina's hair. "Looks like a clean enough cut. Maybe a razor or a hunting knife?"

"No," said the medical examiner. "The blade was serrated. More like a steak knife, if you ask me."

Isabella nodded, removed the pen, and let the blood-caked hair fall back into place. She then turned to the younger detective. "You know what, Mike? To answer the big question of *who* did this, you and I will first have to start asking some smaller ones."

"Smaller ones?"

"Yes. Remember what I told you yesterday about following procedure, ticking off the boxes in order, and not letting emotion or any other kind of feelings get in the way?"

Mike nodded.

"So," she continued, "let's, for example, start concentrating on *when* exactly this happened. And once we have established that, we will then have to ask the other bread and butter questions like *how* and *why*? I guarantee you, Mike, nine times out of ten, discovering the answers to these questions will set you on the path to finding out precisely *who* it is you are looking for."

"Well, the *when* is an easy one," said Brewster. "Husband says she went to check on the baby just after midnight. He followed about five minutes later and found her like this. Poor bastard."

"Judging by the early rigor in the body," said the medical examiner, "time of death pretty much matches his story."

"Okay," said Isabella. "So it begins." She took a deep, steadying breath as she turned toward her young partner. But on seeing the sickened look on his face, she whispered, "Hey, you okay, Mike? Do you need to go out and get some air?"

"No, no," he replied with a sharp intake of breath. "I'm fine. Really. Hell, I was just thinking of my Julie at home with Mike junior."

Isabella placed a hand on his shoulder and patted it in a comforting fashion as she stepped by him and headed back toward the door and out onto the landing. Looking down over the banisters, she caught sight of Sergeant McGregor and immediately shouted down to him. "Hey, Sarge?"

The older man had been in a heated conversation with two of his younger officers, barking orders about how they should not continue traipsing all over the lawn and patio for fear of contaminating the scene. But on hearing her voice from above, he stopped in mid-sentence and looked up with raised eyebrows. "Yes, sweetheart? What can I do for you?"

"You find the point of entry yet?"

"Aye. Busted patio door in the kitchen," he said. "Lock was jimmied with a knife or screwdriver."

"Prints?"

"Not sure. Forensics are dusting now."

"Can you do me a favor?'

"Aye?"

"Carry out an inventory of the kitchen knives?" she asked. "Try to find out if any of them are missing."

"Right away."

Isabella raised a hand in acknowledgement and then

turned back toward Mike. "Well, that's the *when* and the *how*. Now, all you and I need to find out is the *why*."

Just then, Detective Brewster stepped forward after finishing a conversation on his cell phone. "Hey, Garcia, I just spoke to the captain, and it looks like you're taking the lead on this one."

"That's fine by me," she said.

"So, what do you want me to do?"

Isabella thought about it for a second. "Well, first, get forensics up here to do their stuff. Make sure they give this priority. And find out if they had any luck dusting for prints on the patio door."

"Okay."

"Next, have a talk with the neighbors, family, friends. You know the drill. Try to find out about the state of the marriage. See if there was any trouble between the victim and her husband, anything going on that might give us a clue as to what motive someone might have for doing this."

"Got it."

"Oh, and Brewster, while you're at it," she added, "how about running a background check on the husband. What's his name again?"

"Richie," Brewster said.

"Right. Okay, so find out if he has any priors. Any history of violence—domestic or otherwise. You know the routine."

"And me?" Mike asked enthusiastically.

"For the moment, you stay with me," she said. "Let's you and I sit down with this Richie and try to find out, in his own words, *exactly* what happened tonight."

Before Mike could reply, a voice cried out to them from downstairs. Both he and Isabella rushed onto the landing to find McGregor out of breath, halfway up the stairs with an excited, triumphant look on his face.

"We've got the son-of-a-bitch!" he shouted up to them.

"What are you talking about?" asked Isabella.

"One of the neighbors, a security guard coming home from work, saw the bastard jumping the back fence. Thought he was a burglar and followed him down to the harbor."

≈ ≈ ≈

Tommy Mendoza stood at the entrance to the sprawling Miami harbor parking lot, waving excitedly to the two patrol cars and silver Ford Marauder that had suddenly appeared together from the direction of the I-95 ramp. Truth be told, he had been feeling nervous and vulnerable up to that point, waiting there alone in the darkness. But now he experienced a surge of relief on seeing that the authorities were arriving to take up the chase. When he had first glimpsed the hooded man climbing over the Regazzoni's back fence and getting into a small blue Chevy parked in the alley behind the house, he had simply believed him to be a burglar. He had assumed he was just an opportunist searching out an unlocked door or window in the hunt for cash or easily pawned jewelry. But later, as he had followed the car out of the neighborhood and down Okeechobee Road toward the coast, he had phoned 9-1-1 from his cell phone, only to be promptly told that the man was, in fact, a suspected killer.

Tommy had been exhausted after completing his shift at the Biscayne Plaza Shopping Mall but had quickly gained a second wind and a rush of adrenalin upon hearing the news. The police dispatcher on the phone had told him to keep the car in sight, while remaining at a safe distance. She had advised him not to be a hero under any circumstances, and that help was on its way and would be there in a matter of minutes.

Then, without warning, the Chevy he was following had suddenly turned into the unlit harbor parking lot, away from the yellow streetlights, only to turn off its low beams and disappear from his sight into the darkness. Tommy had been scared. He hadn't been sure if the driver had seen him, so had decided to play it safe and had pulled up to the nearby curb. The dispatcher told him he had done the right thing, to exit the car and to keep an eye out for the approaching police vehicles.

"Here! He's in here!" he exclaimed excitedly.

Sergeant McGregor emerged from the lead patrol car. The other police car did not stop, but instead, headed off at speed toward the parking lot's secondary entrance about a hundred and fifty yards farther up the road.

"Did you manage to get a look at him?" Isabella asked with urgency as she sprang from the Marauder and joined them at the edge of the curb. "Sir, is he armed?"

"Too far away to see," Tommy said with a shake of his head. "But he is wearing a dark hoodie. And he's driving a small blue Chevy. A Sonic, I think."

He realized immediately that the female detective addressing him was in charge, for even before he finished speaking, she turned to the older uniformed officer and directed him to block the entrance with his patrol car before following her and her young partner on foot. She thanked Tommy for his assistance as she headed off, telling him to stay put and to keep an eye out for the other patrol cars that would be arriving shortly.

"Don't worry," he called out enthusiastically as she left. "I'll tell them where you've gone."

"Appreciate it," she said. "Oh, and sir, tell them I said to turn off their damned lights and sirens. We don't need to advertise the fact that we're coming."

With that, Detectives Garcia and Ryan drew their weapons and disappeared into the darkness. Sergeant McGregor followed carrying a pump-action shotgun and a flashlight he had taken from the patrol car after duly parking it across the entrance.

≈ ≈ ≈

"Sarge, you swing around to the right as far as that boathouse," Isabella said quietly when they came across the abandoned Chevrolet. It was empty, the driver's door unlocked, parked beside a line of low concrete bollards that divided the parking lot from the boatyard. "I'll take center."

"And me?" asked Mike.

Isabella was quiet, as if undecided what the young man's role should be. "You move left along the water's edge," she said after a moment's contemplation. Then, as her young partner turned to leave, she said, "Hey, Mike, stay close to me, okay? I mean it. Don't go any farther than that pier. If you reach it without seeing him, just wait there until I do a sweep over to you. Got it?"

"Got it," he said dutifully as they split up and disappeared from each other's sight.

Alone now, Isabella ducked down, squinting as she

searched her surroundings. The air was still and hot about her, the only audible sound was the tide lapping intermittently against the wooden pier at the water's edge. Moving out, she cursed the blackness for not allowing her to see more than ten feet ahead, but on the other hand, was somewhat grateful that it offered cover for her and her companions as they closed in on the killer. Isabella was uncertain if he knew they were coming and did not know if they had the element of surprise. That bothered her. The killer must have turned his car into the harbor parking lot for a reason, she mused. It could not have been by chance.

There were a number of possibilities she considered as she moved forward through the maze of boats with shoulders hunched, head down, and revolver firmly in both hands. One of them was that the guy lived somewhere in the area, perhaps on one of the fishing boats or cruisers moored nearby. Or maybe he was crashing in one of the wooden sheds and boathouses scattered about the harbor? She would welcome either of these scenarios; that would surely mean they were about to catch him unawares. But there was another, more dangerous possibility she had to consider. What if he had, in fact, spotted the Regazzoni's neighbor following and swung in here to shake him off, to ditch his car and make a run for it? Looking around, she realized now that the boatyard beyond the parking lot was an ideal place to hide out, a labyrinth of upturned boats and half-finished hulls, crates and barrels, oil drums and rusted engine parts. If the latter was the case, if this guy was hiding out in here, waiting for them, then they could be walking right into an ambush.

Even as she considered this possibility, a shot rang out in the darkness to her left, breaking her train of thought and sending her speeding off toward Mike's position. She tripped over a discarded plastic fish crate, grazing her palms on the rough concrete. But she quickly scrambled to her feet and kept moving. Seconds later, another shot rang out. Unlike the first, which had just been a loud burst in the distance, this time she saw the flash of a muzzle ahead in the blackness and then heard the crack of splintered wood as a bullet ripped into one of the boat hulls to her right. It was too close for comfort. That second shot had been directed at her! This guy was ready and waiting for them, and he was armed. Her worst fear had become a reality.

Crouching low, she moved under one of the boats raised off the ground on wooden pallets and quickly came out the other side, gun still at the ready. She could see the outline of a large timber boathouse about twenty feet ahead in the blackness and inched cautiously toward it.

There was movement nearby. Someone darted quickly from the shadows to her right, a silhouetted figure that sprang up from behind a stack of oil drums and then ducked into the open door of the boathouse.

"Miami Metro!" she shouted to no avail. "Stop or I will fire!" She waited for a moment or two after the figure disappeared, hearing the unmistakable sound of the boathouse door creaking shut behind him. "Mike?" She shouted anxiously into the surrounding darkness. "Mike, can you hear me?"

She heard another noise to her left and swung around with her gun outstretched, finger anxiously on the trigger. "Sarge, is that you?"

"Aye," replied a familiar voice. "Who the hell fired those shots?"

"I don't know," she said, adrenalin still pumping, relieved to have his support. "But that second one was definitely meant for me."

"Jesus, lassie. Are you okay?"

"Yeah, I'm fine. I'm fine. Have you seen Mike?"

"No, not since we split up," McGregor said, holding the shotgun firmly in both hands. "I thought he was off to your right."

"Shit!" Isabella muttered. She thought about searching for her partner for a moment as the older man looked on, then shook her head and decided to concentrate on the problem at hand. "Well, look, I think our guy has gone into this building."

"What do you want to do?"

"You swing around back and make sure he doesn't slip out," she said. "I am going to go in after him."

"Are you sure you want to do that?"

Isabella nodded. "We have him cornered, Sarge, and I don't want to give him time to slip away while we wait for backup."

"Okay then," McGregor told her as she moved off. "But

be careful, sweetheart."

Reaching the edge of the building a few seconds later, Isabella checked that the safety was released on her revolver before pushing the door inwards with her foot and ducking in through the opening. The smell of tarps and varnish that greeted her inside was overpowering, forcing her to remove one hand from the gun to cover her nose and mouth. She stopped and hunched down in the corner to the right of the door, trying desperately to adjust her eyes to the darkness.

Something moving up ahead in the distance startled her. She could not see much but sensed a presence in the shadows. He was in there somewhere and he was waiting for her. A low voice groaned something indistinguishable followed immediately by a loud creaking noise and a straining of timber floorboards. Seconds later, another shot rang out, reverberating in the confines of the wooden building and sending her scurrying for cover behind some nearby crates.

"Miami Metro!" she screamed again at the top of her voice. "This is your last chance to show yourself. Put down that gun and come out with your hands above your head."

When no response came, she rose and inched around to her right, moving parallel to a long wooden bench that stood against the far wall. Halfway down, a large dust-covered window offered the barest hint of light from outside. It was not much, but in its dim glow, she could just make out an upturned boat hull in the center of the room, partly covered with plastic tarpaulin and smelling of fresh anti-foul paint.

Then another sudden creak of wood alerted her once more to the presence up ahead. He was on the move. A cardboard box was knocked from one of the tall metal shelving units on the far side of the boat, splitting open and spilling its contents out onto the wooden floor.

Isabella moved quickly toward the end of the hull, resting her back against it for cover before inching carefully around toward the other side, trying to outflank her prey without being spotted. When she reached it, she took a deep steadying breath, exhaled slowly, and then sprang out with her gun pointing straight ahead. Nothing. She knew then it was a trap.

The moment she showed herself, a loud creak of straining metal shattered the silence. One of the shelving units to her right groaned and came crashing down upon her. It knocked her to the ground, sending tins of paint and rusted nails scattering across the floor. Winded, Isabella tried desperately to crawl free, only to find her right ankle pinned beneath the heavy metal unit. As she tried to push it off, a loud *whoosh* erupted behind some nearby metal canisters, followed by an immediate explosion of fiery orange light. He had sprung his trap, rendered her immobile, and was now setting fire to the boathouse with her inside.

The blaze took hold in seconds, spreading out across the drums of flammable chemicals until it became an inferno. As Isabella frantically tried to free her ankle, it reached the base of the upturned shelving unit, pinning her down and igniting the spilled alcohol and varnish about her. The heat was intense, almost unbearable. She felt her skin blistering and had to turn her face away to shield herself from the blast. There was no time to waste. She had to free her ankle without delay and get clear before the entire building went up.

Steadying herself in the face of imminent death, she took a deep breath and scanned her surroundings for something to use as a lever. Anything would do. She looked left to right and then back again. Then a length of timber lying nearby caught her eye. Grabbing for it gratefully with both hands, she hurriedly wedged it under the shelving unit and pushed up with all her might. The heavy frame groaned painfully at first as it began to move, and her heart started to beat slower. But then, to her horror, the timber snapped right in the middle and the heavy weight came crashing down again.

"Goddamnit." Isabella cursed furiously at the top of her voice.

Her left sleeve caught on fire and her hair began to singe as the flames drew closer. Undeterred, she patted out the flames, took another deep breath and tried to compose herself, searching the area once more. This time, she found a piece of metal pipe lying in the dust and debris behind her. Grabbing for it with her left hand, she wedged it down into the gap beside her ankle and tried again.

"Move, you son-of-a-bitch!" She roared at the top of her voice, using every ounce of strength and energy she possessed in a desperate attempt to force the heavy metal panel up.

There was another creak and a strained groan as the unit

moved upwards a couple of inches, just enough to allow her to pull her ankle free before her grip failed, and it came crashing down to the floor.

She rolled away a split second before the flames engulfed the entire area where she had been lying, shooting up into the air and taking hold in the dry wooden beams overhead. Without a second to spare, Isabella raced to the nearby wall, grabbed a sheet of cloth sack hanging from a nail, and placed it over her head and shoulders for protection. Without hesitating, she used one of the unturned crates as a step and leaped up onto the workbench, kicking the obstructing paint cans down into the sea of flames below before diving head first through the window.

She hit the hard ground outside with a heavy thud, feeling a sharp pain in her side as she rolled clear of the broken glass. Seconds later, the building exploded behind her, sending chunks of burning wood and splinters in every direction. The corrugated iron roof buckled with the heat and then collapsed inwards, hitting the inferno below and knocking part of the wall down toward the fire.

Out of breath, Isabella crawled painfully away toward the safety of a nearby upturned row boat. She sat on the ground with her back to it for what seemed like an age, sucking in the fresh air, looking out on the now brightly lit boatyard for signs of movement.

"Over here!" She shouted with relief when she eventually saw Sergeant McGregor coming around the side of the burning building with his shotgun in both hands. "Sarge! Sarge, I'm over here!"

The older policeman scurried over to her position with his head bowed low and turned away from the searing wall of heat. He knelt beside her, laid his shotgun on the ground, and frantically examined her for wounds.

"Sweetheart, are you all right?" he asked with concern. "Are ye shot?"

"Just a little singed," she replied with a shake of her head. Then, raising a hand to her side, she said, "I think I might have cracked a rib, though."

Sergeant McGregor placed an affectionate hand on her arm, raised his eyes to hers, but then said nothing. She caught the look of hesitation and squinted in puzzlement.

"What is it?" she asked.

He still said nothing, just lowered his eyes to the ground and shook his head.

"Sarge, for Christ's sake, tell me what's wrong."

"The young lad is dead," he eventually said quietly.

"What?"

"Mike's gone, sweetheart. He's dead."

"No. He can't be. How?"

McGregor put a steadying hand on her shoulder and sighed. "I found him off near the pier. He's been stabbed in the back. There was nothing I could do, sweetheart. I'm sorry."

"Stabbed?" Isabella whispered in disbelief.

"I believe that first shot we heard was probably his," McGregor said. "The poor lad was most likely taken by surprise and didn't even see it coming. I think, after the bastard killed him, he must have taken his gun and turned it on you."

Isabella said nothing, just sat on the ground, holding her side and staring silently at the burning building, hypnotized by the orange and yellow flames and sparks dancing skywards into the blackness. Her body was numb now, her heart heavy with an overwhelming sense of grief.

CHAPTER TWO

THE WILD ROVER

He breathed in the warm, salty air as he stood on the forward deck of the *Wild Rover*, tying off sheets and tightening the mooring lines. Making his final preparations for the coming voyage, he made his way back to the main mast and stood for a moment in contemplation.

Marcus Brophy had worked tirelessly throughout the night, only distracted for a short time as he'd watched one of the boathouses on the other side of the harbor go up in flames. As he'd stood on the cabin roof, viewing the spectacle through a pair of binoculars, a couple of patrol cars had arrived with lights flashing, followed shortly after by a fire engine and an ambulance. Within fifteen minutes of the roof collapsing, the entire building was gone. The firefighters had pumped hundreds of gallons of water onto the mound of smoldering wood and tin. But, by then, it had been too late, and even from the other side of the harbor, it had been obvious to him the damage was irreparable.

Barely five-thirty in the morning, the rising sun already began to cast its heat over the marina. Wiping a bead of sweat from his brow, Marcus stared out across the rows of gleaming white yachts and speedboats on his side of the harbor, letting the morning sea breeze cool his face. The light was already growing intense, reflecting off the corrugated tin roofs of the boathouses and sheds. It glistened off the lacquered white hulls and cabins of the sail boats and motor cruisers bobbing up and down on the outgoing tide.

The sight filled Marcus with a deep sense of excitement. But then, he thought, as he returned to work, it always did. This was the environment he had grown up in, his world of boats and the sea. At twenty-three years of age, this was where he felt most happy and at home. The salty smell of the ocean was sweet to his nostrils, the sounds of sea birds gliding above the bay ever enjoyable. Skimmers, terns, and seagulls hovered low above the fishing boats as they re-turned to port, vying noisily for air space as they watched for discarded scraps and crumbs.

The distinctive sound of the marina was like music to Mar-cus's ears. The squawks of the gulls, the *tink-tink-tink* of loose metal ties banging against swaying masts. He listened to the hum of the *Wild Rover's* diesel engine and knew it was in tip-top condition for the upcoming voyage. He and his father had cleaned the plugs and changed the oil the previous day. And, listening now to the steady purr of the engine, he knew it had been worth it. To him, the low, steady hum was like an or-chestra playing a soothing classical symphony. The tide was going out. He felt the wind's speed and direction on his face as he stood on the deck and knew instinctively what kind of sail-ing conditions could be expected for the coming day.

The *Wild Rover* beneath him was his pride and joy—a for-ty-five-foot-long, ocean-going catamaran. She had two wide hulls that stood side by side in the water with a flat white deck and large cabin joining them together. She was sloop-rigged with a single mast and built for speed and stability. On board, she boasted an eighty horsepower diesel engine, an echo sounder, and a wind generator, as well as a row of solar panels fixed just above the main cabin. A low wooden bath-ing deck was fixed at her stern, above which hung an orange rubber dinghy with a small outboard engine.

"Hello on the *Rover!*" A voice called out from the dock, distracting Marcus from his preparations.

He turned to see a young black couple standing by the boat, holding hands, their eyes wide with excitement and anticipation. They were in their mid-twenties—the man, tall and thin with a pair of Oakley sunglasses sitting atop a shav-en head, the woman, shorter and a little on the plump side. Her long black hair was partially hidden beneath a large, red sun hat, and when she smiled up at him, her teeth were so white they reflected the rising sun like a mirror.

"You must be the Kingstons, my newly-weds from Geor-gia," he said warmly. "I'm Marcus Brophy. Come on board and make yourselves at home."

Beaming with excitement, the couple stepped awkwardly onto the thin wooden walkway. Holding on tight to each other as it rocked beneath them, they made their way on deck pulling a large gray wheelie suitcase.

"Jayden and Brianna Kingston," the man said in a strong Southern accent, taking Marcus's outstretched hand and shaking it vigorously.

Brianna shook his hand too but quickly placed her other around his neck and pulled him down to plant a warm, affectionate kiss on his right cheek.

"Lord Almighty, we are, like, sooo excited about this trip," she gushed. "Why, we have been talking about nothing else for the past two weeks."

"Glad to see you're both so eager. I only hope my other passengers will be as enthusiastic," said Marcus.

"Why, it's such a glorious day, and God's ocean is so calm and blue. Who in their right mind would not be thrilled at the prospect of such an exciting trip?" said Jayden.

"So, when exactly did you two get married?"

"We tied the knot last weekend in Georgia," Jayden said. "At our local church. You know, I am a minister in the First Lighthouse Baptist Church there."

"Really?" said Marcus. "A minister?"

Jayden looked him directly in the eye. "Tell me, Marcus, if it's not too personal, are you a Christian?"

Taken by surprise, Marcus just shrugged. "To be honest, I'm not really much into organized religion."

"Well, that's okay," the young black man said, patting him on the shoulder. "That is okay, my friend. In the end, we all find our own paths toward God's plan. The main thing is that, on the way, we live our lives as He would want."

"So," Marcus asked, turning to the young woman in an effort to change the subject. God, religion, and all the arguments surrounding it were not subjects he normally discussed before breakfast. Besides, he mused, they did not know each other well enough to be talking about their beliefs. "Where have you both been staying since the wedding?"

"We've been living in luxury in a hotel here in Miami for the past week," Jayden said before she could speak.

"The Bahia," Brianna added with a smile. "Five star. Like,

on the beach. You know it?"

"Wow. Fancy place," Marcus said with raised eyebrows and a whistle. "I hope you're not expecting that kind of luxury here on the *Wild Rover*."

Jayden laughed, patted Marcus on the shoulder again, and said, "No sir, not at all. Not at all. We are ready to become sailors, aren't we, honey?"

Brianna smiled and nodded in agreement.

"No, don't you worry about that. Why, I think we've just about had as much five course dinners and hotel swimming pools as we can stand. What we both want now is to get out into God's creation for some real excitement and adventure."

"Good. Well, you have definitely come to the right place for that," Marcus assured them.

Brianna placed a hand gently on Marcus's arm and nodded, motioning back toward the dock, indicating that another of the passengers had just arrived.

The man was in his early forties, heavy set with thinning brown hair. He wore a dark gray hoodie and blue jeans. He carried a small, black canvas sail bag over his right shoulder.

"Hello there," said the young captain. "I am Marcus Brophy. Welcome to the *Wild Rover Training Cruise*. Come on board and make yourself at home."

The new arrival walked up the boarding plank without speaking. He took Marcus's outstretched hand and shook it politely.

"Let me guess," said Marcus. "You are either Harvey Hawkins or Benjamin Goldstein, right?"

"Harvey," the man replied cordially in a British accent, his breath smelling of alcohol and stale tobacco.

"Well, it's good to meet you. I hope you are looking forward to the trip?"

"You know, it has gone five already," the British man grunted impatiently. "Shouldn't we be casting off?"

"Yes, you're right. We should. We are supposed to be setting sail on the outgoing tide," Marcus said with a look of mild concern. "But I'm afraid we are still waiting for two more to arrive."

Harvey nodded without reply.

It was clear from the outset that he was extremely anxious to depart, and he was definitely not a people person.

But that was all right by Marcus. He knew it took all sorts. Deck hands came in all shapes and sizes.

"Well, anyway, this is Jayden and Brianna Kingston from Georgia," Marcus said, stepping aside to let him see the other two passengers standing nearby. "They were married last week. Still on their honeymoon."

Smiling broadly, Jayden leaned forward to shake Harvey's hand, but the British man did not reach out to take it. He simply nodded a cursory greeting back to him.

Jayden and Marcus shared a glance, but nothing was said. They were both aware that Harvey was a strange character. He had come across as being impolite and anti-social, but there was more to it than that. It did not really seem to them that he was being rude intentionally, but rather, he appeared to be more stressed and distracted than anything else. He was edgy and irritated, peeved that they were not setting sail on time.

Pursing his lips, Jayden turned to Marcus and pointed back across the narrow stretch of water separating the marina from the fishing boats and work sheds. "So, what was all that activity we saw on the other side of the harbor as the taxi drove us in? Some kind of fire?"

Marcus looked back out across the bay to where the collapsed boathouse could just be made out, a blackened, smoking shell of its former self. There were still a number of patrol cars surrounding it, but their lights were no longer flashing, and the policemen were now standing around in small groups.

"I don't really know," he said quietly, shrugging.

"Lord, I hope no one was hurt," said Brianna.

"Me too," agreed Marcus. "I guess it must have been some kind of electrical fault in one of the boathouses. With such big amounts of spirits and chemicals lying around, those places can be real deathtraps."

≈ ≈ ≈

The morning sun rose higher as Isabella sipped tentatively from the cardboard coffee cup she was holding in both hands. She sat in the passenger seat of the Ford Marauder with the door half open, resting her feet on the hot, cracked asphalt of the boatyard. Her head was bowed, her mood somber. Mike Ryan had been a nice kid, young and eager, full of promise. But now he was gone. She had watched silently from the sidelines as technicians from the coroner's office zipped him into a rubber body bag and took him away in the back of a black Phoenix Cadillac.

A group of uniformed officers conducting a sweep on the other side of the yard had stopped what they were doing to stand with hands crossed and heads bowed in respect. They began chatting again as soon as the coroner's car pulled away, and Isabella noticed how a couple of them kept glancing over toward her.

It was obvious what they were saying. They were debating her role in Mike's death. She knew some of them would argue she was partly to blame. As his mentor, she should have kept him closer. She could sense the accusations, but what was more, she did not really disagree with any of them.

"So, how are you doing?" A voice spoke from the other side of the car, breaking her train of thought and making her turn.

Captain Franklin stepped into view from around the back of the Marauder in a creased blue suit with arms folded, a look of genuine concern on his wrinkled, suntanned face. He was followed close behind by detective Brewster, who immediately put a hand on Isabella's shoulder and patted it sympathetically.

"McGregor said you might be hurt," he said with concern.

"Me? No, I'm okay."

"Did the paramedics check you out?"

"Yes," she replied. "Bruised ribs, that's all."

"Well, the forensic boys have just found your guy in the boathouse," the captain said after a short pause.

Isabella sat upright, a puzzled look on her face. "A body?"

"Burnt crisper than one of my wife's roast dinners," he said. "Can't ID him right now, of course, but once they get him back to the lab, they will run a full, detailed examination. Dental records, blood analysis, and face reconstruction. Don't worry, Garcia, we will find out who the son-of-a-bitch is, one way or the other."

"But he's not the guy," said Isabella, so out of the blue it took both the captain and detective Brewster by surprise. "The real killer lit that fire deliberately to cover his escape. He didn't get caught up in it. He used it."

The captain sighed. "Look, Garcia, you said yourself the building went up in minutes. Hell, you barely got out yourself. And Sergeant McGregor was covering the back door, remember?"

"He could have gone out the front after he pinned me down," she continued.

"Listen, you need to go home now and get some sleep," said the captain.

"I'm serious," she persisted. "Captain, this guy is smarter than that."

"Go home, Detective," he said a little louder. "That is an order."

"What about the Chevy?"

"Forensics are towing it to the pound as we speak," said Brewster. "But I can tell you it was stolen yesterday afternoon off Sunrise Boulevard."

"And Mike's gun?" she asked as the two men began walking away from her.

The captain stopped, turned around, and sighed wearily. "No sign of it yet, but we're still looking. We found a blood-stained kitchen knife about ten yards from the entrance to the boathouse. I'll bet my next paycheck it's the same one that killed Mike and the Regazzoni woman."

"You won't find Mike's gun," Isabella said as he turned to walk away again. "Because I am telling you here and now, Captain, the body you pulled out of that building is not our guy."

"No? Then who is it?"

Isabella shrugged. "I can't say for sure. But it is definitely not Mike's killer."

"Go home and sleep."

"Captain, I'm not going anywhere until I find this guy."

The older man took a deep breath and sighed loudly. "Jesus Christ, Garcia, why are you always so goddamned stubborn? Do you really want to do this here? Now?"

"Huh? Do what?"

"Look, you need to go home and sleep. You need rest, and lots of it. Because, believe me, Detective, later on today, you are going to have to sit before an IA investigation board and go through every minute detail of what happened here. You understand what I'm saying, don't you? You are going to have to justify your actions and explain to them what exactly Mike Ryan was doing over there at the pier instead of being by your side where he was supposed to be."

"But—"

"I mean it, Garcia. You are going to have some tough questions to answer, explaining to them why you decided to send a rookie detective into such a dangerous situation alone."

Isabella said nothing, just blinked her eyes and nodded slowly.

"Now, please, listen to what I'm saying and go home. Shit, I've got to go break the news to Mike's wife."

When he and Brewster left, she sat there for the longest time, deep in thought, staring out across the bay toward the yachts and cruisers in the marina on the other side. Mike had been so eager when they set off from the station last night, she remembered with a twinge of sadness. He had been looking forward to learning the ins and outs of homicide, little realizing, by the time the sun came up, he would be a victim in their latest case. Isabella sighed, the tragic irony hitting hard that he was now just another statistic on the whiteboard in Captain Franklin's office.

But then a glint of sunlight reflecting off one of the taller masts in the marina in the distance caught her eye and got her thinking. A theory quickly formulated, took shape, and then her mind began to focus more and more until it was calculating like a finely tuned instrument. Seconds after it did, she knocked back the dregs of her coffee, cold by now, tossed the empty cup onto the passenger seat of the Marauder, and fired up its engine.

She passed by the uniformed officers without looking at them, muttering to herself as she drove. Once at the edge of the yard, she swung the car out of the parking lot and followed the narrow road that led around to the other side of the harbor. It did not take very long. Soon she had crossed the small wooden bridge that spanned the narrow stretch of water, turned off the road, and then drove straight through the marina's entrance.

She brought the car to a sharp stop on the gravel, then stepped out and headed straight through the pedestrian security gate where the comparison between the two sides of the harbor immediately became apparent. Unlike the junkyard feel of the boatyard and fisherman's area she had just been in—full of sheds, upturned boats, and nets—the marina complex had a much more affluent feel about it. Everything was crisp and clean, freshly painted, and polished. There were international flags fluttering above the entrance gate, signs posted in five languages directing visitors toward the toilets and washrooms, laundry area, and supply shop.

"Hey there, young lady. Can I help you?" A voice called out from behind as Isabella stepped onto the varnished wooden pier leading down toward the boats.

She turned to see a withered old man in blue overalls with a tin of white paint in one hand and a small brush in the other. His face was windswept, his thin gray hair receded so much there was almost nothing left to comb. But he was a friendly-looking old guy with a warm, welcoming smile. Isabella took out her badge and held it up for him to examine through squinted eyes.

"My name is Detective Garcia," she said quietly. "Are you the manager here?"

"Odd job man, security guard, manager. Cleary is the name. Ben Cleary."

Isabella shook his outstretched hand while looking past him toward the office area.

"You been here all night?"

"That I have. Since yesterday evening in fact," he said with a nod. "Graveyard shift. Off in a couple of minutes, then it's home, feed the dog, and bed for me."

"I wonder if I could ask you a few questions?"

"Is this regarding that fire on the other side of the harbor?" asked Cleary.

Isabella said nothing.

"Sure, ask away."

"First off, has anyone come through here in the past three or four hours?" she asked. "Anyone moving around during the night?"

Ben Cleary thought for a moment, pursed his lips, and nodded again. "Five people came through here in the past few hours."

"Oh?"

"Passengers, arriving for the *Wild Rover*."

"The what?" she asked with interest.

"The *Wild Rover*," he said. "She's a catamaran that moors here for about six months of the year. Takes passengers out on working cruises to the Bahamas and the Virgin Islands, I think."

"Cruises? What kind of cruises?"

"Well, more like training voyages, I suppose. You know, young land-loving folks with a hankering to become sailors? They kind of work their passage there and back. Get stuck in, learn how it's done, and get a real taste for the sea life."

"I see."

"Hey, you interested in sailing?"

"So where would I find this boat?" Isabella asked, ignoring the question as she slipped her badge back into her pocket.

"The *Wild Rover*? You won't," said Cleary. "At least not for another few days. She set sail first thing this morning. Saw her heading out with the tide about two hours ago. Not sure where they've gone this time, though."

"Do they at least have a radio?" she asked, visibly disappointed. "And what about a passenger manifest?"

"A what now?"

"A record of who came through here this morning and went out on the boat?"

Cleary put down the can of paint and ran a hand thoughtfully across his stubbled chin. He was silent for the longest time while Isabella looked on in growing frustration. She was playing a hunch but needed more information than she was getting from him to see if it led anywhere. To ascertain if the killer had, in fact, made his escape to this side of the harbor, she needed to know who the five arrivals were and where they had gone. She needed names, addresses and descriptions. She needed facts, and she needed them now.

"You know what?" said Cleary.

"What?"

"I think you need to see Brophy."

"Brophy?"

"Yes, Patrick Brophy. He owns the *Wild Rover*."

"Okay. So, how do I get in contact with him? You wouldn't happen to have his phone number, would you?"

Cleary scratched the back of his neck for the longest time, shrugged his shoulders, and then said, "Naw, afraid I don't have his number."

Isabella sighed.

"But I can do one better."

"Oh?"

"Yes, if you just follow those signs down to pier seven, young lady, you should find him working there on his other boat."

CHAPTER THREE

THE DIRTY NELLIE

Marcus began his safety talk on the deck of the *Wild Rover* shortly after they had chugged out of the harbor. Keeping the powerful diesel engine running steadily, he guided the large catamaran through the maze of gleaming white yachts and motor cruisers bobbing about them in the swell. He waved to the crew of a small fishing boat passing by, returning from a two-day trip down around the Florida Keys, smiling to himself at the sight of their red sunburned faces and arms. Soon after that, he cleared the mouth of the inlet with ease while his passengers sat on deck admiring the view, and then continued on for about a mile before cutting off the engine.

The moment he hoisted the mainsail, the wind filled it and she began moving effortlessly at speed. He tightened the slack on the sheets until there was no give in the canvas, tied them off on spring cleats in the cockpit, and then turned due south, running at a steady six-knots toward open water and the Virgin Islands. The wind was blowing just right for the first leg of their journey, south-southeast toward the nearby coastline of Miami and South Dade.

It was a glorious morning and, apart from a trailing pod of dolphins, they had the ocean to themselves. He waited until everything was set before tying down the wheel and stepping up out of the cockpit. His five passengers were there waiting eagerly on the forward deck, the breeze blowing through their hair. Ready to get started, they were sitting about in a small semi-circle with life jackets on and a light blue plastic folder in each of their hands.

"All right then, first things first," Marcus said with a smile as he took his position standing with his back to the mast. "I would like to officially welcome each and every one of you to the *Wild Rover*, your home for the next four days and nights."

There was a general murmur of excited conversation, and someone in the group whistled enthusiastically.

"As you all know by now, my name is Marcus Brophy. I am your captain on our training voyage to the Virgin Islands and back. Now, please do not let my age and boyish good looks fool you. I actually do know what I am doing."

"Exactly what kind of experience do you have?" Harvey, the British man asked a little skeptically, not as ready to accept the word of their young captain as the others seemed to be.

"Well, let's just say I have been around the block a few times."

"Can you be more specific?"

Marcus looked at him without speaking for a moment, not in anger, just a little surprised he was being asked to elaborate. "Okay. Well, I have been sailing my whole life. When I was sixteen, I crossed the Atlantic Ocean single-handed. I have been taking training crews out on the *Wild Rover* for the past three years and also recently circumnavigated the globe with my father on this very boat."

"Lord Almighty, it sounds to me like you certainly do know your stuff," Jayden said with a laugh as Harvey simply shrugged and nodded.

"Now then," Marcus continued, "my job over the next couple of days is to guide us safely to and from our destination which, as you all know, is the port of Saint Thomas in the US Virgin Islands. But that is only half of it, guys. While at sea, I will be teaching you how to handle this ocean-going catamaran. You will learn how to sail her, take bearings from the sun, make tropical landfall, and guide a vessel of her size safely in and out of port." He stopped for a second, waited for them to take in the information before continuing. "So, before we get started, I would just like to say a few important words about safety. Now, the first and most important rule of sailing is one hand for yourself and one for the boat. In case you do not understand what this means, it means that you do not let go of the boat. *Ever*. Otherwise, you will most likely find yourself floating alone out here in the middle of the sea, watching your only lifeline sail away over the horizon. Now, has everybody got that?"

All five passengers nodded.

"You're sure?"

Again, a general murmuring and combined head nodding.

"All right then, so, here is how we are going to do things. We will work and rest in shifts. That means, two people on deck at all times during the day. Each crew member..." Marcus paused for a moment, smiled, and said, "Guys, that's you by the way."

There was another burst of enthusiastic chatter combined with excited laughter and clapping. As this happened, a larger than normal wave hit the starboard hull side, and the *Wild Rover* shuddered a little. Marcus jumped back into the cockpit and wound one of the winches tighter, adjusting the Genoa sail before coming back to rejoin the group.

"Anyway," he continued, "each of you *crew members* will get a chance to steer and navigate, plot a course, hoist the mainsail and jib, and then, let out the spinnaker. But unfortunately, as this is not a luxury cruise liner, you will each have to take a turn on watch for about two hours at night. We will also share the cooking, my friends. So that means, whether you are a gourmet chef or can just about boil an egg, each one of you guys will have to prepare one dinner and one lunch for the others. Breakfast is a free for all. Any questions?"

"Just one," asked the small, black-haired man wearing spectacles who was sitting at the end of the group. The lenses of his glasses were like bottle caps, so thick they magnified his eyes and reflected the intense sunlight-like beacons. "Have you ever had a mutiny on one of these trips?"

As the rest of the group laughed out loud, he shot a mischievous smile in Marcus's direction. Benjamin Goldstein was an IT consultant from New York City who had been the last to arrive that morning, a few minutes after the pretty young red-haired woman sitting directly to his left had appeared on the jetty. Benjamin did not seem the athletic type to Marcus. No, not in any way. He was short, stubby, and looked comical in a multi-colored Hawaiian shirt that was tucked into a pair of over-sized Bermuda shorts. To add to the ridiculousness of his garb, he also wore thick black ankle socks beneath his heavy leather sandals, so cumbersome that they clunked on the wooden deck when he walked.

"I *have* come close to a mutiny once or twice," Marcus said when the laughter died down. "But just to make you all aware, we still practice keel-hauling out here in the Caribbean."

"What on earth is that?" asked the red haired woman beside Benjamin. Grace Logan was a freelance journalist from Pittsburgh who wore faded blue jeans and a tight white t-shirt that flaunted her breasts to maximum effect. Lightly tanned and with all her curves in the right places, she was a good-looking woman. But nevertheless, despite the fact that she would have looked more at home on a catwalk, she did not appear aloof or standoffish to the rest of the group and actually seemed genuinely excited to be there. Friendly and out-going from the moment she had come onboard, she had shaken everyone's hand with vigor, even warmly returning Brianna's kiss on the cheek.

"Keel hauling?" asked Marcus. "Well, I have to tell you, back in the days of the tall ships, that was a pretty gruesome punishment mutinous sailors in the British navy received. The unfortunate victim would have a rope tied to his waist before being thrown overboard. He would then have to endure being dragged the length of the ship, under the keel and then out the other side before eventually being pulled back up on deck again."

"Well, that sounds just horrible," Grace said with a shudder. "The poor souls must have been terrified."

"Horrible and deadly, love," Harvey interjected in his distinctive British accent. "I have never heard of anyone surviving to tell about it."

"Really?" said Grace.

"Too right. If the sharks didn't get them, they would surely drown."

"Okay, okay, so forget I said anything about mutiny," Benjamin said with his hands up in a gesture of surrender.

Marcus nodded and smiled as everyone laughed. He felt things were going nicely and that this new group of passengers would work well together. They all seemed willing, enthusiastic, and sociable, apart for Harvey, who was older than the rest and still appeared a little standoffish even now that they were out at sea. But then, Marcus knew every group had its own different and distinct characteristics. There was always a joker, he had found, usually a chatty one and, more often than not, someone who rubbed everyone else the wrong way. The trick was to identify the different personalities from the start so he, as captain, could handle them correctly and get the best out of each and every one of them. Marcus was not just a born sailor but a skilled crew manager as well. Although his youth disguised the fact, he had years of experience at this sort of thing, handling boats and people alike. But the real truth was that sometimes keeping the peace among a group at sea was harder than any storm he had ever faced.

"All right then," he continued after a short pause. "Before we get started with the first lesson, I would like you all to take a look inside the folder I gave you when you boarded. Somewhere in there among the notes and charts, you will find a small plastic envelope."

There was a pause, a combined rustling, and murmur of conversation as everyone searched their folders and eventually produced their envelope.

"Now that envelope you are holding is for your passports and any valuables you might like put in the safe in my cabin."

"What about our phones and tablets?" Harvey asked suspiciously. "I suppose you want us to give you them as well?"

Marcus raised a palm in a calming gesture. "First of all, Harvey, relax, man. Putting your passports and valuables in the safe is simply an offer and is not in any way compulsory. If, for any reason, you want to keep them on you, that is perfectly fine by me."

Harvey did not reply, just muttered something beneath his breath.

"But I can guarantee, between here and the Virgin Islands, you are going to get wet a number of times. And you might very well also get thrown around a bit if the wind picks up. So, that being said, I would advise you all to put your valuables in the safe to avoid them getting soaked or broken." He looked back at the British man. "And secondly, Harvey, as far as your phone is concerned, I think you will find your signal went dead as soon as we left Miami harbor."

As if on cue, the boat dipped into a small trough and they were covered by a light, misty spray that enveloped the deck. Without speaking, the British man pulled out his phone and examined it.

"Phones, iPods, tablets...every electronic device that connects you back on land is useless out here. All those little gadgets you thought you just couldn't live without, well, they are now just lumps of plastic and wiring. You see, out here, they are—quite literally—dead in the water."

"Bollox." Harvey muttered bitterly as he put his phone back in his pocket.

"But again, all of you technophiles can relax. I promise, you will get a signal once we near Saint Thomas." After a brief pause to let the information sink in, Marcus continued. "Guys, my advice to all of you is to look on the bright side and enjoy the peace. Really, that is what I always do. With no distractions from the outside world, you will find you can focus better and enjoy the experience far more. Oh, and by the way, if any of you don't have a digital watch, I will be happy to lend you one for the duration of the voyage."

"A digital watch?" Benjamin asked, looking puzzled.

"Yes. You will need it for celestial navigation."

"Wait a second, this was definitely not in the bloody brochure, mate," Harvey snapped with a scowl. "Having no phone signal? I mean, totally unacceptable. I bloody well need my phone for work."

"Well, I'm sorry if it's an inconvenience," Marcus said with an air of authority. "But, like it or not, Harvey, it was explained in the email sent to each of you when you signed up."

"Okay, Marcus, but how are we going keep in touch with shore?" Grace asked with a hint of concern. "In case of an emergency, I mean?"

"Don't worry about that. There is a VHF radio in the main cabin for emergencies," Marcus said with a comforting smile. "Starting tomorrow, I will be checking in with our office back in Miami at six o' clock every morning."

"Just, like, once a day?" asked Brianna, sitting next to Jayden with her arm hooked lovingly around his waist.

"Sure, that is really all we need," said Marcus. "Out here, we are on our own. We just check in to let them know our position and course for the coming day. That's it."

"But what about weather forecasts and shipping reports?" Harvey asked sarcastically, still not looking happy at all that he was being forced to do without his phone. "I take it you do at least check them?"

Marcus took a deep breath and nodded an affirmative. He

had met the British man's type before and already knew how he would have to handle him. Harvey was some sort of su-permarket chain manager back in England. He was used to giving instructions to his underlings, not taking them. He was also too used to getting his own way, so Marcus felt it was vitally important he showed him who was boss from the start. Not in a rude or aggressive manner, of course. After all, this was supposed to be a fun holiday. He would show him in a firm, authoritative way. A captain needed to be in charge, plain and simple.

"Harvey, this is not the North Sea or the English Chan-nel," Marcus said commandingly. "The weather out here in the Caribbean is not as changeable as you might be used to back home. Apart from hurricane season, of course, you will find that the wind out here is pretty constant and sailing conditions fairly routine. But, as it happens, I do use the VHF to listen to the coastguard weather report every morning at six-thirty. Apart from that, as a rule, the radio only stays in standby mode for incoming calls. And, as for your phone, like I said before, you can keep it on you or put it in the safe. That is totally up to you."

Harvey did not look happy but said nothing. He shrugged and muttered something beneath his breath as he slipped his phone out of his pocket and dropped it into his envelope. Marcus kept an eye on him as he did, wondering if he was going to be this confrontational throughout the rest of the voyage. He watched as he licked and sealed the envelope before writing his name on it with a black felt-tip pen that was handed around the group. When this was completed, he leaned forward and dropped it into the plastic bag Marcus held out before them.

"Okay," Marcus said when it was done. "I am going below to store these in the safe. I made a pot of fresh coffee in the galley, and there is fruit, croissants, and a few different cere-als on the counter for you to help yourselves. If anyone would like breakfast, I suggest now is the time to get it. We will meet back up here on deck in thirty minutes to start the first lesson."

As the group rose and began to split up, Jayden and Bri-anna were the first to leave, holding hands. Shortly after that, Grace and Benjamin moved out, chatting and laughing like two old friends as they headed below for coffee. And then, almost as if he was reluctant to rise, Harvey finally got up and moved slowly toward the bathing platform at the stern to light up a cigarette and sit alone.

As Marcus stepped aside to let them all pass by, he spotted something on Benjamin's arm that caught his attention.

"Hey, man, is that blood?"

The small, black-haired New Yorker stopped, turned, and raised his eyebrows questioningly. "Excuse me?"

"There," said Marcus, pointing to the thin trickle of dried blood visible on Benjamin's left forearm below his short sleeve. "I think you have a cut there."

"Oh that?" asked Benjamin, immediately raising his right hand up to cover it. "Nope, it's nothing. Nothing at all. I just scratched my shoulder at work yesterday. Snagged it on the corner of a mainframe computer while I was replacing the motherboard. It's really just a paper cut, that's all. Nothing to worry about. Probably should have put a bigger dressing on it."

"Well, look," Marcus said. "If you do need another bandage or some antiseptic, the first aid kit is in the forward storage locker on the port side." Then, when he saw the puzzled look on Benjamin's face, he said, "That's the small storeroom on the left, beside the galley."

"Oh, okay," said Benjamin. "Thank you, Marcus. I think I will just have my coffee first, then head on down there and see to it."

"You should," Marcus advised. "Really, man, the last thing you need out here is for a cut to become infected."

Grace glanced at Marcus with a little mischievous wink and a knowing smile as she and Benjamin passed him on their way into the cabin. "Don't worry, Captain. He will be fine," she assured him quietly. "I promise you, I will stay with him and make sure he doesn't forget."

≈ ≈ ≈

Isabella moved quickly along the floating dock until she reached a multilingual directional sign. Reading it, she turned right and walked down one of the narrow wooden piers toward the far end. About halfway there, something caught her eye and she stopped, lowered to a crouch, and slipped a small penknife from her jacket pocket. She proceeded to scratch at the brittle wood near the water's edge, raising the blade up to the light to examine it more carefully.

"Blood," she whispered, taking a small clear evidence bag from her inside pocket and scraping the red splinters into it. She sealed the plastic zip lock and placed it and the penknife back into her jacket.

When she stood up, she continued down the pier, scanning the ground carefully as she went. At the end, she found an empty berth to her left with a large hand-painted sign that read *Wild Rover Training Cruises*.

"You okay there?" a voice asked from her right.

Isabella turned to see a man emerging from the cabin of a small wooden yacht moored on the other side of the pier. The name *Dirty Nellie* was painted in bright red script across her bow. Shirtless, the man held a large wrench and had a broad oil smudge across his chest. Tanned and good-looking, she guessed he was in his late thirties or early forties.

"Hi, I'm looking for Patrick Brophy," she said.

"Well, you've found him," he said with a hint of an Irish accent and a friendly smile. "What can I do for you?"

"Mr. Brophy, I believe you own the *Wild Rover* ship?"

"You mean a sailing catamaran," he corrected her, still smiling politely. "But yes, I own her all right. At least, I should say I own half of her. My son, Marcus, owns the other."

"Oh, and where is he?"

"What's this about?" asked Brophy, obviously deciding to find out a little more before parting with any further information.

Isabella showed him her badge. "I am Detective Garcia from Miami Metro."

"Shit, I hope you're not here about those parking tickets."

Isabella was not amused by the remark. This was a serious situation. She was feeling under pressure and was growing more and more impatient as the clock ticked down. "Mr. Brophy, where is your son?"

"He's not here."

"Where has he gone?"

"Out to sea," Brophy said with a shrug. "Set sail this morning for the Virgin Islands with a fresh group of trainees.

They're on a four day competent crew course."

Isabella pursed her lips, cursing to herself. Although the old man said he saw them leave, she had somehow been hoping he was mistaken, that maybe they had simply moved to another part of the marina or were just setting out for an hour or two on a short trip.

"Look, what's going on here, Detective? Is my Marcus in some kind of trouble?"

"Can you reach him by radio?" she asked, ignoring his questions.

"No."

"No?"

"No. Not before you tell me why you are here and what exactly is going on."

Isabella considered her options for a moment, and then, realizing the best course of action was simply to level with him, decided to come right out and tell him what had happened.

"Well?" he asked impatiently.

"Did you by any chance see the fire on the other side of the bay last night?" she asked.

"Of course I did. Couldn't miss it. I was woken by the sirens."

"Well, we chased a suspected murderer into the boatyard around midnight, cornered him in the shed that went up in flames after he killed one of our detectives."

"You don't say? Shit, I'm sorry to hear that."

"They found human remains in the ashes this morning, Mr. Brophy. My colleagues think we got him, but I am not so sure it is the same guy we were chasing."

"You don't think it's him?"

"No."

"Okay, so who could it be?" asked Brophy.

"I really don't know. A bum, a security guard, a fisherman?"

"Then, that would mean this murderer escaped you?"

"Yes, I am almost certain he did," she replied. "Mr. Brophy, I believe he set that fire as a diversion. I think there is a chance he gave us the slip in the darkness and confusion, and that he somehow managed to reach the water's edge and make his way over here to this side of the marina."

"Hell, then maybe you should be talking to old Ben Cleary at the main office," said Brophy. "He was working last night. If anyone was knocking around, he would definitely have seen them."

"I have already spoken to him," she said. "He told me to come see you."

"Me?"

"Yes. He said five people came through here around that time. He said they were all passengers for your boat."

"That's right," Brophy said thoughtfully. He rubbed a hand across his stubbled chin. "Marcus took them out this morning, like I said. There should have been six of them by the way."

"Six?"

"Yes, we took six bookings, but one was a no show."

"Oh, really?"

"If I were you, I would not read too much into it, though. It's really no big deal. We get no shows all the time. Our clients sign up through the website. They pay one third up front and then pay the remainder when they turn up on the day of the cruise." He shrugged. "If they are not here when the boat sets sail, they lose their deposit. Unfortunately for us, it happens at least once or twice a season."

"I see. Well, what would the chances be of us taking this boat out and maybe catching up to them?"

"Lady, are you serious?" Brophy ran his hand across his chin once more. "You have got to be kidding if you think the old *Nellie* here would stand any chance of outrunning a craft like the *Wild Rover*."

"Why? What's so special about it?"

"What's so special about the *Wild Rover*? Well, let me see," he said in a slightly sarcastic tone. "First of all, there is the little matter of her having a two-and-a-half hour head start on us, as well as more than twice the sail power. Then, and not to put too fine a point on it, comparing the *Wild Rover* to this old girl here is like comparing an Olympic athlete to an arthritic old lady out for a morning stroll."

"So how about that radio call then?" she asked. "If I could just talk to your son, perhaps I could warn him, maybe find out if any of his passengers are acting strange or appear wounded."

"Wounded? Hey, you didn't mention anything about that."

"The detective who was killed last night may have gotten a shot off before he died. Up until now, I had not considered the possibility that he may have hit anything, but on the way down here, I found traces of dried blood at the edge of the pier." She took out the small plastic evidence bag and showed him the red-stained splinters inside. "I can't be sure, of course, but there is a chance my partner wounded the guy, or at least winged him enough to draw blood."

Brophy was not as impressed as she thought he would be. Looking at the bag, he grunted his disapproval. "Detective, let me tell you something about life in a harbor. This here is a working marina. People get scratched and cut all the time around these parts." As if to prove the point, he held out his right hand to show her a gash on his palm. It was fresh but not too deep and had stopped bleeding. "I got this one the other day while Marcus and I were changing a fuel line on the *Dirty Nellie*."

"Oh?"

"And look, who's to say what you found there isn't just fish blood? It's not unusual to see the occasional pier angler out here or returning sailors carrying their catch back to their cars and pickups."

Isabella shrugged. He had a point. *Shit.* Although she did not want to admit it to herself, in her mind, there was now a bit of doubt setting in regarding her find.

"Look, I want to help you. I really do. So, if it will make you happy, I will raise Marcus on the radio and see what he has to say about it."

"Thank you," Isabella said with a sigh of relief. "I do appreciate your cooperation."

Brophy motioned for her to come onboard the small yacht, leading her through the hatch and down the four wooden steps into the cabin. Unlike the *Wild Rover*, the *Dirty Nellie* was a mono hull, a smaller, single hull vessel. She bobbed up and down and seemed to lurch from side to side as they moved about. The cabin lay below deck. The inside was quite cramped but clean and surprisingly cozy, boasting a polished oak table to one side with red cushioned seating. There was a small sink and a two-ring burner to the left of the steps and a navigation table with a VHF radio to their right. The ceiling and wall panels had been freshly varnished. It was neat and tidy and offered a cool refuge from the intense heat outside.

"Hey, this is actually pretty nice," Isabella said with a hint of surprise as she scanned the surroundings. She had never set foot on a boat before and had never imagined it could be so homey.

"Well, thanks for saying so," Brophy said, seeming genuinely pleased with the compliment. "Marcus and I have been working on her for a couple of weeks."

"Really?"

"Sure. She was full of holes when we bought her. Got her cheap at auction last month. In fact, you should have seen the inside of this cabin when we first brought her in. Looked like a gang of hobos had been partying in here. Smelled like it, too."

Isabella smiled a little.

"I'm still working on the bilge, though," Brophy continued with a serious look on his face. "We've definitely got a problem there, still got a few hairline cracks below the waterline. But hell, as long as I keep the pump running while I seal them, it's not a big deal."

Totally mystified by what he had just told her, Isabella simply shook her head and raised her eyebrows.

Brophy smiled, no doubt realizing she did not have the slightest clue what he had been talking about. "I take it you don't know too much about pumps and bilges then?" he said teasingly.

She shot him a glance to indicate she knew the joke was at her expense, then motioned toward the radio to remind him why in fact they were there. As she stood beside him, he sat down at the navigation table. Within seconds, he had the VHF switched on.

"Miami calling the *Wild Rover*," he began, keeping his gaze on hers as he raised the small handheld microphone to his mouth. "This is Miami marina calling the *Wild Rover*. Do you read me, Marcus? Over."

Nothing came back across the radio, just a gentle crackle of white background noise when he released the transmit button. He tried again. "This is Miami marina calling the *Wild Rover*. Marcus, do you read me? Over."

After a couple more attempts, he finally lowered the mike and turned back to Isabella with a look of resignation. "I'm sorry, Detective, but it doesn't look like he is manning the radio at the moment. Maybe they are all up on deck. You see, we have a standing agreement to only communicate at six each morning, starting tomorrow. That is, of course, unless there is an emergency."

"But it should still be switched on?" she asked suspiciously. "Shouldn't it? For emergencies, I mean?"

"Of course, it should," he said a bit irritably, at last showing a little concern. "It's called standby mode. And I really can't explain it. But yes, it is very unusual that he, or one of the crew, did not hear our broadcast and get back to us."

Isabella checked her watch, noting it was only nine a.m.

"So, is it possible their radio has been sabotaged in some way?" she asked with concern.

"Lady, are you trying to frighten me?"

"Well, Mr. Brophy, if I am, I am not going to apologize for doing so. Because, sir, the truth is this guy frightens the hell out of me. He is not your usual killer. Trust me. He is a clever son-of-a-bitch. And dangerous, too. He has already shown he will not hesitate to deal with anything or anyone who gets in his way."

"Well, look, Marcus is no idiot, Detective. He really is a strong, independent kid. Street-wise. Tough by nature. Been taking care of himself for most of his life. If there is any hint of trouble onboard the *Wild Rover*, I am confident he will be able to handle it accordingly."

"I hope you are right, Mr. Brophy. I really do. But if this killer is on board that boat, as I suspect, your son and the other passengers will have no reason to be on their guard. And if we can't alert them to the situation, I believe they are in even graver danger. I swear to you, this guy is too clever to show his hand. He is a predator, a ruthless animal. So believe me when I tell you, if he thinks for a second his true nature has been discovered, or if he even suspects your son or anyone else is on to him, there is no telling what he is capable of doing."

This struck a chord with Brophy. He fell silent for a while, appearing lost in his own thoughts. "All right then, Detective," he said after a short pause, switching the radio back to standby and rising to his feet.

Isabella looked puzzled. "All right then, what?"

"All right then, we will do it your way. If you really are serious about what could be happening on the *Wild Rover*, I guess I have no option but to take you out after her."

Isabella was surprised by his sudden change of heart. "After the *Wild Rover*? But didn't you say there was no way you could catch them? Something about an Olympic athlete and an old lady?"

"Yeah well, shit, let's just say I am willing to give it a shot now. And, by the way, if you want to come with me, that's fine. If not, that's fine, too. I'll go alone."

"How soon can we leave?" she asked without hesitation.

"Say, about fifteen minutes. Just enough time for me to top up the fuel tank and load some extra food and a spare battery."

"Fine," she replied, turning for the steps to head back up on deck. "I have just got to make a phone call."

While Brophy milled about between the *Dirty Nellie* and a large wooden storage box fixed to the pier, carrying water, a spare battery, and other supplies on board, Isabella stepped toward the bow of the boat and took out her cell. Leaning against the side rail, she flipped it open, quickly thumbing down through her contacts until she came across the one she wanted.

"Garcia?" said the gruff voice of Captain Franklin. "You had better be calling me from your apartment."

"Captain, I've got a lead," she said, turning to make sure Brophy was not listening. When she saw he was back on the pier, still busy making preparations, she continued. "After you left, I had a hunch and made my way over to the marina on the other side of the harbor."

"A hunch, you say?"

"Yes. You see, I got to thinking. If our guy did use the fire to cover his escape, there is really only one place he could have gone without passing me or McGregor, and that was across the water to the other side of the bay. The boatyard is completely fenced in and the parking lot's two entrances were blocked by patrol cars."

"You're saying he swam all that way?"

"Sure, it is possible, isn't it?" She paused for a second but got no reply. "Or hell, he may have paddled a small boat. Who knows? There are plenty of them tied up around the harbor wall."

Still no reply.

"Anyway, I spoke to the marina manager here on the other side of the bay. He saw five people arrive in the couple of hours following the fire. It seems they left at around six to go off on some sort of training cruise to the Virgin Islands. The problem is they will be gone for about a week."

She paused for a second, but again there was still no reply, only a stony silence on the other end of the phone.

"Anyway," she continued, ignoring the lack of response. "After I found small traces of blood on the dock here, I made contact with the boat's owner and got him to try them on the radio."

"Don't tell me," interrupted Captain Franklin. "No answer?"

"Not only that, it now seems the owner is starting to have his doubts, too. He has offered to take me out on his other boat to see if we can catch up to them. I was thinking, if you could make a call to the coast guard for me, see if they have a ship in the area that could—"

"Garcia, I want you to listen to me," said the captain. "And I want you to listen good."

Isabella knew what was coming by the tone of his voice. Franklin was a good guy, a sympathetic boss who usually stood up for his detectives whenever necessary. But he had his limits, of course, and could only be pushed so far.

"I want you to leave that marina and go home right now. That is a direct order. You understand? And, as far as the coast guard is concerned, under no circumstances are you to contact them or anybody else about this half-baked hunch of yours. Mike Ryan is dead, you got that? And his killer is lying beside him on a table in the Medical Examiner's office."

"Captain, you are making a mistake."

"No, Garcia, you are the one making a mistake. Now, once again, let me be clear. This is a direct order. Go home and get some sleep. Take a shower, change your clothes, and then report back to the station this afternoon."

As soon as the call was over, she immediately made another, waiting until she heard detective Brewster's voice before speaking.

"Hey, Byron, it's me."

"Garcia?" Then, in a low whisper, he said, "You know, girl, I am sitting here outside Franklin's office, and his door is open. He sounded *really* pissed off."

"Yeah? No, he's not that pissed off."

"Don't bullshit me. I heard every word he just said to you."

"Okay," she conceded. "But forget about that for a minute. I need a favor."

"Uh-huh?" he said guardedly.

"I am going to leave something for you in the manager's office in the Miami marina. You know the one opposite where we were this morning?"

"What are you leaving?"

"It's a blood sample I found here on one of the piers. I want you to get the lab to run a check on it. See if it matches anything in their database. Or, at the very least, get a blood type and run it against the Regazzoni woman and Mike Ryan."

"Shit, that could take days," whispered Brewster.

"Then ask them to put a rush on it for me," she said. "But most important of all, Byron, don't let the captain find out or there will be hell to pay."

"Why can't you do it yourself?" he asked.

"Let's just say I am going to be out of town for a few days."

"You know, Garcia, for a woman, you have got one hell of a set on you."

"You'll do it?"

Brewster was silent for a long moment, then whispered, "You owe me, Garcia. I mean that."

As she closed her phone and slipped it back into her pocket, Brophy approached her on deck with a look of concern on his face.

"Hey, everything okay?" he asked quietly. "You still coming with me?"

"Sure, I am. But I've just got to leave something back in the marina office first."

"Well, I will be casting off in five minutes."

"Five minutes? That's fine by me," Isabella said. "I'll be back in four."

CHAPTER FOUR

THE NORTH STAR

Marcus stood behind Benjamin Goldstein in the cockpit as he gripped the *Wild Rover's* wheel for the first time, patting him on the back to calm his nerves and confirm he was doing just fine. Benjamin seemed a mild-mannered individual, not too quick to voice an opinion but open to the ideas and suggestions of others. He was a friendly guy who always seemed to have a smile on his face, and Marcus took a liking to him from the start. He did, however, suspect Benjamin did not have too many friends back in New York. He probably spent most of his time at work. Marcus could almost picture the stubby bespectacled man going home each night to his apartment, empty, except for his computer games and cats.

When Benjamin first arrived, he told the group he was an IT technician for a large bank in Manhattan, and his job was all consuming, but he said it had become boring and routine of late. He needed to get out and meet *real* people, to inject some adventure into his mundane, non-eventful life. That is why he signed up for this cruise, he had explained to those standing around the galley eating blueberry muffins and drinking coffee that morning. To get away from work for a while and experience an adventure firsthand, rather than reading about it in a magazine, or watching it unfold in one of his games.

After breakfast, Marcus had conducted their first lesson about safety and the basic principles of sailing. As always, he had gone through the fundamentals, teaching everyone about running and reaching, the different points of sail which describe a boat's course in relation to the wind. He had explained how running downwind was when the boat sailed with the wind coming directly from behind. To do this, they had to ease the mainsail out as far as it would go, he told them. And because this would block the forward jib sail or Genoa, they would then either have to lower it and replace it with the spinnaker, or set it out on the windward side of the boat, a position known as gull-wing or butter flying.

Reaching, the other point of sail, he went on to explain, was when the boat travelled perpendicular to the wind. A close reach was when she sailed toward it, a broad one, when she sailed away, and a beam reach was when she sailed at a right angle to it. The latter was a precise point of sail, he explained, one in which they would have to put the sails out at approximately forty-five degrees.

When he was satisfied everyone understood what was being explained, Marcus went on to show them how to hoist and lower the mainsail and jib and then taught them how to quickly deploy the spinnaker to gain more speed on a run. It was an interesting and fun morning for the crew to be out on the ocean in the sunshine and fresh air, getting stuck in, feeling the thrill and satisfaction of being free and moving across the ocean under sail.

Later that afternoon, Marcus had a one-on-one, personal lesson with Benjamin, so he could take control of the wheel and learn how to steer a course. It was going well, and the small bespectacled New Yorker seemed to be genuinely having fun. During the lesson, Grace, Jayden, and Brianna took a short break below deck. Harvey remained in the cockpit as an observer, smoking cigarette after cigarette and looking on with mild interest as the lesson unfolded. While Marcus and Benjamin chatted at the wheel, the British man sat without speaking, leaning back on the cushioned seating with his legs crossed and arms folded. He was being his usual, anti-social self, eyeing the other two with a smug look on his face with that now familiar air of aloofness about him.

Marcus did not usually mind or feel uncomfortable with someone watching. But, in this particular instance, he could sense the older man sitting in judgment of his teaching methods. Harvey's problem was that he had a bit of a superiority complex, Marcus had concluded. Since he had sailed before on a small Heron dingy in the Lake District back in England, he seemed to fancy himself as an expert on the subject. More than that, and more annoying as far as Marcus was concerned, he had also been drinking alcohol alone in his cabin while the others ate lunch earlier that afternoon. Marcus could smell it on his breath and, although he decided not to mention it, was not happy about it. A few beers on board a boat at night was something to be looked forward to and enjoyed, but drinking during the day was not to be condoned or recommended. Due to the dangerous nature of moving under sail in the middle of the ocean, it was very important to keep a clear head and have your wits about you at all times.

Harvey's most annoying attribute that day was that he was simply bored by the basic maneuvers Marcus was teaching and was not at all shy about hiding the fact. He had interrupted him on a number of occasions during his talk that morning with little side notes and comments to show everyone he already knew what was being explained. He blatantly up and told them how he felt he was not getting his money's worth, wanting Marcus to hurry up and move on to the more complicated stuff. But that was not how it worked. Marcus was too experienced to be bullied or harassed into skipping ahead for his sake. He was a good teacher who took his time, making sure that everyone on board understood what was going on and, more importantly, were having a fun time.

By seven in the evening, although the sun would not go down for another couple of hours, the sea was calmer and the air noticeably cooler. It was a welcome shift after the intense heat of the day, and some of the passengers had begun wearing light sweaters and cardigans. While Marcus and Benjamin guided the *Wild Rover* from the cockpit, Jayden and Brianna had gone to their cabin to shower and rest before dinner. Harvey had teased them when they announced this. Sniggering like a teenager, he had bid them farewell with a knowing smile and a wink, embarrassing the newlyweds by telling them not to make too much noise when they were "at it," and not to overexert themselves.

Grace was down in the galley preparing dinner. She had happily volunteered to be the first, saying how much she enjoyed cooking for friends back in Pittsburgh and would try her best to make their first evening meal on board a special one. As the afternoon wore on, she spent quite a while searching the cabinets and lockers for ingredients and utensils, banging pots and plates, muttering aloud on a couple of occasions about how she was not accustomed to working in such cramped conditions.

She eventually got the situation under control apparently, growing more acclimated to the layout and kitchenware at her disposal. She noticeably became more organized and finally got things up and running. Within a short time after this breakthrough, a mouth-watering aroma of simmering pasta and frying steaks and peppers filled the boat, wafting up through the vents and open deck hatches. While it cooked away, Grace informed them all it would be ready in another thirty minutes or so, before freshening herself up and then getting busy setting the table in the main cabin. That proved to be no easy task, for as she did so, she had to contend with the constant pitching and rolling of the boat.

Up on deck, Marcus continued to advise Benjamin. "That is perfect. Really, really good. Turn the wheel slowly until you feel it start to resist." Marcus gestured for him to keep his left hand on the wheel while reaching for one of the nearby self-tailing winches with his right. "Now, as soon as you feel that resistance…" He waited for a few seconds, eyes on Benjamin. "Feel it?"

Benjamin nodded.

"Okay, good, now grab the winch handle and turn it clockwise until you feel the main sail tighten. Be careful, though. You don't want to see any give or flapping."

Benjamin acknowledged the instruction with an eager nod, his face full of concentration and excitement as he turned the wheel. Marcus had warned them not to point the boat directly into the wind, explaining how the mainsail would flap uselessly and the catamaran would come to a stop. So Benjamin kept one eye above as he proceeded, waited until it looked just right before reaching forward and winding the handle to tighten the sheet.

"Very good!" exclaimed Marcus. "You know, man, I am beginning to think you are a natural at this."

Benjamin's eyes beamed with pride. He took a deep, visible breath, and Marcus knew he was letting his lungs fill with the warm salty breeze. As he turned with a smile, there was a loud grinding *crunch* from above and the winch handle slipped and began spinning wildly. The cable ran back down with a screech until the main sail lost all of its tension and started flapping wildly in the heavy breeze.

"Way-hay!" Harvey gave a loud burst of laughter. "You forgot to lock down the winch, you plonker."

Ignoring him, Marcus sprang into action, moving quickly to Benjamin's left and grabbing the spinning winch handle with both hands. Seconds later, he managed to get it back under control and began winding it up again. As soon as he finished, he locked it down, stood back, and then examined the friction burns on his palms.

"Oh shit, I am so, so sorry," Benjamin gasped, sounding like he was about to cry. "Marcus, I hope you're okay. I hope I haven't broken anything."

"Broken anything? You could have ripped the whole damn mechanism out of its bracket," said Harvey.

"No, no, it's fine," Marcus assured him, blowing on his hands to cool them down. He cast an irritated glace in Harvey's direction.

"Are you sure? How do you know the winch is not damaged? Oh crap, I am so goddamned, fucking stupid."

"Look, Benjamin, everything is fine. This is how you learn," Marcus said, placing a steadying hand on his shoulder. He smiled reassuringly. "Now chill out, man. Come on, you are on vacation, remember? Believe me, I did much worse when I was learning to sail."

"Really?"

"Yeah, so stop being so hard on yourself. You are here to learn and to enjoy the trip. But you really won't do either if you don't start to lighten up a little."

Although still in shock, the small stubby New Yorker breathed a visible sigh of relief and, after a few seconds, even managed to return a weak smile. It was clear he felt better about the situation.

"Hey, Popeye, keep your damned eyes open," Harvey said a few seconds later from the seating area behind them, pointing up at the main sail that was showing signs it was losing tension once more. "You are fucking it up again."

Looking panicked by the remark, Benjamin adjusted the wheel to correct the situation. As he did, Marcus saw that, although his feelings were hurt, he was too engrossed in keeping the *Wild Rover* on course to defend himself against

Harvey's sharp tongue. Either that, Marcus decided, or he was just too mild-mannered to stand up to the older man. But Marcus was not, and he had just about had enough of the British man's bullshit. He did not like people like Harvey and was beginning to feel he was just an out-and-out bully who needed to be brought down a peg or two. So Marcus decided it was time to intervene, to put Harvey straight about his attitude and behavior.

"Hey, you know, you need to lighten up," he told the British man. "Everyone is here to have a good time, and we have all got to at least make an effort to get along. Tone it down, Harvey, okay? For your own sake and everyone else's."

"Tone what down?"

"You *know* what I'm talking about," Marcus said as he helped Benjamin keep the wheel steady. They had hit a small squall and the *Wild Rover* was starting to pitch and roll with the waves. "You need to quit the smart remarks and tone down that superior-than-thou attitude."

"Excuse me?" Harvey snapped back with a look of surprise, appearing offended by the remark.

Benjamin said nothing, keeping his eyes on the sea ahead.

"And while we are on the subject, I don't have a problem with anyone having a few beers at night, but your drinking during the afternoon has got to stop."

Harvey sat bolt upright with indignation, his eyes burning with rage. "Hey, you stop right there, mister. Who the bloody hell do you think you are talking to me like that? I will have you know I am a very powerful and influential man back on land. My word and opinion carries weight. But you, you are nothing but a kid with a big boat."

"Now listen—"

"And I will also have you know I paid damned good money to be here. So don't you think, for one second, that you can speak down to me or give me orders like that. I expect to be treated with respect while I am here. I will drink any time of the bloody day or night I damn well choose, regardless of what you say. Because, you know what, I am on my holidays and you are just the hired fucking help."

The cockpit fell silent for a moment, with both men staring intently at one another. Eventually Marcus spoke up, breathing a deep sigh before saying, "Okay, Harvey, look, I really don't want to fight with you. And I am definitely not speaking down to you."

"Oh no?"

"No, I am just trying to—"

"You are speaking to me like a bloody child."

"No, Harvey, I am not. Really. I am simply telling you that, for the next few days while we are all here together on this boat, you need to stop being so confrontational and at least try to get on more with the team."

"Bollox to that," Harvey muttered beneath his breath. "Bollox to you, and bollox to your team."

"Well, maybe if you stopped acting like a child, he wouldn't have to treat you like one," Benjamin said without turning around. It was clear he could not listen to any more.

There was a tense pause as Harvey cast his gaze angrily in Benjamin's direction. Marcus inhaled with a grinding of teeth, waiting for the backlash. Benjamin's comment, although true, was like adding coal to a fire and not really welcomed by Marcus now. He had been trying to get the British man to see sense, to tone down his behavior and join in the spirit of the voyage. But the fuse had been well and truly lit now. Benjamin's jibe merely served to ignite the already smoldering fire.

"Why you fat, incompetent twat," snapped Harvey. "How dare you—"

"Enough!" Marcus exclaimed. "That is enough. I mean it."

"And as for you," the British man spat, glaring back toward Marcus with eyes inflamed. "If you *really* knew what you were doing, you would have split us up into groups based on our experience. At least, that way, after paying so much money, I would not have to sit here and endure such an inept novice like him."

"Harvey, I have far more experience than you. Going through the basics together is supposed to be an enjoyable bonding process for the crew. It is all part of the vacation."

"Oh, I see. Is that right? So, how come I don't feel very bonded right now then?"

Marcus stared him directly in the eye and shook his head with a sigh. He wanted nothing more than to grab the obnoxious old prick and throw him overboard. But, realizing that was not an option, he raised a hand to try to settle things down. He needed to steady the ship and get them back on course. Otherwise, it was going to be a very long and uncomfortable voyage.

"Okay, okay, look. Calm down."

"Don't tell me to calm down," snapped Harvey. Then, jabbing his thumb in Benjamin's direction, he said, "I want an apology from that fat little smartarse."

"Look, how about this? What do you say we put this conversation on hold for a couple of hours? How about we all sit down to dinner together and, afterwards, you and I can go somewhere more private and talk this out in a calmer, more constructive manner? If you have any complaints or suggestions, I promise, Harvey, I will be happy to listen to them."

But Harvey seemed in no mood to calm down and stood up to face him. "Complaints? Oh, don't make me laugh. I *do* have complaints, mister, but I bloody well won't be discussing them with you after the way you have just spoken to me."

"Harvey—"

"No, when we get to the Virgin Islands, I am going ashore and telephone your company back in Miami. This whole setup is a joke. You are far too young and inexperienced to be doing this. I am going to inform them how you have spoken to me and I am going to demand a full refund and compensation for—"

Before he could finish his sentence, Benjamin suddenly released his grip on the wheel and stepped away as it spun violently back around. With her rudder turned to port, the *Wild Rover* immediately lurched to starboard and the heavy wooden boom came swinging around from the other side of the boat. It hit Harvey on the side of the head with a loud, ear-splitting *crack*, knocking him off his feet and sending him sprawling backwards over the side rail.

He let out a terrified scream as he fell, but somehow, against all the odds, he managed to grab hold of the rail with his right hand. Within seconds he was gone from their sight, left hanging precariously over the starboard side.

Marcus sprang into action with lightening reflexes. Although a few seconds earlier, he had actually wanted to throw the older man overboard himself, he now dove headfirst toward the side in a desperate attempt to grab his wrist.

Whimpering with fright, Harvey reached up to him with his left hand but was immediately knocked about by the motion of the boat. He attempted to gain a foothold, only to find the lacquered white hull too slick. A split second later, legs scrambling like a spider stuck in a bathtub, he lost his grasp on the rail and fell straight down.

"I've got you!" Marcus again lunged forward and managed to grab hold of his flaying right arm just in time.

The British man's feet entered the water, and he was going under when Marcus pulled him up by his wrist until he could finally reach it with his other hand. With a firmer grip now, he grimaced and groaned with the strain as he tried desperately to pull Harvey back up onto the deck by his right arm. But it was excruciatingly hard. He turned to Benjamin for assistance. "Grab his other hand and help me pull him back up!"

Benjamin made no reply. He appeared rooted to the spot like a rabbit caught in a car's headlights.

"Benjamin, what are you doing?" Marcus shouted. "Get over here and help me pull him up."

Once again, the short New Yorker looked on without speaking, a spectator, watching events unfold as if they were happening before him on a TV screen.

Marcus could not wait any longer. He summoned every ounce of energy and strength he had left and gave one last superhuman pull. Harvey's feet came out of the water, and he managed to swing his body up enough so Marcus was able to get a hold of his shirt. With a better grip, he pulled him up level with the rail. Marcus held him there long enough for Harvey to get his legs back in and roll his body over and back on board. The two men remained there on deck for a few minutes, side by side, both out of breath and panting with exhaustion.

"You...you bloody well did that on purpose," Harvey finally stammered in Benjamin's direction when the wind returned to his lungs. His face was pale and he was clearly shaken from his ordeal.

The bespectacled man simply shook his head, raising his eyebrows and turning his palms up in a gesture of innocence.

Marcus looked over at him too, not in accusation but simply searching for some sort of explanation as to what the hell had happened.

"The wheel, it just slipped right out of my grasp," Benjamin said with a gasp. "Honestly, guys. I swear to you. One second, I had it under control, the next...well, it just jerked suddenly and started spinning. There was nothing I could do."

≈   ≈   ≈

Miami Metro's aged medical examiner, Doctor Leo Walker, glanced up over the top of his bifocals to see Detective Brewster entering his autopsy room. Mike Ryan's body lay before him on the cold metal examination table, but on seeing Brewster approach, Walker pulled the light blue plastic sheet up over the dead detective's face out of respect.

"Evening, Doc. Any news yet?"

The older man looked past him with eyebrows raised in puzzlement. "Where is detective Garcia? I expected her here hours ago."

"Oh, she asked me to drop by and report back with the findings." Brewster replied as nonchalantly as he could. He knew well that, under normal circumstances, Isabella would have been hounding Walker for his report. Not wanting to spill the beans about what was going with her, he shrugged off the question.

"Not like her," Walker muttered with a shake of his head. He lifted a clipboard from the table and wrote on it. "Not like her at all. She is usually here before I make my first incision, almost standing over me and breathing down my neck as I conduct my autopsies."

"She is a pretty eager woman all right," Brewster said.

"Eager? Hah! Eager is one thing. But in her case, I think the word obsessive is far more appropriate."

Brewster shrugged. "Well, Doc, she is out following up on a lead. What can I tell you?"

"I suppose you want my initial report on these bodies? Detective Ryan, Mrs. Regazzoni, and the John Doe from the harbor?"

"If you would be so kind."

"You do know, of course, it is not procedure to divulge

any information until I have finished the full autopsies and until all the lab reports have come back?" He stopped writing and glanced up over his glasses again. "I could be struck off, you know."

"I doubt that," Brewster replied. He knew what was going on, that the older man was simply having a moan. Over the years it had become a bit of a ritual for him. All the detectives were aware of it. To get any information from Walker, you had to play along, to feign sympathy and show your appreciation that he was going out of his way regardless of the fact that there could be serious repercussions.

"Well then, let's just say I could get into a lot of trouble."

Brewster sighed wearily. It had been a long day and he was tired. "Shit, Doc, please, don't give me the run around on this. Not on *this* case. Just tell me what you've found so far and let me get back to it. Okay?"

"Off the record?"

"Of course. I just need something to start with. That's all."

"All right then. Follow me."

Doctor Walker laid down the clipboard and peeled off his white surgical gloves.

"Where are we going?" asked Brewster. "Can't you just tell me here?"

"Detective, I will have you know I have been in the same underwear for nearly forty-eight hours now. I have been up all night and have not eaten since God knows when. And what is more, to top it all off, my assistant called in sick, and I have had to spend the past eight hours poking around inside three dead bodies by myself."

"Hey," Brewster exclaimed disapprovingly, gesturing down at Mike Ryan's covered corpse.

Walker suddenly remembered the sensitive nature of the situation and breathed a deep, apologetic sigh. "I'm sorry, Detective. I know he was one of yours. But I really am tired and desperately need a cigarette and a cup of coffee. So, will you *please* just do me the courtesy of following me outside?"

A few minutes later, they sat side by side on the low brick wall outside the rear entrance of the ME building, their paper coffee cups perched between them. Walker lit a cigarette and furiously puffed on it, blowing clouds of swirling smoke up into the grayish blue sky. The sun was going down, but the evening was still quite pleasant, a gentle breeze blowing across the adjacent half empty car lot.

"You married?" the older man asked Brewster after a few minutes of silence.

"Yes I am, Doc. Got a small house up there in Oakland Park."

"Kids?"

"Two girls. Nine and six."

"That's nice. So, do they take after you or their mother?"

"Me? No, not at all, thank goodness. They have their mom's good looks. And they're really smart, too, like her. Heck, it's getting so I can't keep up with any of them."

"You happy?"

Brewster raised his eyebrows at such an unexpected and unusual question. But then, he thought about it for a moment and shrugged. "I guess I was, Doc, as much as anyone can be doing *this* lousy job."

"Was?"

Brewster sighed with a heavy heart. "Tish, my wife, took the girls to their grandma's a few weeks ago. She said she was sick and tired of spending so much time alone, not knowing whether I was coming home from one night to the next."

"It is a tough job," Walker offered sympathetically.

"Yeah, it sure is. You know, she said we need to take a break from each other. Can you believe that? She says she wants to give it a few weeks and then see where we go from there."

"Detective, you need to make a decision," the older man said with a quick drag of his cigarette. "You need to choose what is most important to you before it is too late."

"I already have," Brewster said as he knocked back the last of his coffee. "As soon as this case is done, I am planning to hand in my badge. I figure there has got to be something else I can do to make a living. Security maybe. Something that won't suck the life and soul out of me every goddamned day of the week."

"Well, good for you," said Walker. He took another drag of his cigarette and blew the smoke down toward his shoes. "You know, I was married once."

"Yeah?"

"Oh yes. But she left me about eight years ago."

"Shit, I'm really sorry to hear that, Doc," Brewster said sympathetically.

Walker waved it off nonchalantly with a hand gesture. "Don't be," he said quietly. "She was the biggest, meanest, most selfish bitch I have ever had the displeasure to meet. And I am sure as heck glad she's gone."

"Jesus, where did that come from?"

"Just telling it like it is," said the older man.

"Well then," said Brewster. "If you don't mind me asking, if she was that bad, why the hell did you marry her in the first place?"

"Darned if I know." Walker shrugged with a rueful sigh. He dropped his cigarette butt to the ground and squashed it beneath his foot. "Strange, isn't it? I suppose she must have had some good points when I met her. But you know what, Detective? I sure can't recall a single one of them now."

Brewster shook his head, not knowing whether to laugh or sympathize. "Doc, you are an odd old fish. You do know that, don't you?"

Walker nodded and then paused thoughtfully for a moment before saying, "You want me to give you those initial findings now?"

"Hell, yes. Yes, please. That would be good."

"Well, first off," Walker began with a sniffle. "Young Detective Ryan was killed by a single stab wound to the back of his right shoulder. It must have been one hell of a powerful blow, because it went clean through his collarbone, punctured his lung, and then severed his left ventricle. Death would have been instantaneous."

"Any match to that kitchen knife we found nearby?"

"Yes indeed, that was the murder weapon. No doubt about it. A serrated twelve inch steak knife. And, by the way, it was also the same blade that severed the Regazzoni woman's carotid artery. A perfect match."

"So, at least we can be sure it was the same guy," Brewster said with a degree of satisfaction.

"Most definitely. And, if you want my opinion, I would say he is probably a big man. Or at least a strong individual, judging by the amount of force it would have taken to puncture through to Detective Ryan's heart like that."

Both men fell silent for a moment, thinking back on the tragic events which had occurred.

"And the other one?" Brewster eventually asked. "The guy we pulled out of that boathouse?"

"Now that one is more challenging," Walker replied, unable to hide his keen interest and sense of excitement at the task of identifying the body. "He was burned pretty badly. Fingers and toes melted clean off. Ears, nose, even his genitalia."

Brewster winced but said nothing.

"I am having his dental x-rays checked at the moment, but don't expect any word back for at least a couple of days."

"Well, what about cause of death? Have you had a chance to establish any?"

"This is strictly off the record, mind you. Because until the lab work comes back and my final report is filed, nothing I am telling you can be used in court or made public in any way."

"Go ahead," said Brewster, now more intrigued. "I understand."

"Well, I can tell you, for sure, the man did *not* die in that fire."

"What? No shit?"

"That's right, Detective. His lungs were clean. Looks like he never smoked a cigarette in his life. But what's more important is no smoke inhalation. Which, of course, means he was dead before the building went up in flames."

"Shit. So Garcia was right," muttered Brewster. "Who would have thought it?"

"Indeed," said the older man.

"Anything else?"

"I believe he died from a single shot to the chest. At first, the wound was pretty hard to spot due to the fire damage, but the slug I pulled out looks like it came from a Glock thirty-eight."

"Mike Ryan's gun," said Brewster.

"Not conclusive," Walker continued. "Forensics are running tests on it."

"Thanks, Doc. Really, I owe you for this."

"Oh, one other thing, Detective. Your John Doe suffered

from psoriasis of the liver. It is almost twice the normal size."

"A drinker?"

"I would say a big drinker. Probably an alcoholic for many years. And what is more, I doubt if he was a very mobile individual."

"Oh? How do you figure that?"

"Well, he suffered from a medical condition known as limb length deficiency, meaning one of his legs is markedly shorter than the other. About three inches to be exact. Would have been quite noticeable when he was alive. He would definitely have walked with a pronounced limp."

"Thanks again, Doc." Brewster stood to leave but stopped as a thought crossed his mind. "Hey, Doc, promise me something?"

"What's that?" Walker asked with a look of curiosity etched on his weathered face.

"Promise me you will change those underwear?"

≈ ≈ ≈

Their first dinner onboard the *Wild Rover* was not the upbeat, happy occasion everyone had been hoping for. They ate heartily enough, their appetites strong from the fresh air and activity of the day, but there was an uncomfortable atmosphere that was almost impossible to break through. After what happened on deck a few hours earlier, there was now an air of tension and unease surrounding the group that was noticeable, a dark ominous cloud that signaled a looming storm on the horizon. There were a couple of bottles of red and white wine in the center of the table, yet no one was drinking except for Harvey. He was already on his second glass by the time they finished their starter of chowder with brown bread and butter. But instead of mellowing him out as one would expect, the alcohol only served to put him in an even fouler mood.

Jayden and Brianna were seemingly oblivious to what was going on, however. The newlyweds had emerged from their cabin a short time before dinner looking happy and refreshed and were now sitting side by side on the inside seat like two lovebirds. Earlier on, though, Jayden had not been doing so well. Suffering from a bout of seasickness due to the motion of the boat, he had looked pale and said he thought he might throw up. But, after swallowing a couple of Dramamine tablets Marcus had given him, he was now back to himself and full of energy. Marcus had explained how the condition came from changes to his sense of balance and equilibrium in the inner ear. At the time, Jayden acted a little wary of taking the pills, citing concerns about the possible side effects of dizziness, dry mouth, and drowsiness. But Marcus assured him he would be fine, and after a couple of hours of rest, as predicted, he arose like a veteran sailor, moving about on a fresh pair of sea legs.

Marcus and Benjamin sat together at the table to the left of Jayden and Brianna, while Harvey sat opposite them with Grace beside him on the outside so she could move back and forth to the galley as the meal progressed. Now and then, as he drank his wine, the British man would cast a venomous glance in Benjamin's direction. But the mild-mannered New Yorker had been warned by Marcus to ignore him and, following his captain's instructions, kept his head down and did not make eye contact at all.

It was an awkward situation for Marcus as well, since it was one of his main tasks to ensure everyone on the trip was having a good time. He had known his share of tough crews on previous voyages, of course, and had, on occasion, been forced to intervene in various arguments over religion, politics, and the like. But in all his experience at sea, he could not remember ever having to save one of his passengers from imminent death at the hands of another.

"Wow, this food is, like, amazing," Brianna said as she reached across the table to top up her plate with more pasta. "Grace, you must give me your recipe. This meal must have taken forever to prepare."

Moving from side to side with the motion of the boat, Grace brought in the main course. Shrugging as she cut into her steak, she raised her eyes to the young black woman and smiled. "Actually, Brianna, there's nothing really special about it. I just filled mushrooms with peppers and garlic, coated them in olive oil, and then put them in the oven for thirty minutes. That's all."

"Oh, girl, you are too modest." Brianna smiled.

"Well, thank you for the kind words, but it really is quite

simple to prepare. The only thing that was difficult, however, was managing to cook anything at all in that tiny kitchen."

She glanced up at Marcus. He smiled back.

"Well, I agree with Brianna," Harvey said aloud, turning his hate-filled gaze away from Benjamin as he buttered another slice of bread and stared directly into Grace's eyes. "The food is absolutely delicious, my love, and you should be commended for it. The steak, especially, cooked just the way I like it. In fact, love, it seems you are not just a beautiful woman, but you also have extraordinary culinary skills as well."

Grace smiled back awkwardly, looking uncomfortable as Harvey leaned in very close. "Why, thank you, Harvey. That is very kind of you to say."

Marcus breathed a quiet sigh of relief to himself, grateful the British man was being distracted from the tension at hand, even if for only a moment, his anger toward Benjamin being deflected. To hear him pay someone else a compliment was also a surprise to Marcus, since he had not heard him say one good word to anyone about anything since boarding that morning. It was clear the older man had an eye on Grace. He was obviously flirting with her. But, Marcus did not care. He was not about to question Harvey's motives. Not now. Not after what he had gone through and the mood he was in.

"Tell me, Grace," the British man continued. "You said you are a journalist. Is that right?"

"Yes," she said, moving back from him a little on her seat. "I freelance for a couple of small papers in Pittsburgh."

"Anything I might have heard of?"

"No, just trade magazines and a few free sheets. Unfortunately, I haven't gotten in with any of the bigger publications yet. So, until I do, it is a case of writing for anyone who will help me pay the bills."

"You know, I always thought journalism was quite a lucrative business to get into," Jayden said. "I have a friend back in Georgia who makes a pretty good living freelancing for the local papers."

"I think your friend is very fortunate down there in Georgia," Grace said with a shrug. "But, as far as Pittsburgh is concerned, I can assure you it is a dog-eat-dog profession. Unless you can get in with the bigger circulation papers, you are lucky if you can just eke out a living."

"Did you ever consider doing any modeling to supplement your income?" Harvey asked with raised eyebrows.

Grace looked puzzled. "Modeling? Me? What kind of modeling are you talking about?"

"Well, I happen to have a friend back in London who works as a photographer for the tabloids over there. I'm talking glamour photography, love. You know, topless modeling and all that. Very artistic and tasteful, of course."

"You must be joking?" she said with a look of shock.

"Oh no, love, I'm not joking. I am dead serious. Listen, I would gladly put you in touch with him. My friend, that is. You know, a girl like you could make some serious money."

"Like me?"

"Yes," he said nonchalantly, gesturing toward her with a wave of his hand. "You really have a super body, you know, and a great pair of tits. Very sensuous and natural looking."

"Lord Almighty!" Jayden exclaimed disapprovingly. "I really don't think this is very appropriate dinner conversation."

Harvey laughed at his shocked reaction, ignored him, and poured another glass of wine. As he did, an even more awkward silence fell upon the table, everyone looking to each other in disbelief at what Harvey had just proposed. There was no doubt he was disliked by all. He was not only a drunk and a condescending bully, Marcus thought with a sigh, but he had also shown himself to be a sexist to boot.

The young captain rubbed a hand across his chin and exhaled thoughtfully. Seeing how things could get out of hand very quickly and realizing the mood needed a serious lift, he decided to act. He stood up without speaking and disappeared down into the galley before returning a few seconds later with two six-packs of beer in one hand and a bottle of Cuban rum in the other.

"Right, me hearties. Help yourselves," he said as he placed them on the table and took one of the longnecks out. "Come on now, there are plenty more where they came from."

He snapped the bottle cap off on the edge of the table and gestured for the others to dive in and follow suit. Once everyone had a bottle in their hands, including Harvey, he raised his in a salute to them.

"As your captain, I would like to toast you all for helping

guide us safely through our first day under sail," he said. "Here's to the crew of the *Wild Rover*. God bless you all. May you have calm seas and fair winds no matter what course in life you sail."

Everyone raised their bottles and drank. As they did, the *Wild Rover* shuddered beneath them for a few seconds when its prow hit the ridge of an incoming wave and dipped into the trough. The hull creaked with the strain for a moment or two until the boat finally leveled out and once more became steady in the water.

"Hey, do you know any other nautical toasts?" asked Benjamin.

"Nautical?" Brianna repeated in puzzlement.

Jayden turned to her, nodding. "He means something about the sea, honey. You know, old sailor's proverbs and sayings."

"How about this," Marcus said after a short pause. "*Ships are the nearest things to dreams that hands have ever made, for somewhere deep in their oaken hearts the soul of a song is laid.*"

Tapping their bottles together over the center of the table, the crew of the *Wild Rover* said cheers to one another and took another long, thirst-quenching drink. It was a miraculous transformation that was not lost on Marcus. The mood lightened immediately and people began to smile and chat amongst themselves. Benjamin and Jayden started discussing computers and wireless technology but somehow ended up talking about God and the major world religions, while Brianna tried making polite conversation with Harvey about England, telling him how she and Jayden were planning to go there someday.

"You know, that was really beautiful," Grace whispered quietly to Marcus as the others spoke. She locked eyes with him from across the table and held him in her gaze for the longest time. "Did you just make it up?"

"No, he didn't," Harvey said with a smug smile, interrupting Brianna to butt into their conversation. "It's from a poem called *My Ship O'Dreams*, by Robert N. Rose." He had quite clearly set his sights on Grace and was attempting to put Marcus down in her eyes.

"Got any more?" she asked Marcus with a warm smile,

blatantly ignoring Harvey's comment and keeping her eyes fixed on the young captain.

It was becoming obvious to Marcus she was flirting with him. He did not know if she was genuine or not, wondering if she might simply be doing it to brush off Harvey's unwelcome attention. Over the years, Marcus was no stranger to being the target of some of his female crew's advances. It was usually just a holiday romance kind of thing, the fantasy of falling in love with the ship's captain while at sea. Nothing ever came of it, of course. Marcus was too experienced to get involved with any of the young ladies who signed up for his cruise. No, he knew that would not be professional and would surely cause problems.

There was, however, something about Grace he was attracted to. He could not deny it. She was a beautiful young woman and had a pleasant personality, coming across as a warm and kind individual. She seemed to be enjoying every moment of the cruise and was not afraid to jump in and help the rest of the crew when required. He liked that about her. She also did not put on an act or try to impress any of them. She was not a very materialistic individual that he could tell, which he also admired, not like a lot of the young women he had met lately. The majority of them, he found, were superficial, materialistic airheads who were ultimately only after one thing in life—a big wedding, an even bigger house, and a wealthy husband.

"*You cannot change the wind*," Marcus recited to Grace after a moment. "*You can, however, adjust your sails.*"

"Hey, I think I like that one even more." She smiled. "But you do realize you've set a precedent, don't you? We will expect you to give us a new one every night at dinner."

"Hell's bells, I know dozens of those old nautical sayings," Harvey said, butting back into the conversation. "You'll probably be fed up hearing them before the voyage is out."

Grace smiled, ignoring him and keeping her gaze on Marcus. "Don't count on it," she replied softly with a blink of her long black lashes and a glint in her eyes that spoke a thousand words.

"Hey, that reminds me," Benjamin said to her, leaning his elbows on the table, his religious debate with Jayden having come to an end without any clear winner. "I never did ask you about your friend."

"My friend?" asked Grace.

"Yes, I think it was Marcus who said you were supposed to have someone else with you on this trip?"

"Oh," she exclaimed with a sudden look of understanding and a thin, rueful smile. "You are right, Benjamin. I was supposed to come on this cruise with my boyfriend. Alas, unfortunately, he is no more."

"Oh damn, Grace, I am so sorry. Me and my big mouth again. I would not have mentioned it if I had known."

Grace laughed, seeming unfazed by it all. "It's fine, Benjamin, really. He's not dead or anything like that. I just meant that ship has long since sailed, as the sailors would say."

"So, like, what happened?" Brianna interrupted, having been eavesdropping on their conversation. "Did he cheat on you, honey?"

"Don't they all?" Grace replied philosophically.

"Uh-huh," said Brianna in agreement.

"But no, seriously. If you really want to know, I'll tell you." Brianna leaned forward. "Four weeks ago, when I booked this vacation, we were still dating. I thought he was one of the kindest, most attentive men I had ever met. Extremely thoughtful and very romantic."

"Flowers?" Brianna asked with wide eyes.

"Oh yes," said Grace. "Every day for the first two weeks."

"Wow."

"I really thought this trip would be ideal for the two of us. Romantic. You know, an adventure on the high seas and all that? Anyway, by the time the date came around to set sail, we were no longer a couple."

"Aw."

"I decided to come alone. I mean, you have to move on, don't you? You can't live in the past."

"Well, again, I am sorry," Benjamin said with a hint of embarrassment. "I honestly did not mean to stir up any bad memories."

Grace smiled, reached across the tabletop, and patted his hand. "Don't worry about it, my friend. I am a big girl, and I can handle myself."

"Amen, sister," exclaimed Brianna.

"In the end, I suppose my Mr. Perfect turned out to be

just another rat. I can honestly say, though, hand on heart, I am better off without him and am in a really good place at the moment."

"Hey, you know what? I have a toast," Brianna said loudly, reducing everyone to silence. "Now, it's not, like, a nautical one or anything, but how about we drink to Grace for preparing such a wonderful dinner?"

"To Grace!" They knocked their bottles together before gulping back their beers.

Grace smiled and bowed graciously. "Hey, in that case, what about the honeymooners here?"

"Now, that is a great idea," Marcus said, lifting his bottle.

"To Jayden and Brianna!" They all cheered.

"Bless you all," Jayden said, smiling. He wrapped an arm around his new wife lovingly as she snuggled into him with a contented smile. "I would just like to say that Brianna and I are having a ball. This is, hands down, the best vacation we have ever been on. And I guess we both want to thank all of you guys for being so nice and including us in this fantastic adventure."

"Yes. To you all," Brianna said with her own bottle raised, as everyone took another drink.

The conversations resumed above the gentle creaking of the hull, and the beer and rum flowed for over two hours. Marcus glanced toward Harvey at one point during the night and was pleasantly surprised to find him smirking at one of Jayden's stories. He poured himself a glass of rum and sat back in observation of his new-found crew. Benjamin was the joker, he concluded with a little smile, although a bit too meek and mild mannered for his liking. Brianna was, without a doubt, the chatty one among the group. Grace and Jayden? Well, they were just nice, friendly people who were easy to get along with and happy to follow any orders they were given. And then, of course, there was Harvey. The older British man, he decided, was the one to watch out for on the voyage, the one he would have to keep the closest eye on. But despite that, as the mixture of good food and strong rum caused a warm feeling in his belly, perhaps after such a rough start, they had finally hit some calmer waters. Maybe tomorrow would be an easier day, he thought optimistically, now that they had gotten to know each other a little better.

"So, who feels up for the first watch?" he eventually asked, noting it was past ten.

"I'll take it," Jayden offered with a smile.

Marcus liked the black minister from Georgia. As he had concluded a few seconds earlier, he was an out-and-out team player.

"Well, wake me up when you're finished, and I'll take the second," Benjamin said with a little burp as he sat forward and placed his empty bottle on the table.

"Okay," said Marcus. "How about this for a plan then? Tonight, Brianna and I will clean up and wash the dishes. Jayden takes first watch until twelve, Benjamin second until two. Grace, you stand watch until four, and then Harvey takes over for you until six. At that time, I will be up to listen to the morning weather forecast and report back to Miami. Once that's done, I will take over while you all drink your coffee and eat breakfast. Is everybody okay with that?"

Each person at the table nodded their approval. Even Harvey, who was now sitting back having downed the last of the rum.

"Well, if that's it then, I'm beat." Grace yawned as she stood and stretched. "I am definitely heading for bed."

As she did, her fingers locking together behind her head, her half-length t-shirt lifted up to expose her belly and the bottom of her pouting breasts. Marcus noted Harvey's eyes following the line of her body. He licked his lips like a dog eyeing a juicy bone. But Marcus said nothing, deciding it was just harmless ogling. He left the older man to his fantasies.

Minutes later, Grace left them for her cabin. Jayden kissed Brianna full on the lips before heading out into the cockpit to stand first watch. Harvey rose and turned heel toward his own cabin without saying goodnight. When he was gone, Marcus sat back with a sigh of relief and slowly turned around to Benjamin.

"Thanks, man. I owe you."

"For what?" the small bespectacled New Yorker asked with raised eyebrows.

"You know, for not going there with him earlier. When he was eyeballing you like that."

"Oh, I see." Benjamin laughed. "Look, don't worry, Marcus. I would rather not have any more dealings with that grouchy old fart than is absolutely necessary. So you can relax, *Captain Ahab*. I certainly won't make your job any more difficult than it already is."

And with that, he, too, was gone, off to his own cabin to get a couple hours of sleep before second watch.

≈ ≈ ≈

Just before midnight, Patrick Brophy emerged from the small cabin of the *Dirty Nellie*, expertly balancing two plates of scrambled eggs in one hand and two mugs of steaming hot coffee in the other. Isabella took hers from him as he sat down beside her and took a turn on the tiller. The sea was calm as they approached the northwest coast of the Bahamas, a warm southeasterly wind blowing from the island of New Providence, filling their sails, making conditions just right for their journey south in pursuit of the *Wild Rover*.

While Brophy checked their heading on the compass once more, Isabella sipped tentatively at the coffee, raising her eyebrows in surprise at how good it tasted. She then turned her attention to the eggs he had handed her with a hint of suspicion. She dug her fork in and turned them over to check they had been properly cooked.

"Go ahead," he said. "They won't poison you. I may not be a great chef, but I do at least know how to scramble an egg."

"Is that right?" she said as she raised the fork to her mouth.

"Yeah, it's true. Actually, I guess you could say coffee and scrambled eggs are my specialty."

Isabella began eating, swallowed, and then went for some more. "Hey, these aren't half bad," she mumbled while chewing. "I didn't know I was so hungry until now."

Brophy rose to adjust the mainsail while she ate, tightened the jib, and then returned to the small, cramped cockpit to sit beside her again. He polished off his own food in three or four mouthfuls before downing half of his coffee in one gulp.

"You want more?" he asked.

Isabella smiled politely and said, "No, thank you. I'm good."

"By the way, I tried the VHF again," he said after a pause. "Any luck?"

"No, Marcus is still not answering. Damnedest thing. I can't explain it at all."

Isabella nodded.

"I guess the only thing to do now is to wait and try again at six tomorrow morning."

"Your scheduled transmission?"

"Yeah, he should definitely be at that radio then. Same as me. Listening out for the morning shipping forecast."

Isabella nodded again. She sat back and took a deep breath of clean fresh air as she stared up toward the night sky. The stars stretched above to the heavens, a magnificent sight she had never fully had time to observe before now. Back on land, her nights were usually filled with the same stuff as her days. Police business. When she was not on duty, she could usually be found in her Fort Lauderdale apartment, going over files and reports. That was her life these days, but she had no complaints.

Isabella loved her job. She lived for it. She ate, slept, and breathed Miami Metro. It was in her blood. The life of a homicide detective was the one she had chosen many years ago, the one thing she was better at than anything else. Isabella lived for the job and never questioned the cost or the consequences to her personal life.

"They really are spectacular, aren't they?" Brophy commented, joining her in looking up at the stars.

"Mmm," she replied without lowering her eyes. "You know something, I don't think I have ever seen them so clear."

"Well, that's probably true. They always appear brighter out here than on land. Didn't you know that?"

"No, I guess I never thought about it before."

"Yeah, it's something to do with light pollution."

"Light pollution?"

"That's right. You see, on the water there is no reflective glow shining back up from the cities and towns. You get a much better view of things out here at sea." He leaned his head to the left and pointed upwards. "Do you see that really bright one there? That's Polaris, the North Star."

Isabella looked up to where he was pointing and nodded, feeling a sense of amazement. "Oh right. Yes, I see it."

"You know, sailors have been steering by that star for centuries now. It's sometimes called the *Guiding Star*, because it is the brightest one in the constellation Ursa Minor. It's also very close to the North Celestial Pole."

"Right. I think I have heard of Ursa Minor," she said with interest. "That's the bear, isn't it?"

"Yeah, that's the one," said Brophy. "The little bear. But the important thing about it is, because Polaris lies in a direct line with the axis of the earth's rotation above the North Pole, it seems to stand motionless in the sky. All the other stars appear to rotate around it. That's what makes it an ideal fixed point from which to navigate by."

"You love all this stuff, don't you?" she said, lowering her gaze to meet his.

"What stuff?"

"The sea, I mean. The stars, boats, all of this stuff."

"Are you kidding? Of course, I do. Who in their right mind wouldn't?"

Isabella nodded without replying. A few days ago back in Miami, she might not have understood so readily, never having even been on a boat before. But sitting with him out there beneath the stars, she could suddenly see and feel the appeal for herself.

"You see, out here there is *real* freedom," he continued enthusiastically. "Probably the only real freedom left on earth. Back on land, there are nothing but rules and regulations to tie you down. So, to imagine you have found freedom back there is just not true. But out on the water? Out here, things are a hell of a lot simpler, believe me. Out here, right now, there is only the *Nellie*, the sea, and us. That's it. Period. No one or nothing else. No rules or regulations. Just us, Detective. We live or die by our own decisions out here. Now that is freedom. And *that* is what I love about it."

"You're not seriously suggesting that we don't need rules?" she asked. "You do realize laws are what keep civilization from self-destructing."

"On land, sure," he replied. "You are right there. But, out here? On the water, the reality is it's just us against nature and all her beauty and dangers combined."

"That simple?"

"Yeah, really, that simple," he said without hesitation.

"You see, Detective, the ocean can be magnificent, but it can also be crueler than any criminal you have ever known. The trick to survival out here is not to take it for granted and to keep your wits about you when things get rough. Oh, and above all else, to show it the respect it deserves."

Isabella leaned back again and returned her gaze skywards. "I guess it is kind of different out here. Like another world."

"So what's your story then?" Brophy asked after a few minutes of silence.

"Me?"

"Yeah, what is a land-loving detective like yourself doing out here in the middle of the Caribbean?"

"I've already told you," she said, lowering her gaze from the sky. "I am after the murdering animal that got away from me in the boatyard last night."

"Yes, but why you?" he asked.

"What do you mean by that?" she said with a hint of irritation.

"I mean, why you? Where are all the other Miami detectives? How come they are not out here, too? Why is this so personal to you?"

"What makes you think it is?"

"I have eyes, don't I? And a brain?"

"I don't know you well enough to answer that second one," she said.

Brophy chuckled. "Well, it's good to see you still have a sense of humor."

Isabella took a deep breath, blinked slowly, and said, "Look, do you really want to know why it's personal to me?"

He nodded without saying anything.

"Okay then. First of all, this guy is vicious. He is a cold-blooded son-of-a-bitch who cut the throat of a young woman in Hialeah last night. And not in a hot-blooded rage or an act of robbery, mind you. No, this animal murdered her without provocation as she tended to her newborn baby. Her husband slept in the next room for Christ's sake."

"Shit."

"He then went on to kill my partner, Mike, a young, newly promoted detective who was put under my wing. Mike trusted that I knew what I was doing and would keep him safe. This killer I am chasing, Mr. Brophy, stabbed my partner in the back with the same knife he used on that woman. Mike was a good kid. He did not deserve to die like that. You know, his wife and baby did not deserve to lose him like that either."

Brophy remained silent, listening, simply shaking his head in sympathetic understanding.

"So you see, that is why I am so anxious to catch up with him. This animal leaves nothing but death and misery in his wake. I don't know what started it, and right now, I really don't care. All I do know is I am going to find him and finish this before he gets the chance to kill anyone else."

"Okay," said Brophy. "But what makes you so certain he is on the *Wild Rover*?"

"Look, don't ask me how," she said with a shrug. "But I just know he is. Call it instinct. Call it a hunch. But I just *know*. And I am rarely wrong about these things."

"Is that right?"

"I have been doing this for eighteen years now, Mr. Brophy, six in uniform and twelve as a detective. So, you see, for your son's sake and for everyone else's on board that boat, I hope to God we catch up to them before this guy makes it to the Virgin Islands and disappears off the radar, or worse, gets spooked and lets loose again before they know what's happening."

They were silent for a while, both sitting in the tiny cockpit, looking out to sea. Isabella felt drained after letting it all out like that. It was not something she normally did. She usually kept her cards closer to her chest. But she felt she owed Brophy an explanation since he had as much at stake in this as she did, even if she might have scared him a little in the process.

"Hey, why don't you start calling me Patrick?" he eventually said, breaking the silence.

"Huh?"

"Yeah, I think it's probably time you cut the *Mr. Brophy* shit, don't you?"

Isabella nodded with a wry smile. "Okay."

"Okay, what?"

"Okay, Patrick," she said with a hint of a smile.

"That's better. And what about you?" he asked. "Do I still have to call you Detective, Detective?"

"Isabella," she said.

"Cuban?"

"Puerto Rican. My mother and father came over to Miami in the sixties. I take it from your accent, you are Irish?"

"Born and bred," said Brophy. "Came to the US just after Marcus was born."

"So he doesn't have the accent?"

"No, not at all. He's a yank through and through." He was silent for a moment, checking the compass before pulling one of the sheets to tighten the mainsail. "All right then, Isabella," he said when he was finished. "Well, let me tell you how things stand at present." He pointed to one of the numbers on the small LED screen beside the compass. "See that? That is our GPS position, and that other one to the right of it is the *Wild Rover's*."

Isabella leaned in for a better look and then nodded.

"Now, according to it, we are still about a hundred nautical miles behind them. But, assuming they won't be sailing at full speed through the night, and if this south-easterly keeps blowing in our favor, we might just get close enough to make contact with them by tomorrow afternoon."

"Close? How close?"

"Close enough that they can spot one of our flares."

"No," said Isabella. "No flares."

"What?"

"That would alert *him* we are in pursuit."

"Look, let's cross that bridge when we come to it. Right now, I am still hoping we can establish radio contact at six tomorrow. If that happens, I will make sure Marcus is alone before I tell him what is happening. I will explain the situation and tell him of the possible danger they are in. He's a bright lad. He will work with us and slow down enough so as not to be noticed, just enough for us to come alongside and board."

"And if we don't establish contact?"

"If we don't? Well, then we will have no choice. We'll just have to get close enough so he can spot our flare on the horizon behind. I know you don't like the idea, but if that happens, he will immediately turn around and come back to see who is in distress. Your guy, if he is on board, may not even realize what is happening until it's too late to do anything."

"So we are sailing at full speed through the night?" asked Isabella.

"*I* am sailing through the night," Brophy said, stacking the two coffee mugs on the empty plates. "You, Isabella, are going down to get some sleep."

"No, I'm not. If you are staying up, then so am I."

Brophy handed her the plates. "Look, anyone could see you are exhausted. And I really am going to need you in good condition tomorrow when we catch up to them. So, please, don't fight me on this, okay?"

"It *has* been a long day," she conceded, suppressing a yawn. "And I am tired."

"Well, on this boat, I am the captain." He smiled. "And right now, your captain is telling you to go below and sleep."

Isabella stood up with the dishes in her hands, signaled her compliance, and moved toward the cabin hatch. "Hey, mind if I use your radio before I call it a night? I need to run a check on the names of those passengers you gave me."

"Sure, knock yourself out," he said. "Do you want me to show you how to operate it?"

"You are forgetting I'm a cop."

"Oh, yeah," he said with a nod. "Well, in that case, go right ahead then."

"Promise you will wake me up if there are any developments?"

"I promise," he replied. "Oh, and by the way, if you want to take a shower, there are fresh towels in the cabinet above your bed. And if you need a change of clothes tomorrow, you will find some clean t-shirts and tracksuit pants in the side drawer unit."

"So, what time is breakfast on this cruise?" she asked with a little smile as she slid back the hatch and headed down into the main cabin.

"Room service comes on about six," he called after her as she disappeared.

Once inside, Isabella dropped the dishes into the sink and headed straight for the navigation table. She fired up the VHF and tuned into the Miami Metro Operational Control Center.

"This is Detective Isabella Garcia," she said to the young

female controller who answered her call. "Badge number six-eight-nine-three. I repeat, six-eight-nine-three. Over."

"What can I do for you, Detective? Over."

"I need to get a message to Detective Byron Brewster in Metro Homicide," she said. "Tell him I need him to run a check on five names in connection with the Regazzoni murder in Hialeah last night. Over."

"Go ahead, Detective," replied the controller. "Over."

"The names are: Jayden and Brianna Kingston from Georgia. Harvey Hawkins, male, from London, England. Grace Logan, a female, from Pittsburgh, and finally another male, Benjamin Goldstein from New York City. Over."

"Got that," said the controller. "I'll pass your message on to Detective Brewster. Is there anything else? Over."

"No," said Isabella. Then, in a whisper, she said, "Wait. Yes, there are two more names I would like him to check out."

"Go ahead, Detective."

"Ask him to run a background check on Patrick Brophy from Miami and his son, Marcus."

"Okay, anything else?"

"No," said Isabella. "That's it. Just tell Brewster he can reach me on this channel day or night. That is all. Thanks, control. Over and out."

CHAPTER FIVE

THE FLAMINGO CLUB

She woke the next morning with a fright, disturbed by the sound of rustling at the foot of her bed. Still half asleep, Grace sat upright, rubbing her eyes, only to discover Brianna kneeling down before her, going through her large canvas carry-on bag. She watched the young woman in disbelief for a few seconds, unnoticed by her, as she had her head almost down inside the bag and was preoccupied in the search through Grace's belongings.

"What do you think you're doing?" Grace asked, fully awake now, swinging her legs out of the bed and placing her bare feet onto the varnished wooden floor.

"Oh, hi," Brianna said looking up, an innocent smile on her face as if this was a perfectly normal situation. "Why, girl, you startled me."

"I said, what are you doing in my bag?" Grace repeated.

"Oh, it's, like, such a glorious morning. I was just looking to borrow your camera," Brianna said, forcing another weak smile as she stood up. "You know, to take a photo of the sunrise. I didn't think you would mind."

"The sunrise? Are you kidding me?"

"No, honey, it really is beautiful out there. You should come and see. The sun has just come over the horizon, and the orange light is reflecting off the clouds and the water. Jayden said it's as if the Lord, Himself is waking the world for another day."

"But, but why would you sneak in here to take my camera without asking?" Grace demanded, not at all convinced by Brianna's explanation.

"Well, I...I really didn't want to wake you, Grace. It's so

early, you see. I thought you might be, like, exhausted after standing watch last night."

Grace was silent for a few moments, considering what had been said. Eventually, deciding to give the young woman the benefit of the doubt, she took a deep breath and let it out with a sigh. She leaned over and opened the bedside locker, produced a small digital camera, and handed it to her. "Okay then. Here. I'm sorry for getting angry, but you really should have asked first."

Taking it in her hand, Brianna nodded silently, lowering her head like a child who had just been scolded. Grace stepped forward, grabbed hold of the brass door handle, and opened it. But as she did, Brianna suddenly began crying.

"Oh Lord, Grace, I am so confused."

"Hey. What's the matter?" Grace asked, more puzzled than ever by this sudden outburst of emotion.

Brianna swallowed hard without reply and began wiping her eyes with the corner of her sleeve.

"What's wrong?"

"Grace, I wasn't looking for your camera at all. Oh, I feel so ashamed. I am truly sorry for lying to you like that."

"Look, what on earth is going on?"

Brianna emitted a deep sigh and lowered her eyes to her feet, looking embarrassment. "I...I was looking to see if you had any birth control pills in your bag."

"What? You're kidding. Why on earth—?"

"It's Jayden, you see. Oh my Lord. He found mine the other night in the hotel and went crazy, threw them in the trash, and called me all sorts of horrible names. Oh my, it was awful. Just awful. The first fight we have ever had. He stormed out of our room and was gone all night. I was, like, so upset, Grace, crying for hours. But then he called from the marina and said he had calmed down and was sorry. He told me he loved me, and I said I loved him, too. So, he said I should check out of the room and get a taxi to the marina. It was four in the morning, Grace. I was, like, all alone and so scared. We met up with each other there, just before we boarded. But he was, like, hugging me and saying he loved me and asking forgiveness for his temper. I know everyone thinks we are such a happy couple, but the truth is, well, ever since the wedding, he has been having these terrible mood swings. It is truly a side of him I have never seen before."

Grace motioned for her to sit down on the edge of the bed so they could talk. She took a tissue from the locker and handed it to Brianna to dry her eyes. Then she sat beside her with a comforting arm around her shoulder. "I don't really understand what you're telling me, Brianna," she said as the young woman continued sobbing. "Why on earth would Jayden flip out when he found your birth control pills?"

"Oh, you don't know him. He is such a religious man, Grace. I mean, don't get me wrong. I have my faith, too. Lord Almighty, we met at our local Church when we were teenagers. But Jayden, well, he, like, absolutely lives and breathes it. He believes that any form of birth control is an out-and-out sin."

"Oh, I see."

"He wants us to start a family right away, Grace, but I am still young. I'm only twenty, and well, I want to wait a year or two so we can enjoy life as a married couple for a little while. You know?"

"Of course."

"I'm not being selfish, am I?"

"Of course not," said Grace, wrapping her arm tighter around the young woman's shoulder. "But you have got to stand up to him, Brianna. You have just got to. If you don't do it now, he will take control of you for the rest of your life."

"Oh, but I love him, Grace. I really, really do. I don't know what I would do without him."

"I know, honey, but you have to learn to stand up for yourself. Men are controllers by nature. Believe me, I know all about it. You have to stand firm and be yourself. Otherwise, you will lose your identity."

≈ ≈ ≈

Marcus was making his way back from the storage room when he passed Grace's cabin and heard voices. He stopped in the open doorway without the slightest idea of what was going on, looking in with a broad smile on his face. "Morning, ladies. How are the heads after last night? Hey, I hope you two are not plotting a mutiny in here."

But then he saw the tears in Brianna's eyes as she

jumped up and hurriedly brushed past him. She tried to raise a smile as she went by, but it didn't come off. Her eyelids were red and bloodshot.

"Shit, I'm sorry I interrupted you like that," he said to Grace with a look of concern, leaning a hand against the doorframe when Brianna was gone. "Is everything okay? Can I help?"

Grace smiled and shook her head at him. "Girl stuff," she said.

"Oh, right," he said, feeling slightly embarrassed. "Say no more."

"No, really. It's nothing to worry about. Nothing at all."

"All right then, if you say so." Marcus raised his palms to indicate his acceptance of her meager explanation. He was content to leave it alone, whatever the hell it was. The very mention of *girl stuff* was enough to let him know he should not go poking his nose in where it was not wanted. And besides, he had really been hoping for a more peaceful day after the trouble he'd had with Harvey during the previous one. "So, tell me, Grace, how did things go on watch last night?" he asked, switching to a subject he knew a bit more about. "Everything okay?"

"Believe it or not, I really enjoyed myself. You will probably laugh, Marcus, but sitting out there in the darkness with only the stars for company was kind of like a spiritual experience for me."

"Hey, I'm not laughing," Marcus said. "In fact, I understand exactly what you're talking about. Sitting out there really puts things into perspective, doesn't it?"

"Wow, yes, yes it does. You know, two hours alone with my own thoughts was probably worth a year's therapy back in Pittsburgh. I think I really got my goals straight and saw through a lot of the bullshit in my life. Things I had not even contemplated before."

"Well, it is a big part of the sailing experience," Marcus said. "That, coupled with the fresh air and feeling of freedom and adventure. There really is nothing else like it in the world."

"If you had said that to me last week, I think I would have thought it was a sales pitch. You know, trying to get more passengers for your cruise? But now, I really do know what you mean, Marcus. Out here on the ocean is like rising above the rest of the world. Really, I'm not kidding. It feels like we have taken a step back and can see everything more clearly. So thank you for all of it. Because this is more than a vacation for me. It truly is a life changing experience. And I am having the most wonderful time."

"I am glad to hear it," he replied with a smile. "Hey, Grace, since you are up, I'm going down to put on a pot of coffee before I check the forecast on the radio. Why don't you come on up when you're ready and grab a bite of breakfast with me."

"Sure, that sounds great."

"Right so, I'll just leave you to get dressed."

Grace looked down. She was naked except for a pair of white panties and a cut-away t-shirt that barely came down over her breasts.

A few seconds later, Marcus reached the galley to make the pot of coffee only to find Jayden had beaten him to it. He was standing there smiling that warm, friendly smile of his, a steaming cup in one hand and a large blueberry muffin in the other.

"Good morning, Captain," he said cheerfully. "Another glorious day at sea. But I do have a confession to make."

"Oh?"

"Yes, I think I've just beaten you to the last muffin."

"Enjoy. It's all yours." Marcus smiled as he poured himself a cup of the coffee and then followed Jayden up the steps to the main cabin, joining him at the table.

As he sat, the wind outside shifted slightly and the boom swung from port to starboard. As the Wild Rover pitched and then rolled, they were forced to grab the edges of the table to stay erect. It remained like that for a few seconds until the boat leveled and finally became steady again.

"So, how is that seasickness of yours?" Marcus asked.

"Completely gone, thank God," Jayden said with a smile.

"And how was your night? First watch go okay?"

"You know, I saw some dolphins swimming along with us for about fifteen minutes," Jayden said with a smile. "Lord, those creatures can really move, can't they?"

"You know, some sailors believe dolphins swimming alongside their ship is a good thing, an omen sent from Poseidon, the God of the sea. A blessing, if you like. A sign of good luck for the rest of the voyage."

"Oh, that is just pagan superstition," scoffed Jayden.

"Is it?" said Marcus. "I don't know. Given a lot of the rubbish we are asked to swallow nowadays, I can think of worse things than that to believe in."

"Nonsense. As a God-fearing man, I have to tell you that it is foolish to hold sway with any of those kinds of superstitions. I have no time for it. The Bible is clear on such matters. And anyway, surely someone educated like yourself doesn't either."

"Hey, you never know," Marcus said with a shrug. "When things turn bad out here, I mean hurricane bad, I've seen atheists bless themselves and God-fearing men throw salt over their shoulders. You see, Jayden, I think when it comes right down to it, most people will pray to anyone and do just about anything to survive."

"Well, I think we will have to agree to disagree on that one," said Jayden. "Because I believe we are all tested in our lives. True, there are weak individuals among us, but I firmly believe it is at those times of peril when we must embrace our faith more than anything else. Remember, Marcus, the Lord is always watching."

Marcus smiled politely before finishing off his coffee with a gulp. He then moved over to the navigation desk. As Jayden watched from the table, he sat down before the VHF and raised the microphone as he turned one of the dials. While Jayden looked on finishing his coffee, a gradual change of expression appeared on the young captain's face. It was clear that all was not well.

"Hey, is everything okay over there?" Jayden asked with an air of curiosity.

"Damn this piece of junk," Marcus muttered as he flipped the power switch back and forth. He stood up and leaned over the radio to inspect the back, tugging at the wires that went into the unit.

"What's the matter?" asked Jayden.

"I don't know. But there doesn't seem to be any power," Marcus said, perplexed. "I can't get the damn thing to fire up."

"Did you check the main fuse?" A voice spoke from the

galley steps.

Marcus turned to see Benjamin approaching with a carton of orange juice in one hand and a banana in the other. He placed them on the table beside Jayden and came over to take a closer look. Marcus moved aside as the bespectacled man expertly unplugged the wires and turned the small VHF around to inspect the back. He twisted a circular knob to the left of the power unit and popped out the fuse. He held it up to the light for a few seconds before muttering something and returning it to its original position.

"Well, your fuse is okay," he said with an air of confidence. "There could well be a short in the power unit, though."

"You know about radios?" Marcus asked with a look of surprise. "I thought you said you were a computer guy?"

"Computers, radios, if there are circuit boards, transformers, or transistors involved, I am definitely the one to call. You know, I was the president of my college radio club for two years running."

"You see? Ask and the Lord shall provide," Jayden said cheerfully, smiling over at Marcus from the table.

"So, would you like me to take this thing back to my cabin and get it going for you?" Benjamin asked matter-of-factly. "I have a small electronics tool kit in my haversack."

Marcus patted him on the shoulder with genuine gratitude. "You know what? That would be great, man. But for the time being, I would rather you just sit yourself down and have breakfast with us."

"Are you sure? It probably wouldn't take more than a half hour. I can take apart and reassemble these things blindfolded."

"No, I'm sure. Thanks, Benjamin, but I would rather you relax for a while. There is no hurry. Besides, I was only going to tune in to the weather forecast. But, given that the conditions look pretty good today, I think we will be okay for a while."

"But what about checking in with your base in Miami?" asked Benjamin.

"To hell with it. Don't worry. I will do that as soon as you get us up and running. But there really is no immediate panic. If you can just get it working some time before lunch, I will check in with Miami late and explain what has happened."

"That's fine by me," Benjamin said as he returned to the table to drink his juice and eat his banana. "In any case, I'll take a look at it when I'm done. And don't worry, Marcus, I will definitely get you back on air. I promise. Even if I have to rebuild the darn thing from scratch."

"Great. Well, guys, after breakfast, I was thinking we might do a few more hours on celestial navigation. Then, I would like everyone to get another chance at steering a course. It might be nice to work the sails a little more and maybe also get a bit of tacking experience."

"Sounds like we have a busy day ahead," said Benjamin.

"Oh, by the way," Marcus said, pointing toward his shoulder. "How is that arm of yours?"

"My arm?"

"Yeah, did you manage to get the bleeding stopped?"

"Oh, my arm. Why, yes," Benjamin said with a nod and a broad smile. "Grace put antiseptic and a larger bandage on it. My own personal nurse. Once she did that, it was fine."

≈ ≈ ≈

Detective Byron Brewster shifted uncomfortably on the Lewinsky's sitting room couch with his notepad balanced precariously on his lap as Alexander Lewinsky tried in vain to comfort his sobbing young wife. Sarah Jane had not stopped crying since she'd heard the horrific news about her best friend, Gina. She was sitting opposite Brewster on one of the large cushioned chairs with Alexander perched on the armrest beside her, leaning down with his hand gently rubbing her back. He took a box of tissues from the coffee table and pulled one out. He placed it in her trembling hands and then sat back a little as she loudly blew her nose.

"This is a nightmare. I know it's not real. It can't be."

"There, there," Alexander whispered as he leaned closer and placed an arm around her shoulders.

Brewster sat in silence, head bowed, sneaking a quick glance at his watch when they were not looking. Time was against him, and he needed to get this thing wrapped up as soon as possible. He felt bad for the grieving young woman, but he desperately needed to move on with the investigation before the trail went cold. If he was honest about it, up until last night, he had not believed there was a trail to follow at all. As far as he had been concerned, like the rest of his colleagues, Mike Ryan's and Gina Regazzoni's killer was dead, and the only thing worth investigating was why he did it. Brewster had agreed with the captain about the body in the boathouse. At the time, against his better judgment, he had genuinely felt Isabella was wrong about the suspect escaping. And, when she'd asked him to investigate behind the captain's back, he'd felt like she had handed him a poison chalice. But, at the time, that was neither here nor there as far as he was concerned. Regardless of whether he believed her or not, Brewster owed Isabella Garcia for saving his ass on more than one occasion over the years. He was not about to let her down, so he set about the investigation as if it was his own, determined to see it through to the bitter end.

Earlier that morning, when he questioned them, the Regazzoni's neighbors confirmed that they were a lovely, young couple who kept to themselves and never bothered anyone. The husband, Richie, was an affable guy. Sure, he worked a lot, but when he passed them in the street, he always said hello with a warm, friendly smile.

Brewster was beginning to think that this was all just a tragic series of events. The deeper he dug, the more he was convinced that the Regazzoni's were desperately unlucky. They were proving to have been an average, law-abiding couple who, seemingly, did not have an enemy in the world. This was leading him to believe Gina's murder was simply an act of random violence. A break-in gone wrong, he figured, or possibly, the work of a sexual predator who had gotten cold feet and panicked, killing his victim before making his escape.

"I am sorry about this," Alexander said apologetically, his wife still unable to speak through the sobbing. "This has hit Sarah Jane so hard. Heck, it has hit us all hard."

"That's all right," Brewster replied with a wave of his hand. "It is quite understandable. These things are extremely difficult to bear, Mr. Lewinsky. It can be hard to accept the fact that there are people out there who are capable of committing such evil acts."

"Have you any idea who he is?" asked Alexander.

"I'm sorry?" Brewster said, raising his eyebrows in puzzlement, not having fully heard the question over Mrs. Lewinsky's sobbing.

"The killer, I mean. The body that was pulled from that fire down at the harbor?"

"Oh, right."

Sarah Jane blew her nose and stopped crying for a moment, anxious to hear what the detective might have to say. Alexander took the soggy tissue from her and dropped it onto the coffee table.

"Well, so far, the body has not been identified," Brewster said. "But the medical examiner is working on it as we speak."

"Death was too good for him," Sarah Jane said with pure, unadulterated hatred in her voice. "For what he did to our poor Gina, I hope he burns in hell for eternity."

As Alexander squeezed his arm a little tighter around his wife's shoulders, Brewster shifted in his seat and flipped open his notebook. "Would you mind if I asked a couple of questions?" he said quietly. "Just for the file."

"Of course. Go ahead," said Alexander. "Sarah Jane and I are here to help in any way we can."

"Any way," she repeated with a sniffle.

"Good. Thank you," Brewster said. "Well, I guess the first thing I need to know is how was Richie and Gina's marriage?"

"Hmm?" Alexander asked with a hint of surprise.

"I just mean was everything okay between them? Was there any history of trouble? Anything causing them to fight or argue?"

"Of course not," Sarah Jane said irritably. "I cannot believe you would ask that. Poor Richie idolized Gina. And Gina, God rest her soul, well, she loved him back just as much."

"Yes, their marriage was very strong," said Alexander in agreement. "They were both excited to have Joshua home and were looking forward to life as new parents."

"I really am sorry to have to ask these questions. I know it is a painful time for you both, and I don't want to seem insensitive, but I hope you understand I am just doing my job. You see, it is sometimes necessary to ask these sorts of things for the final report on the investigation."

"Of course," said Alexander. "We do understand, as I'm

sure you understand that we are still very raw. But keep going, Detective. Please."

"Let me see," Brewster continued, leafing through his notebook. "Oh yes, have either of you spoken to Richie since this terrible thing happened?"

"I tried calling his cell this morning, but he didn't answer," said Alexander.

Sarah Jane started crying again. "Poor Richie. He must be devastated. What will become of him now? All alone with a little baby to raise?"

"As far as I know, he is staying at his brother's apartment in Homestead while forensics have the house sealed off," said Brewster. "I am meeting with him this afternoon and will pass on your sympathies. And as far as the baby is concerned, I believe Gina's mother is taking care of him for the time being."

"Oh Lord!" said Sarah Jane. "Not Margie!"

At Brewster's puzzled face, Alexander leaned forward to explain. "You see, Detective, Gina's mother, Margie, is not the most responsible person in the world. The thought of her caring for little Joshua is quite difficult for us to take. The thing is she has a bit of a drinking problem."

"She is a lousy drunk is what she is," said Sarah Jane. "Poor Gina would be horrified to think she was looking after little Joshua."

"Well, look," Brewster said thoughtfully. "How about this? I will have social services give her a call to make sure everything is okay. Maybe they can look in on her to keep an eye on how she's doing."

"That would be good," Alexander said. "We would greatly appreciate it."

"Now, just another couple of questions before I go," Brewster said. "Mr. Lewinsky, I believe you are one of Richie's oldest friends. Is that correct?"

"He is his best friend," Sarah Jane said proudly. "He and Richie go all the way back to when they were in high school together."

"And Gina?"

"Oh, Gina met Richie while he was studying nursing in Tallahassee. We all became friends and started going out on double dates. When they got married, I was Gina's matron of honor and Alexander was Richie's best man." She paused for a moment as the tears welled up in her eyes. "Oh my God, I've just remembered something. Gina asked us to be Joshua's godparents."

Alexander handed her another tissue and began rubbing her back again. Brewster waited for a moment while she composed herself.

"I wonder if either of you know anything at all about their finances?" he asked.

"Excuse me?" Alexander said. "Finances?"

"Yes, you wouldn't happen to know if they were having any kind of difficulties? Financially, I mean."

"No, not that I know of. But why would you ask that anyway? Shouldn't you be discussing those sorts of things with Richie?"

"Like I just said, I haven't had a chance to interview him yet," Brewster said. "You see, he was suffering pretty badly from shock the other night, so the doctor gave him a sedative. I decided to give him a day, to talk to friends and colleagues first. You know, just to get a little background information before I sit down with him."

Brewster caught a look on Sarah Jane's face. It was just a fleeting glance toward her husband, one that passed in a split second and would have gone unnoticed by anyone else. But Brewster was not just anyone else. He was damned good at his job and was trained to pick up on such expressions. He knew there was something she was not saying. "It's just that I found their latest bank statement in one of the kitchen drawers," he said, keeping one eye on her to see if her expression changed again.

"Is that legal?" asked Alexander. "I mean to say, without a search warrant and all?"

"Oh, we don't need one when a murder has been committed on the property," Brewster said.

"I see. I never knew that."

"Anyway," Brewster continued. "It is probably nothing, not worth mentioning, but it does seem their account was overdrawn quite a bit."

"Like I said, we wouldn't know about that."

"I contacted the branch manager, and he told me how Richie had recently applied, unsuccessfully, for an increase to their overdraft allowance. You wouldn't happen to know anything about that, would you?"

Alexander took a deep breath, glancing fleetingly down at Sarah Jane. Brewster caught the look again and hoped this time they might be a bit more forthcoming. When he saw Sarah Jane give her husband a nod of approval, he raised his pen to the notebook and sat forward to listen.

"All right then, Detective, I shouldn't really be telling you this, but I suppose you will eventually find out for yourself. When you talk to Richie, I mean."

"Of course. Go on," Brewster said, leaning forward a little more.

"Well, I don't quite know how to put this."

"Richie has a gambling problem," Sarah Jane blurted out. She exhaled sharply on doing so, almost as if she had just unburdened herself of a dark, troubling secret that had been weighing her down.

"Is that right?" said Brewster, jotting *gambler* in capital letters into his notebook.

"Yes, it's true," confirmed Alexander. "It all started when we were in college. He began placing small bets on basketball games to help pay for his tuition, and for a while there, he could not seem to lose even if he wanted to."

"Isn't that the way it always begins," said Brewster.

"It was like Richie was a genius or something. He would look at the spreads and instinctively know which games to bet on."

"And then what happened?"

"I don't know exactly what happened." Alexander shrugged. "I really don't. All I do know is, somewhere along the line, he started losing. Sometime after he and Gina got married, I think."

"Tell him about the loan," Sarah Jane interrupted.

Brewster raised his eyebrows.

"Okay then," Alexander said. "Now please, Detective, don't read anything sinister into this. But two weeks ago he called here looking to borrow money. He was in a bit of a state. Said he owed his bookie and was in a real jam. Said he was being threatened and was scared."

"Really? So, what did you say?"

"Why, we said sure," said Sarah Jane. "We *are* best

friends after all. But then, we learned how much he wanted and had no choice but to say no. As much as we wanted to help, we just don't have that kind of money."

"So, how much does he owe?" asked Brewster.

"Nineteen thousand and change," Alexander said.

Brewster whistled, genuinely taken aback at the sum. Up until then, he had assumed they were only talking about a few hundred. "Wow, nineteen thousand? That *is* a lot of money."

"Please don't tell Richie we told you about it."

"You have my word."

"Detective," Sarah Jane asked with a hint of trepidation as Brewster stood to leave. "You don't think this has anything to do with what happened to Gina, do you?"

≈ ≈ ≈

Just before noon on the *Wild Rover*, Benjamin and Jayden were resting below in their cabins. Marcus and Brianna were in the cockpit, going over the tacking and jibing maneuvers one more time. Brianna was apparently a slow learner, although she seemed to make up for it with enthusiasm and a persistent attitude. The morning had been an enjoyable and constructive one for all of them, learning a bit more about navigation and taking sightings from the sun.

When it concluded and the others went their separate ways, Grace grabbed a bottle of cold water from the galley and then went forward to sit alone in the sun. Wearing a white bikini and a pair of sunglasses, her legs dangled over the side of the hull as she faced the wind, the oncoming warm breeze feeling wonderfully invigorating upon her face.

"Mind if I join you, love?" Harvey asked, sitting down beside her before she could reply. He placed his cigarette pack on the deck between them, slipped on his own sunglasses, and turned his face, like hers, toward the breeze.

"Crikey, that feels good, doesn't it?"

"Yes, yes it does," Grace said, looking out toward the unbroken horizon as she sipped at her water.

"Care to try some of mine?" he asked.

"Huh?"

Smiling mischievously, Harvey slipped a silver hip flask

from his pocket and unscrewed the cap. He waved it beneath her nose.

The smell of vodka was overpowering, forcing her to pull her head back and wince. "No, thank you."

"Too early for you, ay?" He smiled, taking a long gulp before slipping it back into his pocket.

"Isn't it for you?" she asked in amazement.

"Love, it is never too early for me," the older man said with a knowing wink. "And by the way, in case you're wondering, I am not just talking about drinking." He nudged his shoulder against hers in an annoying manner, then turned his attention down and tapped a cigarette from the pack.

Grace did not acknowledge the remark. She took another sip of water and continued staring out to sea as he began talking about some of his previous vacations. She felt uncomfortable in the British man's presence but resolved not to let him spoil her enjoyment of the moment. There was a sense of peace and calm for her sitting there on the forward deck. It was both relaxing and exciting at the same time with the sound and the feel of the ocean pitching and rolling about them, the cooling sensation on her skin each time the prows dipped into a trough, and a light salt spray was thrown up on her legs.

She noticed how Harvey's mood had improved since yesterday and was grateful for it. He had become more chatty and outgoing. She told him so, complimenting him on being so helpful to Brianna earlier that morning. They had all been given a small bronze sextant to use in taking a navigational sighting. But the young Georgia woman had been confused by the whole process, lining up the sun and the horizon incorrectly. Sitting next to her, Harvey had gone out of his way to show her what she was doing wrong and to assist her in taking the correct sighting.

"That was nice of you," Grace said with a polite smile. "And I know Brianna appreciated it, too."

The British man shrugged the compliment off with a wave of his hand. "Crikey, you lot all seem to think I am such a bloody bastard," he said with an air of self-pity. "But I'm not so bad, really. I just do not suffer fools easily. And I certainly do not like having my time wasted like it was yesterday."

Grace did not want to get into that conversation so

changed the subject. "Tell me, Harvey," she asked cheerfully. "What part of England are you from?"

"I live in London, Hackney, but I'm originally from Grasmere in the Lake District. That's on the west coast."

"I've heard of the Lake District," she replied. "I have read it is a lovely part of the British Isles."

"Oh yes, love," he said. "Spectacular scenery and plenty of mountains and lakes. Actually, if you ever fancied paying a visit, you could stay with me as my guest. The old family homestead is still there, rented out to tourists for most of the year. And I would gladly show you the sights."

"That's very kind," she said a little awkwardly. The thought of spending time with the older man was not an appealing one, yet she did not want to insult his hospitality.

"Of course, if you ever did come to stay, you would have your own room," he continued as if having sensed what was going through her mind.

Grace hesitated for a second. "Err...unfortunately, with work and other commitments, I just can't see myself taking another vacation for quite some time."

"Hey, I can understand that completely," he said. "My own job is the same. Wankers are always sending me here and there from one supermarket to the next at a minute's notice. One week I'm down south in Brighton, firing and hiring staff. The next, I'm up in Newcastle or Liverpool setting up a new store. I never seem to have time to hold down a relationship."

"No girlfriend?"

"Crikey, not with my workload. In fact, the last one I had was with a young Thai lady I met online."

"Really?"

As Grace spoke, a sudden squall jolted the *Wild Rover* and forced them to hold on as it lurched sharply to starboard. The sudden movement, due to the increase in wind speed, only lasted a couple of seconds before it quickly subsided and the boat resumed on a steady course.

"Oh yes. We were very serious about one another for a couple of months last year," Harvey said when the vibrations stopped. "Very much in love. Blimey, we even spoke about marriage at one point."

"Wow," Grace said with a hint of surprise. "What happened?"

Harvey slipped out his flask and took another long swig of vodka before sighing wearily. "Well, when she began asking me to send money for her sick mother's operation, alarm bells started ringing. I might be a plonker, but I'm not a total bloody idiot. Thankfully, I saw sense and ended it soon after. I suppose, if you think about it though, I was lucky. These days, you read about so many lonely men suckered into sending money to online women they have never met."

"You mean, you never actually met her?"

"No, love, just emails and Skype."

"Wow." Grace whistled.

"So what about you then?"

"Me?"

"Yes. You are a very attractive young lady. There must be dozens of blokes climbing over each other to take you out."

"No. Not really. I guess I'm just concentrating on my work for the foreseeable future," she said. "After my last relationship, well, let's just say I have decided to take a long break from romance."

"That is a pity." Harvey sighed. "And I had such high hopes for us."

Grace shifted uncomfortably. "You know, Harvey, I think I might go below to get out of this sun for a while. I might even take a quick nap before lunch."

"Well, let me know if you would like company," he said with a smile and a suggestive wink, showing his tobacco stained teeth. "You know, love, a little afternoon work out?"

"Err...no," she said with a shudder, standing up to leave.

"Are you sure? Just because I am older doesn't mean I am any less attentive in the sack. In fact, I'll wager I am probably better at it than most of the younger guys you know out there. Age has granted me plenty of experience. And hey, who knows? You might actually enjoy it."

"I am quite certain I wouldn't," Grace said in a firm manner with a clear note of irritation in her voice. "And, Harvey, in the future, I would prefer if you stayed away from me."

She walked away, leaving him sitting with a puzzled look upon his face. But then she stopped and turned back to look down on him. Still sitting on the edge of the deck, the British man removed his sunglasses and looked up, a hopeful glint in his eyes.

"And one more thing," she said.

"Yes?"

"Please stop calling me *love*."

≈   ≈   ≈

While most of the others were busy up on deck, Benjamin went below to his cabin to fix the radio. He had intended on doing it earlier but simply got caught up in the morning lessons, enjoying every moment and learning so much more about sailing. He liked Marcus's patience and attention to detail and felt he was not only a competent captain but an excellent teacher as well. The boat had tacked to port and was rolling more as it travelled on a beam reach. The waves hit the starboard hull, making it harder to stand without holding onto something.

With the VHF unplugged and under his right arm, Benjamin moved from side to side as he descended the steps into the port hull and moved along the walkway. He had just passed the storage room near his cabin when he heard an unusual sound coming from the other side of the polished oak door. It was not a loud noise, something like a rustling of plastic. It did not alarm him, simply intrigued him enough to step forward and open the door.

"Hello? Is anyone in here?" he asked quietly, stepping through.

Thump! Benjamin shrieked in terror as a flash of blurred metal shot toward him from out of the darkness, only missing his side by an inch before smashing into the wooden panel behind him. He looked down in shock to see a three-foot silver spear lodged in the door, its razor-sharp tip buried deep into the wood. The polished metal shaft was still vibrating, bouncing up and down from the force of the impact. He exhaled with a loud, disbelieving gasp, raising his eyes to see Jayden stepping toward him from the shadows with a spear gun in his hands.

Hearing the commotion, the others rushed in. When they arrived, they found the previously mild-mannered Benjamin shouting a torrent of abuse at Jayden, the two men standing face to face in a loud, heated exchange.

"This lunatic almost killed me," Benjamin exclaimed, turning to the others gathered in the doorway, pointing dramatically toward the metal spear to show them what had happened.

"Lord Almighty, I *said* I was sorry," Jayden said. "It was an accident."

"Ha, bloody ha!" Harvey laughed loudly from the edge of the group to Benjamin's right. "Now *you* know what it's like to be almost killed, you twat."

"What the hell were you doing down here in the first place?" Marcus asked.

"Look, I was simply poking around," said Jayden. "Being nosey, that's all."

"And the spear gun?"

"Lord, I said I was sorry. Okay? I was just looking at the darn thing when Benjamin here opened the door and startled me."

Benjamin grew more livid on hearing this. "I startled you? *I startled you?* Jesus fucking Christ, man, you almost impaled me to the door with that thing."

"Now, now," Brianna said disapprovingly, raising a hand and wagging a finger at him. "Regardless of, like, what happened, there is no need to take the Lord's name in vain. Jayden said he was sorry, so you need to, like, let it go."

≈   ≈   ≈

Benjamin opened his mouth to reply, his eyes burning with rage, when Marcus put a hand across him and tried calming him down. He had not seen this side of Benjamin before. He had pictured him as the quiet one, a meek individual who disliked confrontation. And, although Marcus did not blame him for being angry, realizing he must have gotten one hell of a fright, right now he was anything but mild-mannered and meek. Even as he spoke to calm things down, Marcus could not help remembering the incident in the cockpit the previous day when Benjamin turned the wheel and hit Harvey with the boom. Was it really an accident, like he had said? Or had the timid New Yorker done it on purpose to get revenge on Harvey for his insults? No, he concluded, almost as soon as the thought flashed through his mind. That was just too far-fetched to even consider.

"Look," he said firmly. He was the captain, and it was his job to show authority and to restore order. "Let's all just calm down and go back to the main cabin for lunch. What do you say? What's done is done. It was an accident. What happened was bad, I know, but no one got hurt. That is the main thing. And it is over."

Benjamin went to say something but Marcus continued before he could speak.

"It was a stupid, stupid thing to do, and I think Jayden knows it. Right?"

"I do," Jayden replied. "And again, like I said, Benjamin, I am really sorry."

Marcus turned back to Benjamin. "Look, man, it has been a long morning for all of us. Do you think you can try to put this behind you, if only for the sake of your own, hard earned vacation?"

Jayden put his hand out to Benjamin, who looked as if he thought long and hard about it, before finally taking it.

"All right, then," Marcus said with relief. "Let's all go up and have some lunch. And then, later on this afternoon, we can go on deck and run through the procedures for plotting a course."

Harvey was first to leave, followed closely by Grace, who quickly put a comforting arm around Benjamin's shoulders in a gesture of friendship. Marcus stood aside to let Jayden exit the storage room. They exchanged a relieved, unspoken glance before Brianna hugged her husband and snuggled into him as they followed the others. Marcus remained behind for a moment to catch his breath and let his heart rate settle. Turning to the door, he grabbed the metal spear in both hands and wriggled it up and down before finally managing to work it free from the wooden panel. When it was out, he snapped it back onto the side of the spear gun and placed the deadly weapon out of harm's way on one of the top shelves. It had been a narrow escape, he decided with a sharp intake of breath, and was best forgotten. It was too disturbing to think about what could have been, what would have happened if Benjamin had been standing just a few more inches to his left.

≈ ≈ ≈

Detective Brewster squinted uncomfortably when he entered the Flamingo Club from an alleyway off Sunset Boulevard. The lights were low within, a stark contrast to the intense white sunshine he left outside. Strips of blue neon fluorescents ran around the walls, while large ultra-violet strobes flashed in the darkness about them. The music was loud, the ceiling and floor vibrating to the rhythmic beat. A young woman was dancing topless on the center stage, moving in time with the music while surrounded by tables of ogling men sipping beer and waving dollar bills to attract her attention. And then a smoke machine kicked in behind the stage and the woman's lower legs became lost in a swirling cloud of luminous white gas.

Brewster walked toward the circular bar in the center of the room and sat down, waiting for the bartender to approach before discreetly showing his badge.

"I'm looking for Sal!" he shouted, his voice almost drowned out by the loud, incessant music.

The lanky, young barman with the pockmarked face said nothing, just eyed him with distain and turned his back. He reached for the phone by the register, lifted the receiver, and tapped at the keypad. While he spoke in whispers, Brewster turned his gaze around the smoke-filled club. It was not exactly full to capacity, he noticed, but was nonetheless still doing pretty good business for a Wednesday afternoon. There were handfuls of customers scattered about the room, businessmen taking an extended lunch, loners dropping by to spend a couple of hours indulging their fantasies. Regardless of whom they were or where they were from, all eyes were fixed on the naked, young woman up on the small wooden stage.

"What can I do for you?" a gruff voice suddenly asked from behind.

Brewster turned on his stool to find a large, mean-looking individual standing beside him with one arm leaning on the bar. Salvatore di Maggio's nose was bent in half, broken too many times to ever be reset. Dressed in a dark shirt and trousers, he wore a brown leather jacket and had a deep scar running down his cheek from his right eyebrow.

"You Sal?" Brewster said.

"Who wants to know?" asked the big man.

"Miami Metro," said Brewster, flashing his badge. "I'm investigating a murder that took place down in Hialeah two nights ago. You ever heard of a woman named Gina Regazzoni?"

"Nope, can't say that I have. Is she a stripper?"

"How about Richie Regazzoni?"

"Doesn't ring a bell."

"Is that right?" Then, after a short pause, Brewster said, "Well, look, how about the figure of nineteen thousand dollars and change? Does *that* ring any bells?"

Sal said nothing, just stared back without showing any sign of emotion. This was going to be harder than Brewster thought. It was clear he was in an establishment that did not like or fear the law.

"The only reason I mention that amount is because that is what I believe Richie owes you in gambling debts."

Sal continued to stare without speaking, an angry, contemptuous expression forming across his face. Brewster hoped he might be considering opening up. It was clear to him that the big guy did not like talking to the police and felt unhappy even standing beside one.

"I've got nothing to say to you," Sal eventually said gruffly beneath his breath. "Now, unless you've got a warrant in that pocket of yours, get the fuck out of here and don't come back."

Brewster shook his head. "You know, that's not a very smart move, Sal."

"What is not smart is you coming in here like this, throwing accusations about. Taking book is illegal in this state, and as you can see, I run a licensed, respectable business. So, Officer, unless you want a lawsuit for defamation of character, I would seriously consider getting the fuck out now."

Brewster went to speak but stopped when he felt a sudden presence behind and hot breath on the back of his neck. Turning, he found the lanky, young barman and a bald, heavier set man wielding a baseball bat standing over him. They looked mean, itching for a chance to unleash upon him. Brewster took a deep breath and turned back to Sal.

"Do you *really* want to do this to an officer of the law?"

Sal motioned toward the sign above the bar that announced, *The Management Reserves the Right to Refuse Admission*. When Brewster read it, Sal cast a glance to the two men standing behind him and jerked his thumb backwards toward the door.

Brewster rose from his stool with a heavy sigh. "Okay, Sal, I'll go. But I promise you, when I come back with that warrant, you had better make sure everything is squeaky clean in here. I mean, if I find so much as a turd not flushed down the toilet properly, I will shut you down with everything at my disposal."

As he left, the two men followed on his heels, walking so closely behind he could still feel their breath on the back of his neck. They escorted him outside into the sunlight and then stood mockingly in the doorway to watch him leave.

"Bye bye." The heavy-set, bald man called after him with a sarcastic smile.

"Yeah, so long," said the barman. "Hey, and don't y'all come fucking back now, you hear?"

Brewster was a few feet from them but stopped and turned back around with eyebrows raised. "You know what, guys, you two comedians need to work on your material a little. You've got a good double act going on there, but you might want to get some newer jokes."

The heavy-set man raised the bat to his forehead in a gesture of salute and then waved goodbye with his free hand in a teasing manner. But the younger barman could not resist throwing one more jibe, this time spitting on the ground near Brewster's feet before curling the side of his mouth up and saying, "Hey, you know what, pig? I hear the place around the corner sells a mean fried chicken."

"What was that?"

"Yeah, you might want to call in. Say howdy to all the other Negros there."

Brewster emitted a deep sigh of resignation and stepped back toward the two men. The bald man raised his bat in readiness, but the detective ignored him and went straight toward the barman. Standing face-to-face, he eyed him threateningly for a few seconds. But the young barman was not intimidated and simply stared back defiantly.

"Son, you need to work on that attitude," Brewster said

without blinking.

"What, you gonna make me?" asked the younger man.

Brewster sighed again, lowered his eyes, and then cast a quick glance to the bald man with the bat. The heavier man's eyes were red and almost bulging out of their sockets, his blood pressure visibly increased. He looked like a mean, violent individual, and Brewster could instinctively tell by the way he was standing that he was getting ready to swing the bat. He was balancing his weight on his back leg with both hands clenched tightly around the handle in readiness for the blow.

Brewster had to deal with him first. Lowering his head, he sprang into action, smashing a fist into the man's face and immediately breaking his nose and sending blood spattering up into his eyes. The barman raised his arm to throw a punch, but Brewster grabbed his fist in mid-swing and violently twisted it downwards before he could react. As the younger man's wrist snapped and his body spun sideways, Brewster brought his forehead down onto his face with such force it cracked the bridge of his nose. The barman emitted a painful scream as blood bubbled from both nostrils. He crumpled to the ground like a sack of potatoes at Brewster's feet.

Without pausing, the detective turned back to the bald man, who was nursing his own injured nose, and slammed the base of his palm up into his throat, sending him sprawling backwards with such force his feet left the ground, and he collapsed choking onto the dirty concrete. As he hunched over and retched, Brewster stepped back with clenched fists.

"Hey, Cop!" Sal di Maggio stepped from the club and entered the alley. "How's about you try that again with me?"

Brewster moved away from the two men writhing in agony on the ground and raised his fists. "All right, Sal, if that's the way you want to do this. But, as I said earlier, I only called in to ask a few questions. I really don't give a rat's ass whether this Richie guy owes you money. I don't even care if you are running books or not. That is not my department. All I'm trying to do is find out a little bit about him. That's all. Then I am out of here, brother, and you won't see me again."

"Okay then, I'll tell you what," Sal said, eyes squinted, spitting to the concrete as he circled around his two fallen employees who were now in the process of scrambling shakily to their feet. He moved past them and drew closer to Brewster with his own fists raised. "If you can knock me down, Officer, I will tell you whatever you want to know."

"Jesus," Brewster muttered. "You Italians really make a guy work for it, don't you? But all right, if that is what I've got to do to get some answers from you, then let's get to it."

Sal smiled. He feigned a jab toward Brewster's left jaw, shifted his weight onto his right foot, and then circled around a little bit more. It was clear to Brewster that the big man was enjoying himself, that a confrontation like this, especially with a policeman, was actually making his day.

"Well?" said Brewster. "Are you gonna keep dancing like that, or what?"

Spurred on by the remark, Sal moved closer. Brewster watched his eyes carefully as he drew near, waiting for the telltale sign he was about to strike. It did not take long. Sal's eyes suddenly narrowed, his weight shifting again before he lunged forward with his right fist clenched. Brewster side-stepped a split second before the impact and brought his own elbow up into Sal's chest.

"You'll have to be a lot quicker than that," he told the big man as he stepped back to continue circling.

Without warning, Sal moved to Brewster's left and then came in with a vicious jab to the side of the detective's head. It shook Brewster to the core, sent him stumbling backwards a few feet with his hand covering his throbbing left ear. Sal came at him again, this time with both fists. Brewster ducked a couple of times and replied with a sharp uppercut to the big man's chin. His knuckles stung from the blow, forcing his opponent's head upward, leaving him exposed for the briefest moment to a second strike. Brewster knew it was the chance he had been waiting for. He summoned up all his strength and went in for the kill, smashing his left fist down into Sal's temple before pounding his right one up against his jaw. Seconds later, the big man went onto one knee, holding his head in both hands.

"Want a boost up?" Brewster asked, standing over him with his palms showing.

Sal wiped the corner of his mouth and then spat a mouthful of blood to the ground. Without taking Brewster's outstretched hand, he got to his feet and brushed himself down. Brewster clenched his fists again, convinced the Italian was going to have another go. But he didn't. Instead, he motioned for his two employees to go back inside the club and then turned to face the detective.

"Make it quick," he muttered begrudgingly. "It takes a good man to knock me down, but you did, so ask me whatever it is you need to know and be on your way."

"Shit, if I knew it was going to be *that* easy I would have hit you back in the club," Brewster said, attempting levity.

Not amused, Sal eyed him coldly as he fixed his shirt back into his trousers and motioned with his hand that Brewster should get on with it.

"Okay then, I need you to confirm that you know Richie Regazzoni," Brewster said.

"I know him."

"Well, it was his wife, Gina, who was murdered the other night in Hialeah," Brewster said, hoping it might encourage the Italian to talk a little more.

"Yeah, I know all about it," Sal admitted. "You think I had something to do with it?"

Brewster raised his eyebrows. "Did you?"

Sal shot him another cold stare. "Look, I read about it in the newspaper like everyone else. No, I didn't have anything to do with it."

"Any idea who did?"

"Not the faintest. But it sounds like a psycho if you ask me. Killing a woman like that is bad enough, but doing it in front of her kid? Naw, that is not my style. That is just sick shit."

"Okay then. So, what about Richie?"

Sal shrugged. "What about him? Look, your dime is running out, Detective. Ask me what you need to know and be done with it."

"Well, I suppose all I really want to know is if you have anything on him that might be relevant to the case."

"You think he did it?" Sal asked with a look of surprise.

"No, I didn't say that," said Brewster. "But I would like to find out why his wife was murdered. If it had anything to do with his gambling problem or any other shit he might be in to."

"No, there's not much I can tell you that you probably

don't already know. Richie is one of my best customers, sure. But for the past few months his stock has nosedived. I mean, he has bottomed out big time."

"Huh?"

"Every bet the poor bastard placed in the past two months has lost."

"Oh, right."

"He was like that guy."

"What guy?" asked Brewster.

"You know, *that* guy? The one who touched things and turned them to gold?"

"Oh, you mean, Midas."

"Yeah, that's the fella. Well, Richie was like him for as far back as I can remember. Almost cleaned me out a couple of times over the years. It even got to the point where I had to start laying off some of his bets with other bookies." Sal paused, nodded again and then smiled wryly to himself. "But you know what they say, don't you? All good things come to an end, right? Well, anyway, Richie's winning streak finally bottomed out. Within the space of two and a half months, he has ended up owing me fourteen grand."

"I thought it was nineteen."

"No, fourteen."

Brewster looked puzzled.

"It was nineteen, but he recently came up with five when we—"

"Go on," Brewster prompted when Sal hesitated.

"Well, when we sort of threatened to break his legs."

Sal stared at Brewster as if to gauge his reaction. He was careful to keep a blank expression. As he had promised, Brewster was only interested in learning about Richie right then. And he was learning more about him than he had hoped.

"Go on with your story," he said.

"Well, there ain't much more to tell," said Sal. "We gave him two weeks to come up with another five grand. That's all. The next thing I know, I am reading in the paper about how his wife had been murdered like that. Hey, didn't I hear on TV that you got the guy, that he got burned in a fire?"

"The body is still being identified," Brewster said with a shrug.

Sal turned to leave, casting Brewster a look of begrudging respect as he headed back toward the door.

"By the way, did Richie ever come in here?" Brewster called after him.

"Sure, but only once or twice. Why?"

"I don't know," Brewster said. "I was just wondering if he had anything else going on besides gambling."

"You mean strippers?" asked Sal. He chuckled to himself as he grabbed the handle of the door and opened it. "Shit. Richie doesn't need to come to a place like this to get his rocks off. He's a good-looking guy, Detective. He doesn't need to pay for it."

"How do you mean?"

"I mean, Richie Regazzoni is a ladies' man."

Brewster raised his eyebrows in surprise.

"You didn't know? Hell, the way I hear it, he has them lined up around the block."

"You're kidding me?" said Brewster, genuinely taken aback.

"No, I ain't," muttered Sal. "He seems so straight and clean cut, doesn't he? But let me tell you something. I heard your man, Richie, has been boning one of them nurses over at that hospital where he works."

≈   ≈   ≈

She sat in the cockpit of the *Dirty Nellie*, steering the small craft with both hands on the tiller, the warm trade wind blowing hot on her face. Isabella wore one of the white t-shirts she had found in a drawer in the tiny forward cabin, and had also managed to locate a pair of light gray tracksuit pants that only stayed up when she folded the waistband down over itself. Earlier that morning, she had washed her clothes in the half-sized sink using a bar of soap and hot water before hanging them out to dry from the jib-stay on the forward deck.

Brophy was below in the cabin, attempting to raise his son on the radio. It was shortly after six a.m. He had assured her the *Wild Rover's* radio would be live for the shipping forecast.

Isabella flipped out her sunglasses and slipped them on.

She sat back and stared out at the rolling blue ocean on all sides. She took a deep, satisfying breath and marveled at the peace and beauty of it all. This was another world from the one she knew, far removed from the ugliness and violence she dealt with back in Miami every day.

When Brophy had woken her that morning, it had been with a smile and a cup of coffee. They had chatted for a few minutes, her sitting in bed with the sheet pulled up to her breasts, him standing in the doorway with his shoulder against the frame.

He'd seemed amazed when she'd informed him she had never been on a boat before then. "That's just crazy," he had said with a shake of his head. "Really, I can't believe you have never been on a boat before."

"Well, crazy or not, it's true."

"So, how are you liking it so far?" he had asked with a smile.

"I have got to admit, if we were here for any other reason than we are, I think I would be having a good time. Does that make sense?"

"I think I know what you mean," he had said. "So anyway, how did you sleep?"

"Like a log. Must be something to do with the fresh air and the rolling of the boat."

"That will do it every time." He had grinned cheerfully. "Well anyway, the good news is we have made some serious progress during the night."

"Really?"

"I estimate we can't be more than fifty nautical miles behind them now," he had said as he turned to leave. "If we keep up this pace through the morning, we should be within sight by early this afternoon."

After he'd left, Isabella had taken her revolver from under her pillow and put it safely away in the bedside locker. Old habits died hard. She was used to sleeping with a weapon close to hand. She had then quickly showered and dressed before going up on deck to take over at the tiller while he went below to the radio.

Now, as she sat admiring the magnificent view, she remembered the task at hand and felt a little guilty for having forgotten it. She wondered what Mike Ryan's wife was doing at that moment, if she had any family or friends in Miami to comfort her. She also wondered what her own colleagues were saying about her back at the station. They must have missed her by now, she concluded, and would more than likely have guessed where she had gone after her phone conversation with the captain.

Captain Franklin was furious, of course. She might, in all probability, be out of a job when she returned. But Isabella did not really care about that right now. If bringing Mike's killer to justice meant she was out of a job, then so be it. Seeing that animal burn would be worth it a hundred times over.

"Nothing!" Brophy growled when he swung open the hatch and emerged from the cabin. His raised voice startled her a little, making her sit upright. "Not a goddamned thing from the *Wild Rover*."

"Maybe he just hasn't turned his radio on for the forecast?" she said, not really believing it, but feeling sympathy toward Brophy for the first time on the voyage. After all, his son was on board the other boat, and the thought of what could be happening over there must have been troubling for him. She could see the anguish and worry beginning to spread across his face.

"No, that's not it," he replied with a sigh of resignation. "You know, up until now, I really didn't believe what you were proposing. To be honest, I thought you were just chasing shadows. But now? Well, now I am beginning to have my doubts. And, hell, I am goddamned worried about it. Really concerned about what could be happening out there."

Before she could reply, a loud crackle erupted from the radio in the cabin and a voice could be heard trying to get their attention. Believing it to be Marcus, Brophy jumped up and raced down to take the call, only to appear back at the cabin hatch a few seconds later with a look of disappointment on his face. "It's Miami," he said with a sigh. "They want to speak to you."

Detective Brewster was waiting in the Metro Control Center when Isabella depressed the microphone's transmit button to acknowledge his call.

"Byron, thanks for getting back," she said a little awkwardly. "Any success with the blood and those names? Or are you calling to tell me I am out of a job? Over."

"You know, Garcia, there *was* talk about suspending you for disobeying orders," Brewster said. "But, right now, I think the captain has other things on his mind. It looks like you were right about that body we pulled out of the boathouse. Seems the killer may still be out there after all."

Isabella exhaled sharply, relieved she was being vindicated, or at least, she was being taken seriously. She had taken a chance, a big one. Up to that moment, she had not known if she was about to lose her career because of it.

"The suspect's body was burned beyond recognition, but Doc Walker says he had been shot point blank in the chest by a Glock thirty-eight," said Brewster. He paused for a second before continuing. "That's right, Garcia, the same gun Mike used. The one that is still missing. But there is something else. The Doc has put John Doe's age somewhere in his sixties. Says he suffered from some sort of medical disorder which meant he would have walked with a pronounced limp. You getting all this, Garcia? Over."

"Uh-huh," she replied. "I am reading you loud and clear. Keep going. Over."

"Well, I talked to your friend Tommy Mendoza. You know, that neighbor who followed him down to the harbor? Anyway, although he didn't get a good enough look to even guess the guy's age, he is adamant he did not walk with a limp. Even said he was running at one point. And one other thing, they need to run more tests, but Doc is now saying it looks like the guy was definitely dead when the fire took hold. Seems there wasn't enough carbon in his lungs, so he could not have set it."

Isabella concluded, even before he had finished speaking, the body was definitely *not* the killer's as she had maintained all along. She felt a wave of relief, coupled with a renewed determination to continue the chase.

"Looks like a bunch of people back here owe you an apology," Brewster said. "You were right about him. Over."

"Save it," she said. "Let's just move on and try to catch this guy. For Mike. Over."

"Yeah, I read that," he said quietly. "We also had a bit of a break regarding the victim's husband. After interviewing some of his friends and associates, I discovered that our man, Richie Regazzoni, was not quite the stand-up guy and devoted husband he led us all to believe. Seems he has a big gambling problem and is in deep with the wrong people. Fourteen thousand dollars' worth to be precise. And one more thing. It may be nothing, but I also heard a rumor that his marriage may not have been as solid as we first thought. It seems Richie was running around with one of the nurses at the hospital while his wife was pregnant. But look, I will have to get back to you on all that. We have called him in for an interview later today. Over."

"Any word back on the blood or those names I asked you to run? Over."

"The blood work is not back from the lab yet, and we are still running a check on the names. But, to be honest, Garcia, without more details, other than just names and cities, it is going to take a bit of time. Here's what I have so far. Jayden and Brianna Kingston appear squeaky clean. He is a minister in the Baptist Church up there in Georgia, and she is the daughter of a local doctor. Their friends and colleagues speak very highly of them. And, as far as I can tell, neither has a record or has been in any kind of trouble. Same for the Logan woman. Pittsburgh PD can't find anything on her except for a couple of unpaid parking tickets. Regarding your British guy, though, Scotland Yard in England does have a file on a Harvey Nigel Hawkins, who apparently did time in Wormwood Prison a few years back for sexual assault. Again, without any additional information on him, we can't even be certain it is the same guy. Patrick and Marcus Brophy are still going through the Miami database. As for the Goldstein guy, not a whisper back from the NYPD yet. I will just have to get back to you when we get more. Over."

"Thanks, Byron. I appreciate what you are doing for me." Then, after a short pause, she ventured to something more personal. "By the way, have you heard anything from Tish or the girls yet?"

"She finally returned one of my calls," Brewster replied with a heavy sigh.

"That's good, right?"

"Not sure. When she finally called, I was out working the case. Wouldn't you know it? Just my luck. Anyway, she left a message saying she wants to meet face-to-face tomorrow night. So, as I said, I'm not really sure whether that is a good thing or not."

"I'm sure it will be okay," she told him, trying to raise his spirits. "Well, look, keep me posted, okay? You know where I am. Over."

"Yeah, regarding that," said Brewster. "How are things going for you out there? Somehow, Garcia, I cannot imagine you on a sailing boat. Over."

"You know, it's really not that bad," she said cheerfully. "And we are making good progress. Patrick Brophy, the owner of the boat we are following, says we should have them in sight by this afternoon. Over."

"Well then, be careful out there," advised Brewster. "And look, when you catch up to them, remember who it is you are dealing with. Don't take any chances. Over."

"I read you loud and clear. Over."

"I am going to talk to the captain about contacting the chief of police on Saint Thomas in the Virgins for you," Brewster said. "I'm going to ask him if he can get them to be on alert when you guys arrive. Meanwhile, I will also have a talk with this Richie character and get back to you. Over and out."

As she replaced the microphone and returned the VHF to standby, Isabella felt a deep sense of gratitude toward Brewster. She knew without him fighting the cause for her back in Miami, she would probably have nothing to return home to. With this on her mind, her thoughts wandered back a few years to the time when they were partners. She had liked him from the start. He was a nice guy and they had always worked well together, sharing information and thoughts, combining their own individual talents to help solve an impressive number of cases. And Brewster had always been upfront with her, sharing everything and never trying to take credit for solving an investigation without her. Sadly, that was not always the case with some of the other detectives in Miami Metro. Over the years, she had learned to be selective in whom she trusted, realizing not everyone in the department was a team player like Brewster.

Her mind wandered again for a moment and she recalled a case they worked together down in Little Havana. A young woman's body had been found in a dumpster near Riverside

Park, her head bashed in and almost every rib broken. It was a horrible, disturbing sight, her delicate young arms and legs twisted and contorted in a hideous manner as she lay face up among the garbage. It was a gruesome memory, and one Isabella had not been able to shake off. But she particularly remembered how Brewster had been enraged at the brutality of the crime, throwing himself headfirst into the investigation as if he knew the girl, as if it had been a personal matter to him. Then, as now, the golden rule of detective work was not to let the job get to you. To do so, the department psychiatrist constantly warned, frequently led to depression and breakdown, and more often than not, alcoholism. But, at the time, these dangers did not concern Brewster in the slightest, nor did they stop him. He was very single-minded. And it made her smile a little when she remembered how, like a dog with a bone, he had refused to let go, thinking about nothing else until they'd eventually brought the young girl's killer to justice.

But Isabella also recalled how, in the early days of the investigation, they had hit a brick wall, discovering that none of the woman's friends were willing to talk or be associated in any way. It had been obvious they were afraid of someone. Someone powerful. They had clearly been worried that, if they came forward, they, too, might have ended up the same way as their friend. But Brewster had persevered. That was his nature, his personality, following, harassing, and even threatening reluctant witnesses until a co-worker of the dead woman had eventually broken and given them the information they had wanted. That had led to their first lead, and that, in turn, had set them off on the path to finding the killer. Within a couple of days of that first breakthrough, they had put enough of the pieces together to establish a motive and a suspect.

They had discovered the victim's name was Eva Morales from Pompano Beach, barely twenty-one years old. They also learned that she had worked as a hostess at a seedy nightclub owned by two Cuban businessmen, Oscar Mendoza and his son Diego. The word on the street had been they were peddling drugs and running a prostitution ring from the club. Diego, in particular, had a reputation for becoming violent with any of the girls who dared to step out of line. It had been clear from their investigation that the two Cubans believed themselves to be above the law, untouchable due to the fact that they had a few of the local uniforms on their payroll. That part had only been rumor. They'd had no hard evidence to support it.

During their initial meeting with the Mendozas one afternoon while the club had been empty, it had become patently clear that the two men were definitely involved. Brewster had taken the lead in the conversation, she remembered, with her pretty much sitting back as an observer.

They had entered the club to find Oscar and Diego eating lunch in one of the booths near the main circular, glass bar, looking like kings of all they surveyed. She and Brewster had been wearing suits that day, she recalled, and they flashed their badges before sitting.

"Hey, guys, I hope we're not disturbing your lunch," Brewster had said with a hint of sarcasm. He had left his jacket open just enough to let them see his shoulder holster and revolver, an old, but sometimes effective trick aimed at intimidating suspects, showing them who was in charge. "I am Detective Brewster and this is my partner, Detective Garcia, from Metro Homicide."

"We know why you are here," Oscar had said sharply, unable to hide his feeling of disdain. He had finished his food and was drinking thick, black coffee and smoking a cigar. "You are here about that waitress, the dead girl who worked for us at the club, yes?"

"So you know about her murder?" Isabella had asked with suspicion. "Anything you would like to share with us?"

"It has been all over the news, Detective. Don't get so melodramatic. The whole city knows about it. Now look, whatever it is you are here for, please, make it quick. We are busy men with a busy nightclub to run."

Brewster had leaned forward with his hands on the table while she'd remained sitting back. He had paused for a moment, looking directly at the two Cubans with an expression of contempt. "Cut the bullshit, Oscar, we know all about your business. You and your son here are just evil little pimps, taking advantage of vulnerable young girls to turn a buck."

Visibly filled with rage, Diego had started to rise as if to attack him for the insult, but his father had quickly placed a hand on his arm to stop him.

"Look," the older man had snapped irritably. "What exactly is it you want to know?"

"What we want to know, Oscar, is why your boy here killed Eva Morales?" Brewster had cut straight to the chase, pouncing upon it like a wolf. Both he and Isabella knew from experience that people generally let their guard down when their blood was up. Brewster had obviously decided to turn up the heat. If you found a suspect with a fiery temper you used it to your advantage. That was the game. But Oscar had been clever, more level-headed than his son. He had simply shrugged and shook his head, keeping his hand on Diego's arm to stop him from doing something rash. Isabella still remembered how his fingers had dug deeper into the younger man's arm.

"She *did* work for you, didn't she?" Brewster said. "We know she was one of your girls. A prostitute. We have a witness who confirms it."

"A witness? Well, Detective, if you would like to give me the name of this so-called witness, I can pass it on to our lawyer along with yours. Oh yes, I am quite certain the character defamation case he will file is going to be very profitable for us."

"So, you're not talking then?" Brewster asked angrily.

"Detective, do me a favor." Oscar had flashed a smug grin. As they had watched, he had removed his hand from Diego's arm, sat back, and then had folded his own arms across his chest. "Please, close the door on your way out."

"You think this is over?" Brewster had asked with a snarl. "No, Oscar, this is only just beginning. Believe me. We know Diego killed that young girl, and I will bet, if we get our guys to do a swab, his DNA will match some of the hairs and fluids found on her body. That, with the testimony of our witness? Well, let's just say you two will be speaking to each other through bars for the next fifteen years."

Isabella had known at the time he was only bluffing, because the body taken from the dumpster had been there for days, and forensics had produced very little from it. But Oscar and Diego did not know that. They had remained silent, eyeing them suspiciously as she and Brewster stood up to leave.

"We will be back with that warrant," Brewster had said as they went. "I am going to see to it personally that this club is shut down and you both face charges of murder and running prostitution."

Back in their car, however, he had slammed both palms onto the steering wheel in frustration. "Shit! Did you see their eyes? Those bastards were laughing at us. That little runt, Diego, killed her. I'm sure of it now."

"You want to try and get a search warrant for the club?" Isabella had asked.

"On what grounds?" He'd muttered beneath his breath. "Nah, there's no point. By the time we do, they will have made sure there is nothing there to incriminate them."

But that had not been the end of it. That evening, Brewster's witness, the young woman who had first spoken out, had called him wanting to meet. She had been terrified. She'd said she had more information, but had been scared to death of Diego and of what he might do, saying she did not trust the police since he had so many of them on his payroll. Brewster had calmed her down and had agreed to meet her in the parking lot behind the Sun Life stadium in Miami Gardens, assuring her he would come alone. Isabella had protested, saying it might be a trap, but he'd insisted she stay behind, not wanting to rattle the young woman any more than she had been. Of course, Isabella had paid no attention to his instructions, and she'd followed him.

Two hours later, she had watched what had happened. What she hadn't been able to see, Brewster had told her about later. He'd turned his car into the huge parking lot and pull up at the far end, close to the main stadium entrance. He had waited for what seemed like hours until finally the woman's battered red pickup had turned in and had rolled to a stop beside him with her window down. Brewster had rolled down his window to speak to her. Suddenly, Diego had sprung up from the passenger seat brandishing a Kalashnikov rifle. Before Brewster could utter a word, the Cuban had leaned across the young woman in the driver's seat and had fired down upon him. Brewster had quickly ducked his head, narrowly avoiding being hit by the ferocious hail of bullets ripping into his car. He'd shoved the car into reverse and gotten the hell out of there. Unable to see clearly with his head lowered and bullets flying everywhere, he had only gone back a few yards before hitting a low, concrete bollard. The sudden jolt had released the driver's airbag and had knocked the wind from his lungs, dazing him for a moment.

When he had come to his senses, he'd looked through the now smashed passenger window of his car to see Diego standing there staring in at him, loading another clip into his weapon with a victorious grin on his face. He had snapped the replacement clip into place, pulled back the firing pin, and then had slowly pointed the muzzle in through the window. Brewster could have done nothing. Trapped in his seat by the airbag, he'd watched in resignation as the Cuban had slipped his finger over the trigger and had prepared to fire. And then, a single shot had rung out from one of the pedestrian gates nearby.

Isabella remembered the look on Diego's face when he had turned to find her standing behind him, revolver held firmly in both her hands. His eyes had been wide and full of questions, but before he could do or say anything, they had rolled back in his head, and he had collapsed against Brewster's car. Seconds later, he'd slid off the hood onto the hot asphalt below. Keeping her gun on him, Isabella had walked over to kick the Kalashnikov away before holstering her revolver and then leaning down to look in the shattered window.

"You okay in there?" she'd asked with concern.

"Jesus," Brewster had muttered back to her. "That was close. Man, am I glad you didn't listen to me and stay at home."

"You hurt?" she'd asked again, prying open the passenger door as broken glass fell everywhere. She'd leaned in to help deflate the airbag pinning him to his seat.

"Nah." He had sighed. "Just a few cuts and scrapes. But I owe you, Garcia. Shit, girl, I owe you big time."

CHAPTER SIX

THE BILGE

She found his body when she emerged from her cabin that afternoon. Stretching and yawning, Brianna was making her way down the narrow hall, past the galley, and toward the steps leading up to the main seating area. When she reached the end of the corridor, however, she stopped for a moment, alerted by an unusual noise. Listening above the creaking and groaning of the hull, she could just make out an intermittent banging sound coming from one of the adjacent storage rooms. She assumed something had worked itself loose inside. The wind had shifted from the south that afternoon, and the sea around had become rougher with the *Wild Rover* now rolling and pitching more dramatically on the incoming waves. Intending to tether the unsecured object, she opened the door and stepped inside. Immediately, she froze when she saw him lying there.

Brianna screamed at the top of her lungs, a blood-curdling shriek that filled the entire boat and brought everyone rushing down from deck or out of their cabins. With Jayden's arm wrapped tightly around her shoulders for support, she buried her head deep into his chest and sobbed hysterically, pointing a trembling finger back through the open doorway.

Benjamin's neck was most definitely broken, twisted sideways in a quite unnatural way. His glasses were hanging from one ear, eyes half open, his body slumped backwards over a wooden bench in the center of the room. The sock on his right foot appeared to be caught on a protruding screw in the metal shelving unit fixed to the wall. Bundles of rope, canvas sail bags, and lifejackets were lying across him, scattered everywhere about the floor.

Marcus took control.

"Jayden, take her back to your cabin," he instructed Brianna's husband on seeing how distressed she was.

He was trying desperately to hold himself together, his legs going weak as the shock began to set in. Marcus's heart was pounding furiously in his chest, his mind racing in turmoil. In all his sailing experience, he had never faced *anything* like this. Not even close. There had been moments of danger, of course. He had fought storms and squalls that had threatened the lives of everyone on board. He had dealt with broken arms and legs, cracked ribs, and on one occasion, even a mild heart attack. But nothing compared to this. In all his experience, Marcus had never dealt with the death of a passenger at sea.

Jayden followed Marcus's instructions and left with Brianna. The storage room fell strangely quiet for a few minutes. Grace was the first to act. She went to Benjamin's body and checked his pulse. Then she examined the back of his head. Harvey remained beside Marcus at the door.

"I don't see any blood," she said quietly. "There is a large lump at the base of his skull. You can feel it quite clearly."

Marcus turned to Harvey with a somber, pale expression. "How could this happen?" he asked in a low murmur, still reeling from the tragedy. "I just don't understand. He was up on deck with you less than an hour ago, wasn't he?"

"It looks to me like he was getting something down from that shelf," Harvey observed. "Must have been using the lower one as a step when he fell backwards and caught his foot. Probably hit his head on the corner of the bench there."

Marcus nodded. It occurred to him how distant and unmoved the British man seemed, how he did not appear to be fazed by the sight of the dead body. Harvey may have been in shock as well, of course, but on the outside, he was maintaining his composure remarkably well.

"Don't you think we should move him back to his cabin?" asked Grace.

"We certainly cannot leave him lying here," Harvey said.

Marcus dropped to his hunkers and placed his face in his hands, swallowing hard. "Shit, I don't know what we should do," he said quietly. "I...I'm still trying to get my head around this. Trying to make sense of it all."

Grace knelt down beside him, moved in close, and placed a comforting arm around his shoulders. "Marcus, are you all right?"

"All right? No, I'm not. Not at all."

"Hey, hey. It's not your fault," she whispered supportively.

"It *is* my fault," he said. "Everyone on board this boat is *my* responsibility. My job is to keep you all safe."

"But you can't be held responsible for an accident like this."

"I hold myself responsible."

Grace squeezed his shoulders. "No, you mustn't. Look, you just have to accept the fact that, no matter what you do, bad things happen. You can't wrap people in cotton wool and watch them every minute of every day."

"Blimey, the boat just rolled with a wave while he was standing on the shelf reaching up," muttered Harvey. "Poor bugger simply lost his grip and fell backwards. That was nothing to do with you."

"Do you really think that is what happened?" Marcus asked, removing his hands from his face and trying to compose himself a little more.

"Of course, I do. It's bloody obvious," said Harvey. "What else could have happened? Look, he simply forgot the golden rule of keeping one hand for himself and the other for the boat. You did tell him that the first day, remember?"

"It was one of the first things you told us," Grace agreed.

Marcus took a deep breath, held it for a few seconds, and then exhaled with a sigh. He patted Grace's arm in a gesture of gratitude for her support, took it away from his shoulders, and stood up with renewed purpose.

"Okay," he said with a sigh of resignation. "Let's wrap him up in something and carry him down to his cabin. We should be sighting Saint Thomas by this evening. So I think the best thing to do now is to make landfall as quickly as possible and report the accident to the authorities. They can take it from there."

≈   ≈   ≈

Brewster sat at his desk in Miami Metro working on some

overdue reports when he spotted a familiar face across the busy room. Alexander Lewinsky was standing in the open doorway leading to the hall, talking to one of the other detectives by the elevator. Brewster saw the detective turn and point back in his direction.

Alexander looked over, spotted him, and then waved to attract his attention. Brewster beckoned him over, and seconds later, Alexander was sitting opposite him at the desk.

"So, tell me, what brings you down here, Mr. Lewinsky?" the detective asked, pushing aside a stack of manila folders.

Alexander shifted uncomfortably in his chair, glancing around nervously.

"Well?"

"Look, this is a bit delicate," Alexander said quietly, leaning forward with his elbows on the desk. It was clear he did not want anyone else to hear what he was about to say. "Detective, I need to tell you something, but you have to promise me you won't tell my wife."

"Mr. Lewinsky, this is a murder investigation. I cannot possibly make that promise. I think you must know that."

"Okay then," Alexander said, sitting back with a sigh of resignation. "But I am imploring you not to repeat this to her unless you feel it is absolutely necessary."

"Okay."

"*Absolutely*," Alexander reiterated.

"You have my word, Mr. Lewinsky."

On hearing this, the younger man took a deep, steadying breath. "Well, here goes. Look, I wanted to tell you this morning, but Sarah Jane was there when you called, so I couldn't. At least, not in front of her."

"Tell me what?" Brewster asked, sounding intrigued, sitting forward a bit more.

"It's about Richie and Gina," he said. "Well, to be more accurate, it's about Gina and me."

"Mother fucker," Brewster muttered beneath his breath, knowing immediately where this was going. "You and she?"

"Yes," Alexander said, lowering his eyes in shame. "We had an affair."

"You should have told me."

"How could I? You saw how upset my wife was. Something like this would destroy her."

"For how long?" asked Brewster.

"Oh, just for a couple of weeks. I mean, she ended it before she got pregnant. By the way, the baby was definitely not mine, if that's what you're thinking."

"That thought had occurred to me. But go on."

"Well, you see, I own a small bakery in Hialeah and used to call to their house every Saturday evening on the way home from work. I would usually drop in with a box of cakes and donuts. It's kind of an old tradition of ours. Since our college days. You know, sitting around for a few hours every Saturday night, playing cards, eating cakes and drinking beer. Just a bit of fun, a way to relax after a hard day's work. Quite harmless."

"Go on."

"Well, last year, Richie's roster was changed, and he began working graveyard shift at the hospital. Gina and I found ourselves alone every Saturday, and it just sort of happened. I won't go into the details, but we started the affair sometime in August and then decided to end it by mid-October. Only a couple of weeks really."

"Christ," said Brewster. "Don't tell me Richie found out?"

"I'm not sure if he did."

"What? How can you not know? After all, he is your friend, isn't he?"

"Yes," Alexander admitted, running a hand across his chin. "I'm sure Gina didn't tell him at the time. No, I would have known if she did. But then, she called me two weeks ago, the day after Richie came to our house looking for money, threatening to tell him and Sarah Jane about us if I didn't help them out. I could only manage to raise five thousand for them. Sarah Jane knows nothing about it, Detective. As for Richie, after I gave Gina the money, I'm just not sure if she ever told him or not."

"But Gina definitely did know about Richie's gambling debts?"

"Yes. I mean, no. I mean, eventually. You see, things became so bad when Richie got in deep that she knew something was going on. He was being threatened, receiving phone calls in the middle of the night. In the end, I think he just came out and told her about his problem. She wasn't happy about it, obviously, but stuck by him regardless. She supported him like a wife should, I suppose. That is what Gina was like, you see. She was a beautiful, loving human being."

"Except when she started blackmailing you," muttered Brewster.

"I didn't really blame her for that," said Alexander. "I mean, she was just trying to protect her family."

"Wait a second," Brewster interrupted. "Back it up a little."

"Huh? I don't follow."

"You and Gina had an affair, right? Well, I mean, hell, if a guy finds out his best friend is banging his wife, it is not something he generally keeps to himself now, is it?"

"No, I suppose not."

"So, once again, think hard. Did Richie know about the affair?"

"No, I suppose he didn't," said Alexander. "Or, at least, all I can tell you is he never said anything to me."

Brewster nodded with a thoughtful sigh and then watched as Alexander stood to leave. "Just one more thing while you're here," he said, stopping the younger man. "You wouldn't happen to know anything about Richie and one of the nurses at the hospital?"

Alexander appeared puzzled by the question. "Richie? Cheating on Gina? Are you serious?"

"So I take that as a no?"

"Look, Detective, all I can tell you is, once again, if he was up to anything like that, he never said a word to me about it."

≈   ≈   ≈

Isabella greeted Brophy when he emerged from the cabin just after two. She was back at the tiller again, keeping the *Dirty Nellie* on course while he caught a few hours' sleep. Squinting his eyes in the afternoon sunlight, he rubbed his unshaved chin and came out into the cockpit to sit beside her, handing her one of the two bottles of water he was carrying under his arm. He was also carrying a few pieces of fruit and placed them on the bench between them.

"How did you sleep?" she asked as she took a sip of the ice cold liquid.

"Not bad. I didn't realize I was so tired."

"Well, you were sailing through the night."

"I know," he said. "But I've done that a dozen times and stayed at the helm all the next day without so much as a yawn. Must be getting old, I guess."

"It happens to the best of us." She smiled.

"Hey, did you get something to eat?" he asked. "I could fix you some eggs if you like?"

"Nah, I'm good. While you were sleeping, I had a couple of those chocolate muffins I found in a tin below the counter. That will keep me going until this evening."

"You liked them, did you?"

"Sure," said Isabella. "Why?"

"It's just that, well, I made them myself."

"No way."

"Now, don't go spreading it around for Christ sakes, but I have been known to bake a pie from time to time."

"Well, those muffins are delicious."

"Thanks. The first time I ever tried was when Marcus was in junior high," he said. "Kid came home upset one day because they had been told to ask their moms to help them bake something. Well, it kind of struck a chord with him, since his mom passed away from cancer the previous year."

"Oh, I'm sorry to hear that."

Brophy shrugged. "Anyway, I told Marcus to dry his eyes and go fetch his mom's old recipe book. Took his mind right off things and kept us both occupied for the rest of the evening. We made a hell of a mess, though. But I swear we baked the biggest damn apple pie you have ever seen. Marcus took it into school the next day, the proudest kid on the bus."

"Was it good?" she asked.

"No, it tasted like shit." Brophy laughed. "I think it was probably the most disgusting thing anyone had ever tasted. The base and crust were still doughy, and we had sliced the apples whole instead of peeling them and cutting out the core first, so there were pips and lumps of peel in every slice. But Marcus didn't care one bit. He carried it into school that day and gave a big slice to his teacher."

Isabella smiled. "Oh shit, what did she say?"

"Not much, as far as I know. To hear him tell it, she just chewed for a minute or two, smiled awkwardly, and then swallowed hard while he watched. He never did see what became of the rest of it, but if I was asked to guess, I would say she threw it in the trash the minute his back was turned."

Isabella laughed. "Wow, it must have been difficult for you," she said. "I mean, raising a kid on your own like that."

"You know something?" he said. "It *was* difficult. I have fought hurricanes in the South Atlantic and tropical storms in the Pacific. I have even constructed a makeshift mast and rigging after mine was washed overboard off Cape Horn, but I swear to you, raising a kid was ten times harder than any of those things. But it was also more rewarding than anything else I have ever done in my life. I have loved every goddamned minute of it and wouldn't trade one of those years for anything. You see, Marcus was a great kid, full of fun and adventure, questioning everything. Hell, he is still like that."

"He sounds a lot like you," Isabella said quietly.

"Why, thank you, Detective." Brophy nodded with a smile. He raised his bottle in a gesture of appreciation and took a drink. "So, what about you?"

"Me?"

"Yeah. Are you married? Do you have any kids?"

"No kids," she replied with a shake of her head. "Just never had the time with my police work. But I was married for a while back there. Nine years to be precise."

"Oh yeah? So what happened?"

"Oh, it just didn't work out," she said. "After a few years pretending everything was okay, we finally decided to go our separate ways."

"Still friends?"

"Well, I wouldn't say that exactly. But we certainly never fell out. Oh, he's married somewhere up near Jacksonville. Last I heard, he runs his own accounting firm and has a couple of kids and a few dogs."

Brophy sat back. He took a drink of his water, breathed in the salt air, and leaned his head back to glance up at the sail. "Well, you have certainly got her nice and taut," he said after a pause. "Good to know you were paying attention when I showed you."

"And I have also been keeping us on course like you said," Isabella told him with a hint of pride, gesturing toward the compass. "South, south east. About an hour ago, the wind changed a little and the sails went a bit limp, so I pulled on the lines and tightened them like you instructed."

"Well, I'll be damned." He grunted, seemingly impressed as he looked at both sails with critical eyes.

"What?" she asked. "Did I do it wrong?"

"No," he said. "On the contrary, you did it just right."

Isabella could not help smiling at the compliment. She was the type of person who prided herself on doing things right and felt a deep sense of satisfaction that he was pleased.

"Damn, I'm beginning to think you are a natural at this."

"We must be almost on them now?" she said after a pause.

"I'd say about forty-five miles off," he said, checking the GPS. "We should be within sight in a couple of hours. Should be able to get Marcus's attention then."

Before Isabella could reply, however, a loud bang erupted from below deck, a grinding of metal and an ear-splitting screech that shook the entire wooden boat to its keel. Isabella bolted upright, worried as she turned to Brophy for an explanation.

"Christ, it's the damn pump," he growled angrily. "You stay here and keep us pointing due south while I try to get it going again."

She nodded, watching with concern as he rushed below again to carry out his repairs. Patrick Brophy was a strange man, she thought as she kept one eye on the compass to maintain their course. He was rough and ready, not shy about giving orders when the need arose. But he had also shown himself to be a kind, considerate man, one who cared deeply for his son. She had not met many men like him in her line of work. He didn't seem to be aware of the fine qualities he possessed and definitely did not put on an act or try to impress her. He was also quite handsome.

"Well?" she asked with raised eyebrows when he came back on deck about twenty minutes later, a large wrench in one hand, shirt off, covered in black grease and oil. "How does it look down there?"

"The motor's brushes have worn down and broken up in the blades," he said, shaking his head in frustration as he wiped his hands on an oil-stained cloth. "One of them snapped off and tore up the inside of the pump."

"Oh?"

"It's not good," he said, translating the technical details. "That pump is the only thing keeping the bilge dry."

"What does all that mean in English?" she asked in puzzlement.

Brophy dropped the cloth, rubbed his hands together, and sighed. "Loosely translated, I'm afraid it means we are sinking."

≈ ≈ ≈

While Grace went up on deck to man the wheel, Marcus and Harvey carried Benjamin's body, wrapped in tarpaulin from the storage room to his cabin, placing it on his bed and covering it with a sheet. They didn't speak as they worked. Harvey had unhooked the dead man's foot from the shelf, and both of them had then lifted him off the wooden bench and down onto a precut square of tarpaulin. With one at each end, they had tucked Benjamin's arms in by his sides, then had rolled him over a couple of times until he had been completely wrapped in the plastic.

To ensure his body had been sealed properly, Marcus had used silver duct tape to fasten both ends down after folding them over. The Saint Thomas Police would open it up when they arrived at the Virgin Islands. That would be when they would conduct an autopsy on Benjamin's body to determine the exact cause of death. There would be forms to fill out and questions to answer, of course. Lots and lots of questions. But, until then, Marcus just wanted to keep the dead New Yorker's body safe and out of sight.

"I need another drink," Harvey muttered gruffly as he shuffled away toward the seating area.

Marcus let him go, then turned to examine the radio which was lying dismantled on Benjamin's locker. Various scattered pieces caught his attention, and he began sifting through them for the transformer. It was strange. He couldn't find the small black transformer that powered the radio. He searched again, but it was nowhere to be found. Something odd was going on that he could not explain. He knew the transformer could not just disappear like that, but he was not in the right frame of mind to get his head around it at that moment in time. Whatever was going on, he decided, would have to wait until they were on dry land again.

After closing the cabin door, Marcus moved down the walkway and slipped into his own cabin. He knelt down, opened the small, metal safe beneath his bunk, and removed the bag containing his passengers' personal belongings. Examining its contents for a few seconds, he came across the plastic envelope that bore Benjamin's name. He sighed deeply as he removed it and then placed it back into the safe for the Saint Thomas police to examine. When the door was secure again, he stood up with the bag of remaining envelopes in his hand and then made his way out to rejoin the others.

Jayden was sitting at the table with an arm around Brianna's shoulder, holding her close. She had finally stopped crying, but her eyes were red and her face was ashen from the trauma she had experienced.

Brianna seemed to be a timid creature who, until now, had led a sheltered life. The sight of Benjamin's corpse seemed to have hit her hard. She could not be blamed for feeling that way, he mused. It was something she would never forget, something that would most likely haunt her dreams for many years to come.

Harvey was sitting opposite them at the table in the process of pouring two glasses of rum. He slid one across to the young black woman.

"There you go, love. Get that into you. Knock it back in one go and it will help calm you down."

"Brianna doesn't drink hard liquor," Jayden said with an air of disapproval. But even as he spoke, his young wife took the glass, raised it to her lips with a trembling hand, and downed it all in one loud gulp.

"Hey, go easy on that stuff," Marcus told them as Harvey followed suit and immediately began pouring another. "The Saint Thomas Police will want to question all of us about what happened. I don't think it will look too good if they come on board to find we have been drinking."

"To hell with the Saint Thomas Police," Harvey muttered with contempt. "Crikey, after what we've been through, we are entitled to have a couple of nips to calm our nerves."

"Well, I want everyone to take their belongings back,"

Marcus said, emptying the contents of the bag onto the tabletop. "Power up your phones and see if you can get a signal."

"Really?" said Jayden. "Out here at sea?"

"As we get closer to the Virgin Islands, there is a chance someone might pick one up," he said. "If anyone does, let me know, and I will call the harbor master to advise him of our arrival. If the police are there waiting for us, it should speed up the process for you guys, let you get ashore quicker so you can check into your hotels."

"What about you?" asked Jayden. "What are your plans for when we arrive?"

Marcus shook his head and sighed. "Me? Oh, I imagine I will be spending the next couple of days in the police station. I will also have to try to find out who Benjamin's next of kin is. I guess it will be up to me to break the news and probably organize returning his body back to the mainland."

"Well, if there is anything we can do, let us know," said Jayden.

"Thank you, man. I appreciate that."

"Of course, I assume we will all be getting a full refund," Harvey said as he opened his envelope and emptied its contents onto the table. He slipped his passport and wallet into his pocket and powered up his phone.

Marcus eyed him with distain. "All right then, I will arrange it as soon as I get a chance."

"Well, don't you worry about us," Jayden said. "Brianna and I aren't looking for our money back. With God's help, we just want to move on from this. Don't we, honey?"

Brianna nodded silently.

"Are you feeling any better?" Marcus asked.

"A little," she replied in a whisper. "Lord, I just got such a shock. I wasn't expecting anything like that."

"None of us were, love," Harvey muttered as he knocked back his second glass of rum. "But then, maybe we should have been. As your hubby so wisely pointed out on a number of occasions, the Lord works in mysterious ways, right?"

"And just what do you mean by that?" Marcus asked irritably.

"Well," continued the British man. "We all saw how incompetent Benjamin was when it came to sailing and manual labor."

"That's enough," snapped Marcus, fed up with him bad-mouthing everything and everyone all of the time. "I think you had better stop talking now."

"No, I am entitled to voice my opinion. And I am serious when I say that Benjamin had no business signing up for a trip like this. He was a weak little man, awkward and clumsy. We all saw it. You can't deny it. He almost killed me, for Christ's sake. So I mean it when I say he was quite literally an accident waiting to happen."

"Oh, that is just nonsense," said Jayden.

"Is that, like, what you two were arguing about this afternoon?" Brianna asked quietly.

The cabin fell silent for a moment, all attention focusing on Harvey.

"What do you mean?" Marcus asked Brianna. "Did you just say they were arguing?"

"No, we were not," snapped Harvey.

"Why, yes, yes you were," said Brianna. "Don't you remember, Harvey? I was going into my cabin to take a nap, and I saw you two arguing in the walkway by the storage room. You seemed extremely angry. You had him back against the wall and were, like, tapping at his chest with your finger."

"Oh, that is just out and out rubbish," exclaimed Harvey. "You don't know what the hell you are talking about, stupid woman."

"Hey, hey," said Jayden. "I will ask you *not* to talk to my wife like that."

"Well, I will ask you to ask your wife *not* to go around making up stories," said Harvey. "I think that glass of rum has gone to her head already."

Marcus sat forward, placed his elbows on the table, and clasped his fingers together. "Look, Harvey, don't play games here. Were you or were you not arguing with Benjamin today? It's a simple question."

"Oh, I see what is going on," Harvey said with a wave of his hand. "This is utterly ridiculous. What on earth are you all implying? Ay? That I had an argument with the man and then bashed his head in?"

Brianna winced visibly.

"Look, no one is implying anything of the sort," Marcus assured him. "I am simply asking whether or not you and Benjamin were arguing this afternoon. It's a simple question."

"Okay, so we had words, yes. But I definitely wouldn't call it an argument." And then, looking accusingly toward Brianna, "And I *certainly* did not have him pinned against the wall, nor was I jabbing my finger into his chest."

"So what was it all about then?" asked Marcus.

"Nothing. Really. It was nothing. Just a silly discussion about nothing."

"I heard you threatening him," said Brianna.

"I did not threaten him!" Harvey shouted at the top of his voice. He fell silent for a second, then muttered, "Well, not really."

"Well then, what did you do?" Marcus asked, growing impatient.

Harvey sat back with a rueful expression and a quick shrug of his shoulders. He finished the last drop of rum in his second glass and sighed loudly as he poured a third. "Look, if I tell you what happened, you are going to think all kinds of crazy stuff."

"Just tell us," said Marcus. "We will believe whatever you have to say."

"Okay, okay. Well, what happened was that Benjamin stopped me in the walkway this afternoon and accused me of sabotaging the radio."

"The radio?" Marcus asked in surprise.

"Yes, can you believe that nonsense? He opened it up in his cabin while the rest of us were busy on deck. Then he came storming out and happened to catch me passing by in the hallway. He claimed I removed some sort of transformer mechanism from it."

"Removed? Are you sure he said removed?"

"Why? Don't tell me you are buying into this—"

"Just think for a second. Did he actually say it had been removed?"

"Yes. That is definitely what he said. Removed."

"But why would he accuse you?" Marcus asked, shaking his head. Benjamin must have had a reason to suspect Harvey. Why else would he make such an accusation?

"It was stupid, really. He caught me messing around with it the other night while I was supposed to be up on deck keeping watch."

"Messing around? How do you mean?"

"Oh, this is just silly. I know what you are all thinking."

"No, please go on. I want to hear it."

"Well, the truth is, I simply wanted to find out who had won an important soccer match played that evening. The Champions League Final, to be exact. I support Chelsea, and they were playing Barcelona."

"Go on."

"Well, Benjamin walked in while I was trying to get the damned thing working. Which I never did, by the way. Like you, I could not get it to turn on."

"So, Benjamin accused you of meddling with it?"

"Not meddling," replied Harvey. "He was very precise in his accusation. He downright said I purposefully sabotaged it."

"And did you?" Jayden asked.

Harvey did not answer. He just shot Jayden an angry glance.

"So, what was it you were saying to him when Brianna saw you two together?" asked Marcus.

"Oh, here we go. As soon as I tell you, you are all going to get crazy."

"Please, Harvey," said Marcus. "You have already told us what really happened. We just need to know what you said in response to Benjamin's accusation."

"Okay then, if you must know."

"Go on."

"I told him he was a sniveling little prick—"

"Oh my Lord," Brianna exclaimed.

"And I told him if he ever accused me of anything like that again, I would—"

"Go on," Marcus prompted him when he hesitated.

"All right then, if you really must know. I told him if he ever accused me of anything like that again, I would break his bloody neck!"

≈   ≈   ≈

Captain Franklin was talking on the telephone, sitting on the edge of his polished teak desk when Brewster entered his office. He motioned for the detective to take a seat, as he continued speaking to someone in a low voice. Brewster scanned the room while he waited, fixing first on the various marksmanship trophies in a glass cabinet to his left, then to a neat row of framed photographs lining the main wall. The majority of them were of the captain in the company of other police officials and politicians, as well as some minor local celebrities. Award ceremonies and charity functions mainly, it seemed Captain Franklin was not shy about getting his name in the paper.

"That was the medical examiner," he said when he finally hung up the phone. He returned to the comfort of his reclining leather chair on the other side of the desk. "Doctor Walker."

"Any more news?" asked Brewster.

"Just official confirmation that the John Doe from the harbor is not our killer."

"So, it seems Garcia was right."

"It seems so," the captain agreed with a sigh, keeping his eyes fixed on Brewster for any sign of mockery or triumphalism. But none came. "You know where she is?" he asked after a few seconds. "Internal affairs are still trying to set up a meeting with her."

Brewster sat forward in his chair. "Look, all I can tell you is she is somewhere in the Caribbean."

"Christ on a bike," muttered the captain. "Why the hell does that not surprise me?"

"I don't think anything that woman does can surprise me anymore," agreed Brewster.

"So, you know what she's up to down there? The last time I spoke to her, I seem to recall she had some hare-brained hunch about the suspect making his escape on a cruise ship."

"I don't think it was a ship." Brewster corrected him. "More like a sailing yacht of some sort."

"Whatever," Captain Franklin said dismissively. "If it doesn't fly or run on wheels, I couldn't care less if it was the goddamned Titanic itself."

Brewster pursed his lips and nodded. "Well, anyway, it seems she hitched a ride with some sailor she met at the marina and is now on her way down to the Virgin Islands after the other boat. She asked me to run the names of the passengers on board, but so far, I have not had much luck at all."

"She asked you to run names?" The captain's eyes narrowed, and he looked accusingly at the detective sitting before him. "When exactly did she do that?"

Brewster knew he had spilled the beans on himself but decided to keep going. He had been conducting the investigation behind the captain's back, but there was no point in beating around the bush now.

"She radioed me after they set sail, asked me to run the names and a blood sample she found."

"Ah yes," said the captain. "The infamous blood sample she found at the marina. I had forgotten about that. Did you log it in as evidence?"

Brewster winced a little. "No. No, I didn't."

"Christ," muttered the captain. "That's a rookie's mistake. If you don't log it in, it won't be admissible if this goes to court."

"Okay. I'll do it as soon as we are done."

"Did you at least send it to the lab?"

"Yes, but nothing back yet."

"Well, I will get on to forensics and tell them to get the finger out."

"Captain, could you also put a call through to the Saint Thomas police and ask them to be on standby for Garcia's arrival?" asked Brewster.

"I suppose I could do that."

"And could you ask them to be on the lookout for the other boat?" He checked his notebook for a second. "It's a catamaran called the *Wild Rover*."

"Anything else?" the captain asked sarcastically.

Brewster shook his head. Under the circumstances, things were not going too bad, so he did not want to push his luck with the captain any more than he needed to.

"What about you?" Franklin asked after a pause.

"Sir?"

"Do you think this guy is on that boat too? Like Garcia?"

"Hell, sir, I don't know. But if that woman has a hunch, I have learned over the years it is worth following up."

"You find out anything else of interest while you were out there conducting this investigation behind my back? Like, for example, who this guy could be and why in God's name he would murder a pretty young mother like that?"

"I did discover a few truths about the husband, Richie Regazzoni."

"Oh? Go on."

"I found out he is into Sal di Maggio for fourteen thousand."

"You don't say? Gambling?"

"Yes."

"Di Maggio and his crew are dangerous people to owe money to."

"I know. I had a few words with him this morning and—"

"Is that how you got that cauliflower ear?" the captain asked, interrupting him.

Brewster pursed his lips again and nodded.

"Go on," Captain Franklin said with a little smile.

"Well, after a little bit of, err, *persuasion*, Sal opened up and told me all about it. Richie actually owed nineteen thousand, but after Sal's boys threatened to break his legs, he came up with five to buy himself a little time."

"Where did he get it?"

"That is the other interesting thing I learned," said Brewster. "He got it from his friend, Andrew Lewinsky, who I discovered had an affair with the dead woman, Gina. It seems she threatened to tell Richie and Lewinsky's wife about them if he didn't come up with the money."

"Hell, this just gets better and better," said the captain. "Tell me, have you spoken to this Richie character yet?"

"He's coming in this afternoon. But I am taking a trip to Fort Lauderdale before that to visit the hospital where he works and have a chat with some of his coworkers. According to Sal, he has been having an affair of his own with one of the nurses there."

"Okay then," said the captain. "You go ahead and do that. But then, I want you to get back here and really put the screws on this Richie character. There is something odd about all of this, something that is not right. And, in my experience, that old saying about *no smoke without fire* is usually true. As for big Sal di Maggio, we'll get back to him later."

"You want to sit in on the interview with Richie?"

"The husband? Hell yes. Wild horses couldn't stop me."

CHAPTER SEVEN

HARMLESS FUN

Patrick Brophy's head emerged from the foam at the stern of the *Dirty Nellie* as Isabella reached down to help him climb back on board. Wearing nothing but a pair of shorts, he scrambled up the three wooden steps leading back into the small cockpit and collapsed down for a while to catch his breath. Isabella picked up a towel and draped it over his shoulders.

With the mainsail and jib lowered, the small craft was now still and unmoving, except for an intermittent bobbing motion with every ebb and flow of the waves. Thirty minutes earlier, Brophy had gone over the side while Isabella had waited anxiously for him to reappear. He had explained to her that if he could seal up the hairline gaps in the wooden keel, he might be able to buy them some time before sinking. It had been a long shot, but they'd had no other choice. A difficult task on dry land at the best of times, but out there in the middle of the ocean, almost impossible. Without oxygen or diving gear, he'd had no option but to hold his breath each time he went under. He had carried a tin of waterproof sealant, and each time he'd made his way beneath the keel, he had dug some out with his hand and worked it into the rough cracked wood with his fingers.

While he had been gone, Isabella had sat at the stern, waiting for his return. His head had broken the surface every three of four minutes, and he had gasped loudly as oxygen had filled his lungs, before disappearing again beneath the swirling foam. She'd found herself wondering what the hell she was doing out there. Until two days ago, she had never even been on a boat before, and now, here she was drifting in the middle of the Caribbean with a man she had only just met, waiting to sink.

"Oh my God!" She suddenly rose to her feet and cupped her hands around her mouth to make her voice even louder. She had spotted a telltale black fin circling about twenty yards out that immediately sent a shiver of fear down her spine. "Get out of the water, Brophy! Get out of the water!"

Brophy's head emerged from the foam. He looked in the direction she pointed, twisting around to see the encircling shark. She heard him curse. He quickly tried to swim around toward the steps. But things did not go according to plan. As he kicked off to move around to the stern, the left leg of his shorts caught on a protruding nail, pulling him back. He thrashed his hands out in an effort to break free.

Isabella watched the shark closely and saw it turn suddenly, alerted by Brophy's movement. It had been swimming parallel to the *Dirty Nellie* but suddenly turned head on and began drawing nearer. Isabella wasted no time. Moving like lightening, she ducked down through the hatch and disappeared into the cabin, reappearing moments later.

When the material of Brophy's shorts finally ripped, he broke free, the approaching shark almost upon him. In obvious desperation, he reached out a hand and grabbed the nearby rail, pulling himself toward it. His other hand scrambled for the farther side rail, and he tried to get his right foot up onto the lowest step. Too late, however, for even as he did so, the long, gray shark opened its mouth and moved in for the kill.

Isabella raised her revolver, took aim, and fired a series of shots. Without a second to spare, she put one foot up on the stern post and leaned over, firing directly down into the gaping mouth of razor-sharp teeth. The shark twisted and turned violently as the bullets ripped into it, before falling backwards with a splash and disappearing almost instantly beneath the bubbling red foam. A few seconds later, she helped Brophy up the steps and back into the safety of the cockpit.

"Wow." He gasped, still hunched over trying to catch his breath, water dripping from his body. "That was a close call."

Isabella sat on the seat and placed her own head in her hands.

"You okay?" he asked through squinted eyes.

"Me? Hell yeah, I'm just fine. Couldn't be better."

"Are you sure?" he asked.

"I mean, Brophy, why wouldn't I be?" she asked. "Considering I have just shot my first great white and all."

Brophy was silent for the longest time before saying, "Hey, don't get mad or anything, but it was actually a Caribbean Reef Shark."

"Well, whatever the hell it was, I just put six bullets down its throat, so it won't be coming back any time soon."

They both laughed, relieving the tension and trauma of what they had just endured. There was a growing chemistry between them, an undeniable bond forming. Eventually, Isabella sat back with a deep sigh and turned to him.

"Well, how are things looking down there?"

"It's not as bad as I thought," Brophy said when his breath finally came back to him. "There were a couple of cracks I couldn't get to, but I did manage to seal most of them up. At least enough to buy us some time."

"How much time?" Isabella asked anxiously.

"Well, with the main ones sealed, and if I can put the pump back together, get it working at even a quarter of its capacity, I reckon we could get another one or two hours."

"One or two hours? Is that all? Will that be enough to get us to Saint Thomas?"

"It should be," he replied. "But we will first have to raise these sails and move as fast as we can. We will also have to take shifts bailing out by hand."

"Okay. So, how do we do that?"

Brophy dropped the towel to the deck and slipped his t-shirt and pants back on. "While you raise the sails, I will go and lift up the cabin floor so it will be easier to reach. Then, it is just a matter of scooping out the bilge water by hand. That means you reach in and fill the plastic bailing buckets, then take them up on deck and throw the water over the side. It will be hard, exhausting work, but if we take it in fifteen-minute shifts, it should buy us enough time to get close to Saint Thomas before we go under."

"Okay then," Isabella said with renewed purpose. "Let's get to it as soon as possible."

"Just two other things," Brophy said before leaving her. "I

think we should inflate the dingy and fill it with supplies. If my calculations are wrong, or something unforeseen happens, I think we should be ready to abandon the *Dirty Nellie* at a minute's notice."

"Okay, that makes sense. What's the other thing?"

"Well, apart from you putting on your lifejacket, I think we should send out a distress signal in case there are any ships in the area and then start letting off a flare every fifteen minutes. It's a long shot, now that they have gotten farther ahead of us, but there is an outside chance the *Wild Rover* might just see one and turn back."

"But what about what we discussed?" asked Isabella, trying to keep her composure under the circumstances. "You know, about the killer being alerted by our flares? About what he might do if he realizes we are after him?"

Brophy put his hands on his hips and shook his head. "I'm afraid that can't be helped. Unless you have a better idea, sometimes you just have to do what is needed and hope for the best."

≈   ≈   ≈

Grace sat in the cockpit of the *Wild Rover*, sipping at the mug of hot coffee Marcus had just brought her from the galley. She had been steering the large catamaran for the past hour while he and Harvey had stowed Benjamin's body in his cabin, keeping them on course for the Virgin Islands, which were now less than one hundred miles away. But now, with him at the wheel, she was finally able to sit back and rest for a while, to lift her feet up and fold them under her as she sat back on the comfortable cushioned seating.

As she looked on, Marcus adjusted the main sail for maximum speed and then tightened the jib and tied off the sheet in the cockpit. Watching him, she realized how she had grown to like the young captain in the past couple of days, feeling comfortable in his presence. Unlike most of the guys she had met lately, he did not seem to have an ulterior motive for being friendly toward her. She could tell he also felt an attraction by the way he looked at her. She had a sense for those sorts of things and knew the signs from experience. However, unlike most of the guys she knew back on land, he treated her with respect, with a kindness and warmth that was genuine, not forced. She really liked that about him and was even more attracted to him for it.

"So, how are you holding up, Marcus?" she asked with concern when he finished adjusting the sails and returned to take the wheel.

"Me? Oh, I guess I'm okay, considering," he said. "I am more worried about you, Grace. You were supposed to be here enjoying a vacation, and now you have found yourself caught up in all of this."

"Don't worry about me. I am fine," she said, trying to sound upbeat. "Apart from having to put up with that old dog in heat, Harvey, I was actually having a wonderful time until, of course, what happened to poor Benjamin."

"What happened to Benjamin is something I will never forgive myself for," Marcus said quietly. "I don't think I will ever get over it."

Grace placed a gentle hand on his arm. "Of course, you will, Marcus. Time heals all wounds. Believe me, I know."

"I really do appreciate how strong you have been throughout all of this. You have been a real rock."

"Look, I know it is a tragic, horrible thing to have happened," she said. "It has shaken us all. But honestly, Marcus, I have never been one to panic or get hysterical. Whatever life throws at me, I deal with it the best way I can. I think you have to adopt the same outlook and just get on with it."

"You must be a very strong woman then."

"I think I am," she replied. "At least, emotionally."

"Oh? Why is that, do you think?"

Grace shrugged. "Well, when I was thirteen, my parents died in a car crash."

"My God, I'm so sorry."

"It's okay. I'm over it now. Stronger. But, at the time, I was devastated. I shut myself away for months, afraid to face the future without them. After a while, I came to the conclusion I could either withdraw from the world, becoming sullen and mistrusting, or I could just quit feeling sorry for myself and go out and get on with my life. So, Marcus, I decided to embrace the good and the bad as it came, to live my time to the fullest like my parents would have wanted."

"You know, I lost my mother when I was young, too,"

said Marcus. "She died of cancer when I was ten."

"I'm sorry," Grace said, running her hand up and down his arm, wanting to show him sympathy.

"But at least I had my dad," he said. "It must have been so much harder for you. I really admire the way you have remained so strong."

"Thank you," she said, pausing for a moment before continuing. "So, how are the others doing in there? Is Brianna okay?"

"Harvey is still bitching and complaining, insisting he gets a full refund when the trip is over. He also wants me to pay his hotel bill on Saint Thomas. And Jayden, well, he is doing his best to comfort Brianna after the shock of finding Benjamin like that."

"You know, I am a little bit worried about her," said Grace.

"Oh, I think she will be okay. Harvey gave her a drop of rum, and it seemed to calm her down."

"No, I don't mean that. I mean, I am worried about her mental state."

"I'm sorry. I don't follow."

"Well, this morning, when you saw her leaving my cabin so upset, she had been confiding in me that Jayden was having mood swings since their wedding, trying to control her every move."

"Oh? That is odd. I can't say I noticed anything like that at all. Jayden might be a bit of an uptight bible basher, but he doesn't strike me as the controlling type."

"She told me he stormed out of their hotel room on the night before we set sail after finding a pack of birth control pills in her bag. She said he had become overly religious and would not hear of her taking them."

"Christ, I know he's a bit of a Jesus freak, but—"

"Wait, that's not it at all," said Grace. "You see, I approached him on deck this afternoon while Brianna was taking her nap in their cabin. I thought I might have a discrete word. You know, to try to help them get through it."

"That was very thoughtful of you."

"Maybe, but the strange thing was, Marcus, when I mentioned it to him, he broke down in tears. I mean, a grown man, crying like a baby. He confided in me that he was at his wits end with Brianna and was scared to death she was having some sort of psychotic episode. He told me how she was the one who was having mood swings, and how she was the one who stormed out of their hotel and was gone all night."

"You are kidding. Do you believe him?"

"I'm not sure. I think so. Yes. He seems genuinely worried about her, Marcus. He said he was distraught and almost called the police, but she eventually phoned about three in the morning to say she was sorry and would meet him down at the marina."

"Very, very strange," muttered Marcus. "So which one of them is telling the truth? And why lie about it in the first place?"

"I don't know," said Grace. "But I do know I caught Brianna in my cabin this morning going through my stuff. There is something strange about that girl, Marcus. At first, she said she wanted to borrow my camera and didn't want to wake me. Then, she suddenly changed her story and broke into tears, telling me that tale about looking for birth control pills."

"Odd," said Marcus.

"What is odder still is Jayden confided to me that she has recently been in the hospital after some sort of mental breakdown. He said she was diagnosed as being sterile and went off the deep end. The fact is, if he is telling the truth, Brianna doesn't even need birth control pills on account of not being able to conceive."

"Shit."

"Jayden says the doctors think the news had something to do with her breakdown and her subsequent mood swings. He thought getting married and coming down here would solve all Brianna's problems."

"Wow, the poor girl. I don't know what to say. They seem such a normal, happy couple. And I'm sure finding Benjamin in the storage cabin like that has not helped her state of mind at all."

"I really don't know what is true and what is not," Grace continued quietly. "According to her, he is a controller who has taken his religious calling a little too seriously, but according to him, she has been having these mental problems, and since being released from the hospital, she has flat out refused to attend her scheduled psychiatric appointments. He is also worried because he suspects she is not taking her medication the way she is supposed to."

Marcus fell silent for a moment, looking deep in thought. "You don't think she had anything to do with Benjamin's accident, do you?"

"Oh God, no," said Grace. "I am not suggesting that for one second. Please, don't get me wrong, Marcus. I'm just saying I am worried about her. About what the consequences of all this could do to her."

"Well then, if you think what you have just told me is shocking, wait until you hear what I just heard."

"What's that?"

"While you were out here, the rest of us had a little heart to heart chat in the main cabin, and some very interesting and disturbing facts have come to light."

Grace waited in anticipation.

"A few minutes ago, I learned how Harvey and Benjamin had a violent argument outside the storage room a short time before he died. It seems Harvey was threatening Benjamin with breaking his neck."

"No. Threatening him? But, why?"

"Seemingly, Benjamin claimed the radio had been deliberately sabotaged, and he accused Harvey of doing it."

"None of that makes any sense," said Grace. "Why on earth would Harvey want to break the radio? After all, he was the one giving out about not being able to use it from the start."

Marcus shrugged. "Well, look," he said quietly. "No matter what the outcome of all this is, I would like to say thank you, Grace. We will be in Saint Thomas soon, and once the police board, I may not get another chance."

"Why thank me?"

"Don't think I haven't noticed how you have been helping everyone out these past few days. Me included."

"Well, I am part of the crew, aren't I?"

"You certainly are. But it was more than that. You really have shown yourself to be a kind-hearted person, Grace."

"Shucks, that's just my saintly nature," she said with a big smile. "But don't forget, Marcus, what you call helpful, others might call interfering."

"Well, I wouldn't dream of calling you that," he said with

a chuckle. "You have made friends with everyone here and have been there to offer support and encouragement."

"Oh now, you are embarrassing me."

They fell silent for a few minutes, during which time, Marcus adjusted the wheel to keep them on course. It was an easy silence, one that sat well between two people who felt comfortable in each other's presence.

"Hey, Marcus," Grace said eventually. "Would you mind if I asked you something?"

"Sure, go right ahead."

"When we get to Saint Thomas and you eventually finish your business with the police..."

"Yeah?"

"Well, I was just wondering if you would like to have dinner with me. I know, while we are out here at sea, you are the captain, and I am just another shipmate. There are certain protocols you probably must observe."

"There are."

"But I was wondering, I mean, I was hoping, when this voyage is over, maybe you and I could get to know each other a bit better?"

≈ ≈ ≈

Brewster left his car in the parking lot of the Broward Psychiatric Health Facility on the outskirts of Fort Lauderdale. Slipping his jacket on as he walked, he entered the steel and glass building through a large revolving door. Outside, the sprawling grounds were landscaped with an impressive water fountain shooting spray up from the center of a small, circular lake. The grass was freshly cut, bright green and well cared for, watered against the harsh Florida heat by countless buried sprinklers whose sputtering jets moved in circular motions across the lawn. Beds of brightly colored flowers bordered the inner areas with islands of pink Bougainvillea shrubs and cabbage palms placed at precise intervals around the grounds.

A handful of people outside strolled about the gardens in the midday sun. The patients wore white dressing gowns, while those members of the staff keeping an eye on them were dressed in light blue hospital uniforms. Some of the patients seemed lucid enough to Brewster, chatting amongst themselves in small, intimate groups at the edge of the car lot. But others, he noticed, appeared more sedated. They sat quietly alone on the benches or in wheelchairs, staring blankly off into the distance as if lost in their own troubled worlds.

Once inside, the detective checked in at reception and then walked down a wide, brightly lit corridor leading toward the private wards. There were countless signs to direct visitors, but he knew where he was going. He rode the elevator to the first floor and turned left down the corridor. When he came to an intersection, he kept to the right and walked straight up to a small, circular nurse's station at the end of the hall. The nurse behind the counter greeted him with a warm smile.

"Good afternoon, sir, how may I help you?"

"I'm Detective Brewster from Miami Metro," he said politely. "Doctor Hibbits is expecting me."

When he came down the hall a few minutes later, Doctor Nathan Hibbits welcomed Brewster with a shake of his hand and quickly led him off into a small, side office. Apart from a few polite, introductory words, they did not discuss the detective's reason for being there as they walked. "I am afraid the walls in here have ears," he explained as he closed the door behind them. They were alone in the room, sitting down on either side of a small metal desk by the wall. "When you work with women, especially young nurses, you quickly learn that rumor and gossip are transmitted faster than the internet."

"I can imagine," Brewster said with a polite smile. He took out his notepad and placed it on the desktop. "But I don't think that is unique to young nurses. You should try working in a police station, Doctor. Some of the older guys there are worse than women."

"So, Detective, you said you wished to interview Richie Regazzoni's coworkers on the night shift."

"Just the female ones," Brewster said. "And it really is more like just a couple of questions than an interview."

Doctor Hibbits sighed, clasping his fingers together on the desk. "This is, indeed, such an awkward, terrible time for us all. I cannot even comprehend what poor Richie is going through. We are all still in deep shock after hearing the news."

"I can imagine," said Brewster. "It was a terrible tragedy,

to be sure."

"So, you will be a little sympathetic and understanding with the young ladies? Please try not to upset them too much at such a sensitive time."

"I promise you, Doctor, I will make this as quick and painless as I can."

"I never had the pleasure of meeting Richie's wife," Doctor Hibbits said after a short pause. "But I do believe she was a very nice young woman."

Brewster nodded in agreement, waited a few seconds, and then raised his eyebrows. "Do you happen to have that list?"

"Oh yes, yes of course," said the doctor. "And all three young women are here. They came in especially to see you."

"I really do appreciate their cooperation."

"Detective, would you like me to remain in the room while you talk to them?" asked Doctor Hibbits.

Brewster shook his head without even thinking about it. "No. If you don't mind, Doctor, I would rather you just leave me to it."

"Of course," he said, slipping a small computer printout from his white coat pocket and handing it over. "That is a list of the hospital's current employees. I have highlighted the names of the three nurses who work the night shift with Richie."

"Excellent," said Brewster. "Would you mind asking the first one to come in?"

"Of course," Doctor Hibbits said as he stood up and headed for the door. "I'll leave you to it and send Nurse Torres in immediately."

When he was gone, Brewster examined the names on the list before opening his notepad to the next available blank page. He sat for a few seconds, whistling to himself, surveying the small examination room about him. There was no window, just an old torn poster on the wall of a stream and meadow, which he assumed was supposed to instill calmness and serenity. Brewster raised his eyebrows, not feeling very calm or serene.

Then he cast his gaze around again, noticing that, apart from the desk and two chairs against the wall, there was very little furniture to speak of. There were, of course, the usual hospital bills adorning the notice board by the door, a flyer advising all men over forty to seek a prostate examination, and another showing a mother and father with their two children, all smiling beneath a heading announcing that *mental disease is a silent killer*. Brewster knew of other silent killers. He and Isabella Garcia had put a few of them away over the years. His mind drifted back when a light tapping on the door broke his train of thought.

"Come on in."

The door creaked open a few inches and a woman's head peered nervously around the frame. She was a young, dark-skinned Latina nurse who hesitated for a moment before entering. Brewster waved her in, greeting her with a polite, businesslike smile.

"Hi, I'm Detective Brewster from Miami Metro."

They shook hands.

"Hello," she said shyly. "I am Nurse Torres."

"Nurse Maria Torres?" Brewster asked, consulting the printout. He released her hand when she confirmed it and motioned for her to sit down. He could see she was nervous and tried to put her at ease with another polite smile. But she just stared back at him with a look of trepidation.

"Do you mind if I call you Maria?"

Nurse Torres shook her head to indicate she did not mind.

"You can call me Byron if you like."

"Okay."

"So, Maria, first off, I am really sorry to have called you in like this, but I just have a couple of questions to ask."

The young woman shifted uncomfortably and nodded her understanding again.

"Nothing to worry about," he said reassuringly.

Nurse Torres swallowed hard and returned a weak smile.

"Okay then," Brewster began. "So, I assume you have heard about Richie Regazzoni's wife?"

"We all have," she said. "It is horrible. Just horrible."

"Tell me, Maria, did you happen to know Gina?"

"No, I never met her. But Richie brought in photographs of her and the baby a couple of days ago. Poor Richie. He must be heartbroken."

"I'm sure he is. It's a terrible thing."

"Yes. Yes it is."

"Did you happen to notice if Richie seemed upset or dis-tracted in any way in the past couple of days? You know, be-fore what happened?"

The young woman returned a blank stare, saying nothing.

"I mean, was he acting in any way different than usual?"

"Is Richie in trouble?"

"Good Lord, no, not at all. These are just routine ques-tions, Maria. You understand? For the file."

"Oh, I see," she said, shifting a little in the chair, growing a bit more comfortable in his presence. She placed her hands before her on the desk.

Brewster noticed she was not wearing any rings. "Well? Did you sense anything odd about his behavior?"

"No," she said. "Definitely not. Richie is a very hard work-er. He is good at his job. When he is not tending to the pa-tients, he is usually preparing things for the morning shift. He didn't seem any different than normal as far as I could tell."

"You two spend much time together on the night shift?"

Nurse Torres shrugged. "I guess. About as much as any-one else, I suppose. We have a team meeting before we start work, make our plans regarding the patients for the coming night, then we all go about our duties until we sit down for a coffee break about three hours later. There is always so much to do here, you know. Many of the patients can't sleep, so sometimes, it can be just as busy as the day shift."

"And how long is your coffee break?"

"Fifteen minutes maximum," she said. "We also take a half hour lunch break at five."

Now that he had her relaxed and talking, Brewster looked directly into her eyes and went for the big one. "Maria, I apologize in advance for asking this, but there is really no other way than to just come right out and say it."

"Hmm?" The young nurse raised her eyebrows in curiosity.

"The thing I need to know is, are you aware if any of the nurses here had a relationship with Richie?"

"Relationship? I don't really follow."

"Uh-huh. Now, I don't mean a work relationship, you un-derstand? I mean the other kind."

Norse Torres looked down in embarrassment, and he knew instinctively she was hiding something. He waited patiently while she considered her answer, before eventually saying, "Maria?"

His voice seemed to startle her. She sat upright a bit more and shifted again. "I don't know. You will have to ask the others."

"Maria, I don't think you are being totally honest with me. You do realize I am conducting a murder investigation here? I am afraid I am going to need a more definite answer."

The young woman considered his words for a few more seconds before emitting a sigh.

"Look," he told her. "I know this is difficult and awkward for you. And I am sorry. Really. But you have got to tell me what you know for the sake of poor Gina Regazzoni and that helpless little baby."

Her eyes met his.

"You won't get into trouble," he said. "I promise. This is a strictly confidential discussion between you and me. Your superiors will not be told about any of it, so your job is not at risk in any way. But as I have said before, this is a murder investigation. Serious stuff. So you should think, Maria. Think very carefully about what you are going to say."

"I know it is a very serious investigation," she suddenly said.

"So, would you like to reconsider your answer and tell me what it is you know?"

"Yes."

"Yes, you would like to reconsider your answer?"

"No. I mean, the answer to your question is yes," she said.

"So, one of the nurses on the night shift *did* have a relationship with Richie?"

"No."

Brewster sighed loudly. "I'm sorry," he said, looking up perplexed from his pad. "I have to say, I am getting a bit confused here."

"It wasn't just one nurse. You see, we were all sleeping with him."

"What, all three of you?"

"Yes. Not at the same time, of course, but on different nights."

Brewster raised his eyebrows in amazement. "Richie, Richie, Richie," he whispered beneath his breath.

"Look, it was just a bit of harmless fun," the young nurse said with a meek, innocent shrug. "When you work nights like we do, things can get very boring."

≈ ≈ ≈

Sal di Maggio's back was aching, his ears ringing from the incessant moaning and bickering of his two companions. All three men were cramped into the front of the battered white van they had stolen earlier that day. Sal was in the driver's seat with the stocky bald man on the passenger's side and the younger lanky barman sitting between them in the middle. Both of Sal's companions were nursing the broken noses given to them by Brewster. Vinney, the stocky man, had his nose simply bent out of shape, but Joey, the young barman's was a lot worse, swollen, covered at the bridge by a large plaster with both of his eyes blackened and bruised. The van was parked off the road in an area of waste ground opposite an electrical warehouse in Little Havana, and they had been waiting there for over two hours for the signal to move in.

The surrounding district was rundown with no one in sight, full of old factories, warehouses, and storage lockups. It was a virtual ghost town at that time of the late evening with little or no traffic or pedestrians except for a few workers coming and going from a small lithographic printing company near the end of the block. But Sal and his companions were not looking to have something printed. The unit that interested them was one of the larger buildings closer to the river. Surrounded by a high mesh fence with razor wire on top, it was a two-story warehouse constructed of concrete and aluminum cladding with an overhanging corrugated iron roof. There were no windows on the ground floor, just a wide ramp with a large roll-up bay door for loading. The small office area was situated above this on the second floor with a row of narrow mesh-covered windows running side by side from one end of the building to the other.

Joey had been talking a lot of stick to the other two over the undue length of time they had been waiting. He was the one responsible for bringing them there in the first place, announcing that very afternoon how a contact of his in the warehouse just called. He said the man was working as a temporary security guard and informed him that a shipment of two hundred brand new laptops had arrived and were just sitting on pallets, waiting for a truck to transport them to Jacksonville the next morning. For the first twenty minutes or so, everything inside the van had been fine, but then, as the evening wore on, muscles tired, tempers became frayed, and a number of arguments broke out. The two men with the broken noses were bickering to Sal that they wanted to seek revenge on the black detective, but the older man was having none of it and laid down the law.

"Why don't you two boombots shut the fuck up and just leave it be?" he hollered when he could take no more of their bitching. "You guys started it in the first place, so you two got what you fucking deserved."

Before either of them could respond, the bay door suddenly began to rise, slowly at first, then faster until they could finally see a man standing in the opening. He was dressed as a security guard and switched on and off his flashlight a number of times to attract their attention.

"Yep, that's him," Joey said. "That's my guy."

"What the fuck is he doing with that flashlight?" Vinney asked irritably. "The way he's waving it about, he looks like he's in a fucking James Bond movie."

"That's the fucking signal," Joey said. "I told him to do it."

"Why can't he just wave us in? Why does he have to be so fucking mysterious about it?"

"Jesus Christ, will you two stop bitching," snapped Sal, firing up the engine and guiding the van carefully across the bumpy waste ground and then out onto the tarmac that led toward the gate. "It's like spending the night with two old women."

As they rolled to a stop at the gate, Vinney jumped out and snapped the heavy-duty lock and chain with a bolt cutter. Once the metal links gave way and fell to the ground, he pushed in the gate and held it open while the van passed by. Sal drove up to the ramp and then reversed back until they reached the loading bay. As soon as he did, he switched off the engine, jumped out, and walked around to the back of the van to open the doors and face the security guard standing in the open doorway. Seconds later, Joey exited the van and came around from the other side.

"Hey, are you the guy?" Sal asked him.

≈   ≈   ≈

"Aye, that's me," Sergeant McGregor replied, aware there were three patrol cars and a SWAT van parked just out of sight, watching and listening to everything going on. But he still played his part like a veteran actor, scratching at his oversized belly that was almost bursting out of his tight-fitting security uniform. He squinted his eyes and looked to Sal. "You Joey?"

"I'm Joey," the younger man said as he joined them.

"Right," said the sarge. "Well, I'm sorry it took so long. I had to disable the security cameras before I waved you in."

"Are we good?" asked Sal.

"Sure, there's no one else here. So, are you boys ready to start loading?"

"Hey, you do know you don't see any money until we get paid for the merchandize?" Sal said.

"Aye, I know."

"And that you are only getting twenty-five percent of each sale?" said Joey.

"These things sell like hot cakes," Sal added with a nod. "We should have the lot moved by the end of the week."

"*Och*, the lad there can call me when you have the money," the Sarge told him, pointing toward the young lanky man. "I trust you boys."

Sal cast a glance to Joey and smiled. "You hear that, Joey? It must be your honest face."

"The laptops are in here on pallets," the sarge continued before the lanky man could respond. "We can handle them into the back of your van if you like, or if any of ye know how to operate a forklift, there's one out back."

"Fuck that!" snapped Sal. "Let's just throw them in the van and be on our way. Oh, and by the way, my friend, you do know we are going to have to tie you up before we go? To make it look more believable, I mean."

"You want me to slap him around a bit?" asked Joey. "That way the cops are less likely to suspect an inside job."

"No offense, sonny," said the sarge. "You can tie me up,

sure, but no one is slapping me around."

As the sarge spoke, Vinney joined them in the bay after closing the gate back over and hooking the broken chain across it to avoid suspicion. As he came around the side of the van, however, he stopped dead in his tracks, seemingly lost for words for a second. With eyes bulging and heart racing, he pointed accusingly toward the sarge.

"Sal, I know this guy."

"What?"

"He's a cop!"

"No way."

"I'm telling you. He's a fucking cop!"

All hell broke loose the moment he uttered the words. The sarge acted first, immediately swinging away toward the side of the bay door and reaching for the pump action shotgun he had left leaning against the wall. Vinney jumped into the van and started its engine in an attempt to flee the scene. As he did, Sal and Joey heard the sirens and spotted the approaching patrol cars as they drove straight for the gate and smashed it inwards. Not wanting to get caught in the open, and realizing they would never make their escape in the van, they both raced up the ramp and headed inside the warehouse. Sal passed by the sarge as he turned with the shotgun and, grabbing it by the barrel, punched the policeman square in the face, sending him sprawling backwards.

"This way!" Joey shouted as he ran by Sal and the sarge into the building.

Seconds later, the van was surrounded by patrol cars before it exited the yard. Vinney was forced to climb out at gunpoint and lie flat on the ground.

≈   ≈   ≈

When Sal, now brandishing the shotgun, caught up to Joey, they made their way at speed up a metal staircase and onto the second floor of the building. Looking for a way out, they reached a locked wooden door at the end of the hall and kicked it inwards in a hail of splinters. Seconds later, they ran through into a large open office area. Forcing open another locked door beside a row of desks and filing cabinets, they made their way up a back stairwell and out onto the roof.

Even with the sun going down, the corrugated iron was still hot beneath their feet as they ran from one edge to the next, looking for a way off. When none could be found, Sal grabbed Joey by the arm and pointed the shotgun toward the flat tar roof of the factory next door.

"We've got to make a jump for it," he shouted, panting.

Without another word, the two men ran forward and jumped across the narrow gap toward the nearby building, but as they reached the other rooftop, Joey lost his footing and fell backwards. Reaching out in panic, he grabbed the butt of the shotgun still in Sal's hand, clinging to it for dear life, dangling in space. Sal grasped the barrel tight and tried to pull him back up.

"Don't fucking drop me!" Joey screamed out in terror, reaching his right leg up in an attempt to get a foot onto the roof.

"Then stop fucking moving." Sal grunted, trying desperately to pull him back up, his face contorting with the strain.

Joey swung his hips as he tried once more to get a foothold, but it was a difficult maneuver, and he slipped. As he did so, his finger found the trigger and accidentally pulled down upon it.

Sal saw what was happening as if it were unfolding before him in slow motion, but he could still not react in time. As he opened his mouth to shout a warning, the muzzle exploded upwards and his left ear was blown off in a spray of blood and gristle. His grip automatically released on the barrel as he collapsed in agony onto the hot tar rooftop, leaving Joey to fall, screaming in terror as he hurtled backwards toward the hard concrete below.

CHAPTER EIGHT

THE SPEAR GUN

"Could you pass me that smaller wrench?" Brophy called out from the bottom of the steps in the main cabin. "The one with the red handle."

Isabella was sitting in the cockpit, manning the wooden tiller with her life jacket on. She grabbed the small wrench from the old metal toolbox before her. She stepped through the hatch, leaned forward, and quickly handed it down to him.

Taking it from her, Brophy nodded his thanks before going back to continue his repairs. Thirty minutes earlier, he had left Isabella steering the crippled *Dirty Nellie* while he had set about lifting up the carpet and flooring boards. Within minutes of doing so, he had been lying flat on his stomach, the upper half of his body immersed in the flooded bilge beneath him. As standard on a small craft of the *Dirty Nellie's* design, the faulty pump was situated at the lowest point of the yacht, its one simple task to automatically turn on when the water reached a designated level. A gentle hum would normally indicate it was working, that it was sucking in and then expelling the unwanted brine out through a long plastic hose. But now, the bilge had become a small lake, overflowing with foaming sea water.

Brophy's upper body became completely submerged each time he leaned down, his head and shoulders disappearing beneath the briny liquid for minutes at a time while he tried desperately to reassemble the circular nylon housing. It was not an easy task, but he persevered. The alternative was to give up and let the *Dirty Nellie* sink without a fight. That was not an option for him. If nothing else, he was a fighter.

While he worked tirelessly away trying to keep them afloat

for as long as he could, Isabella maintained their course toward Saint Thomas. As well as manning the tiller, she had loaded the inflated rubber dinghy with whatever supplies she could think of. Brophy had not been specific about what she should put in, only saying not to overfill it for fear of sinking. Isabella tossed in a couple of plastic water bottles, some dry food, and the first aid kit, which she had found clipped onto a small bracket above the navigation table. She also threw in a spare can of diesel for the outboard motor, a flashlight, and a couple of blankets, but only after she had gone down to her own cabin to retrieve her revolver from the bedside locker where she had stowed it after seeing off the shark.

When Brophy eventually appeared back in the cabin doorway, he dropped a handful of tools and wrenches into the box before slipping back into his t-shirt. He cast a quick glance into the dinghy, which was now tied to the stern, bobbing up and down in the swell.

"You did good," he said, gesturing toward the supplies she had loaded.

Isabella nodded.

"Well, it's up and running again," he said quietly.

"The pump? Thank God for that."

"Actually, yes and no," he replied cautiously. "The thing is it is supposed to be pumping four thousand gallons per hour."

"It's not?"

"No, I'm afraid not. Not even close. By the sound of it, it's not even managing an eighth of that."

"Well yes, but at least you managed to get it working," she said, looking for him to confirm it was not all bad. "Anything is better than nothing, right?"

"Yeah, I suppose so. But, carrying all this extra water, our speed won't be worth a damn."

Isabella shrugged, trying to put a brave face on for his sake since she knew he had worked so hard to try and get them going.

"Hey, did you check the GPS?" he asked.

"Not recently," she replied.

Brophy leaned over, placed his hand above the small unit to remove the glare and then reached for the flare gun.

"What's wrong?" she asked, seeing the concerned look on his face.

"While we've been sitting dead in the water, they've gotten farther away than I'd hoped." He snapped another flare into the barrel and cocked it. "They are almost out of range."

He looked down at Isabella as he raised the gun into the air and prepared to fire. "You know, if you are owed any favors up there, now is the time to call them in."

Isabella watched as he pulled the trigger and their last flare arced high up into the clear blue sky, exploding in a burst of luminous sparks that spread out like the petals of a fiery flower.

"Well, that's it," Brophy said as he dropped the gun into the toolbox. "If Marcus doesn't see that one, he is never going to. The *Wild Rover* will be out of range in the next couple of minutes."

"So, what then?"

"Then? Then I suppose our best hope will be to try to make the nearest landfall while we are still afloat. Once we get ashore and make contact with the police, we can set off with them to locate where they have moored."

Isabella said nothing, not wanting to alarm Brophy any more than was necessary. He was doing his best, and scaring him further would serve no purpose. But, deep down, she was worried, and not just about them sinking. If the *Wild Rover* did reach land before them, there was no knowing what might happen to Brophy's son and the others on board. Isabella could not imagine the killer allowing them to contact the Saint Thomas authorities to announce their arrival. No, she decided, that would mean a regulatory customs search of the boat, passports required, and immigration procedures. She just could not see this guy putting himself through all of that. She imagined he would want to get ashore as quickly and quietly as possible, to blend in with the countless vacationers and cruise ship day trippers on the busy island. Once safely among the masses, he would then be free to disappear forever, quietly and unhindered. If that happened, she would have failed, she thought angrily, and he would escape justice, leaving God knows how many dead bodies in his wake.

≈ ≈ ≈

Detective Brewster watched from behind the one way mirror as Richie Regazzoni sat alone in interview room number seven at the Metro Police Station in Miami. He was fidgeting with his phone and looking extremely uncomfortable. Of course, he had every reason to feel uneasy, thought the detective, having found his wife murdered so gruesomely two nights earlier. But Brewster wondered if there might be another reason for his discomfort. When he had phoned Richie a few hours earlier, confirming he was still coming down to the station for a talk, he mentioned that he had been questioning his coworkers at the hospital. That had immediately put Richie on the defensive. Brewster could see how uneasy he was, that he knew there were some tough questions ahead.

When Brewster and Captain Franklin finally entered a few minutes later, they were carrying a couple of manila files and a small digital recorder. They placed them on the tabletop and sat down opposite him, then leaned across the table in turn to shake Richie's hand.

"Thank you for coming down, Mr. Regazzoni," the captain said in a sympathetic, yet authoritative voice. "And once again, our deepest condolences for your loss. This whole thing must seem like a nightmare to you."

"Thank you," Richie said quietly as the handshake ended. "It is a very tough time for us all. And yes, a nightmare, to be sure. But I am just trying to get through it as best I can for the sake of my boy, Joshua. And, of course, I want to help in any way I can."

"How is your son doing?"

"About as well as can be expected," said Richie with a sigh. "I spoke with Gina's mom a few hours ago, and she said he was sleeping. But I am worried about her too. I don't think any of this has fully sunk in for her yet."

Anxious to move ahead, Brewster leaned over and switched on the recorder, positioning it in the center of the table. "May twelfth, four-thirty p.m. Captain Franklin and Detective Byron Brewster, Miami Metro Homicide, interviewing Mr. Richard Regazzoni."

"Richie."

"Interviewing Mr. Richie Regazzoni." Brewster clasped his fingers together on the table in front of him and flashed Richie a polite smile. "Are you ready to begin? Would you like water or a coffee before we start?"

"No, I'm fine," said Richie. "Let's just get it over with."

"So, Richie, you are aware we are still trying to establish a motive for your wife's murder? Do you have any information that might help us in this regard? Any thoughts as to why someone would want to break into your home and kill your wife?"

"No," Richie said with a shake of his head and a weary sigh. It appeared that he was not lying when he said he was having a rough time of it. "Gina really was a lovely person. A genuinely kind-hearted girl. I have no idea who would want to do such a thing. She was so well liked by everyone that knew her and really didn't have an enemy in the world."

"What about you?" Captain Franklin asked. "Is there anyone you can think of who might have a grudge against *you*?"

Again, Richie shook his head. But, this time, there was a hesitation in his voice. "Look, I...I am just an ordinary Joe. I work hard for my family, and I have never been in trouble with the police."

"Come on, Richie," said Brewster. "Are you trying to tell us you are a saint? Because, if I have learned one thing in my time In law enforcement, it is that everyone's shit stinks sooner or later."

Richie looked taken aback by such an insensitive remark, casting his gaze to the captain then back again to Brewster. "Look, I don't think it is right that you should talk to me this way. After what has happened."

Captain Franklin sat forward. "Mr. Regazzoni. Richie. I am sorry if Detective Brewster has upset you. He can be a bit insensitive at times, but he does have to ask these things for the investigation. You do understand we are on your side, that we are trying to help you here?"

"Well, even if I did have enemies," Richie said. "Who in their right mind would think killing Gina in front of our baby would serve any purpose?"

"You are right, of course." Brewster agreed sympathetically, trying to keep Richie calm and relaxed. "And I am sorry if I offended you. Would you like to change your mind about that water or coffee?"

"No. Thank you. I'm fine. It's just that I am still on edge after...well, I still can't believe what has happened." He turned to the captain. "It's like you said, I keep thinking it is all a nightmare, and that I am going to wake up at any moment."

"Unfortunately, all we can do for you is try to catch the animal who did this," said Brewster.

"But didn't I hear you already did?" Richie said, looking confused. "I mean, it has been all over the news and papers about how he was burned to death down at the harbor."

Brewster turned to the captain, deciding he should be the one to respond to that question.

"Unfortunately," said Captain Franklin, "it turns out the body found in the burned boathouse was not the guy we thought. We now think he may have been a hobo sleeping rough in there."

"Jesus," said Richie, looking a little panicked by the news. "Then, that means he got away. That means Gina's killer is still out there."

"Unfortunately, yes," Brewster told him, sitting forward and clasping his fingers together in front of him. It occurred to him that now was the best time to press Richie on some of the more delicate matters, while he was off-guard. "You see, that is why we asked you down here today, Richie. We really need your help in locating this guy."

"Well, like I said, I want to help in any way I can."

"Good," replied Brewster. "So then, as I mentioned on the phone earlier, I paid a visit to the Broward Mental Health Facility and had a little chat with some of your coworkers there."

"Okay?"

"Well, actually it was your friend, Sal di Maggio, who mentioned it might be worth my while going there."

Richie made no reply, just shifted uncomfortably on his chair. His face became paler, and he swallowed hard.

"You *do* know Sal, don't you?"

"Yes, I know him," Richie said reluctantly.

"And that *is* where you work, right? The Broward Mental Health Facility? You are a nurse there, right?

"Uh-huh."

"Well, according to the three pretty young nurses I spoke to this morning, it seems you have all been, how should I put this, bumping privates?"

"Now wait one second—"

"Look, Richie, we are not here to judge you."

"In fact," said the captain. "We have not passed this information on to your employers or the press and are not
planning to."

"So, you can relax, Richie," continued Brewster. "Your job
is perfectly safe. All we are interested in is if you think any of
these young ladies might have a reason to hold a grudge
against you."

"A grudge? No, of course not. That is ridiculous. Look, it
was just a bit of fun. That's all."

"What about angry husbands?" asked Captain Franklin.
"Jealous boyfriends? Jealousy can be a powerful motive, you
know. And playing around with so many young fillies has got
to lead to some sort of trouble somewhere down the line."

"No," said Richie. "Detectives, I swear there was no trouble with husbands or boyfriends."

"Did your wife know what you were up to?" asked
Brewster.

Richie paused, dropped his gaze, and sighed. "Look, for a
while, she and I went through a bad patch. That's all. I kind
of went a bit wild for a couple of months. But there was no
trouble, and no one got hurt. So, once again, I am telling you
there were no jealous husbands or boyfriends involved."

"That you are aware of," the Captain said quietly.

"Okay. Yes. That I am aware of."

"What about outside of work?" Brewster continued.

"Huh?"

"Yes. You know, during this *bad patch,* did you happen to
sleep with anyone other than those nurses you worked with
on the night shift?"

"No. Definitely not."

"You are sure about that?"

"I swear."

"So, what about this number?" Brewster asked, holding
up a sheet of paper and pointing to the dozens of numbers
marked with a yellow highlighter.

"Huh?"

"This is your cell phone record, Richie. So stop playing
games. Can you tell us whose number this is?"

"No, I'm sorry. It doesn't look familiar."

"Well, according to this, you received numerous calls
from this number in the two days leading up to your wife's

death. They didn't last very long from the look of it." Brewster examined the sheet for a moment. "Let's see, the longest one was only about twenty seconds."

"Okay, let me think for a bit."

"Think? Think about what for Christ's sake?"

"Okay, I do know that number."

"Go on."

"Before I say anything else, though, I need to know that what I am about to tell you will be kept strictly between us."

Brewster and the captain shared a glance.

"I mean, I could really lose my job and get into trouble over this."

"Richie, my friend, considering you have already lost your wife," said Brewster, "and that this is a murder investigation into her death, I really think you should just tell us what it is you know and forget about how it might look to your employers."

≈ ≈ ≈

Brianna sat with her back to Harvey as he finished off the last of the bottle of rum in the main cabin. He was drunker now than he had ever been since boarding and was muttering obscenities. His mood had nose-dived dramatically since the others questioned him about his confrontation with Benjamin. He told Marcus, Jayden, and Brianna, in no uncertain terms, that they were ganging up on him, interrogating him and conducting a "bloody witch hunt."

After Marcus went outside to relieve Grace at the helm, she tried to ignore him and not make eye contact. She rested her chin on her hands and sighed with a heavy heart, her elbows leaning on the back of her seat. Still upset over finding Benjamin's dead body, she stared thoughtfully out the forward window. The island of Saint Thomas could just be made out in the distant southern horizon.

Jayden had left her side for the first time since her upsetting, gruesome discovery that afternoon. He was down in the galley fixing her coffee and a sandwich. She knew he was trying to cheer her up and help her pull herself together. The only problem was, to do so, he had no other choice but to leave her alone with the inebriated and bad tempered British man. Before he had left, Jayden had asked Harvey if he wanted a sandwich, too, but the older man had made no reply to the question, simply glared back at him through squinted, hate-filled eyes, holding up his half-empty glass of rum to indicate he had all he needed right there.

Harvey was so drunk now he was slurring his words as he told Brianna about some of his previous, *more professionally run* vacations. Although her back was turned in a blatant effort to ignore him, he continued telling her about the time he went rafting down the Colorado River with a group of thrill-seekers, and how he had also trekked across the Andes with another small group of like-minded adventurers. But she was not paying attention to any of it as he rambled on and on. She was miles away, lost in her own thoughts as she stared out the large cabin window at the untamed vastness of blue ocean heaving and rolling toward the horizon.

Jayden returned a few minutes later and placed her sandwich and a mug of steaming hot coffee on the tabletop in front of her, patting her on the shoulder to get her attention and bring her back to reality. But Brianna did not turn around to thank him. She just continued staring out the window in silence.

"You okay, honey?" he asked with concern as he squeezed around the table and sat beside her again. "Come on now, you've got to eat something."

"Why don't you leave her alone," Harvey blurted out drunkenly. "And if you want to really make yourself useful, how about going down below and fetching me another bottle of that rum, Jayden?"

Jayden knew better than to converse with Harvey while he was in such a state. Ignoring him, he moved his head in closer to his wife's to whisper, "Please, honey, just come back to the cabin if you don't want to eat."

"Can't you see the woman thinks you're a knob?" Harvey muttered, clearly trying to get a reaction. "You, with all your Jesus this and Jesus that. Crikey, it is no wonder the girl has lost her marbles."

Before Jayden could respond, Brianna raised her head from her hand and sat upright. "That's odd," she whispered, more to herself than anyone else.

"What is, honey?" Jayden asked, shooting a disapproving

glance at Harvey.

"I think she means *you*, mate." Harvey laughed. He burped loudly, and even from the other side of the table, his breath reeked of rum.

Ignoring the continuous jibes, Jayden remained focused on his wife. "Brianna? Are you okay, honey? What is odd?"

"You know, I think we have just, like, turned around," she said quietly.

Harvey laughed out loud. "Don't be so damned stupid, woman. Why on earth would we do that?"

"That is *enough*!" Jayden said angrily.

"Blimey," Harvey muttered with a mock pout of his lips. "What the bloody hell is your problem? I'm just saying we wouldn't turn around with Saint Thomas only thirty minutes away."

"Well, you have said enough for one day," snapped Jayden. "And I will thank you to leave my wife and me alone. We do not want to listen to your obscenities anymore."

"Way-hay-hay." The older man laughed, obviously delighted Jayden had finally taken the bait.

"I mean it," said Jayden. "We have both had as much of you as we care to take."

"Yeah? Well, don't worry, your holiness, you won't have to put up with me for much longer. No, sirree, Bob. In thirty minutes, I will be getting off this shit bucket onto dry land again, and then you and your old lady can kiss my hairy white arse."

"Are you sure you are feeling all right?" Jayden asked Brianna again, ignoring Harvey once more and placing a firmer hand on her shoulder.

"I mean it, Jayden," she said persistently. "I really do think we are going back the other way."

"Silly cow." Harvey muttered quietly to himself beneath his breath, shaking his head.

"Brianna, baby, why on earth would you think we have turned around?" Jayden asked, keeping his attention solely on his wife.

"I just do," she said.

"You know, when we did the navigation class this morning, you admitted you didn't really understand what it was all about."

"Understand?" Harvey goaded from the other side of the table. "She didn't have a fucking clue, mate. She was holding the bloody sextant upside down until I showed her how to do it."

"Look there," she said quietly to her husband, meeting his eyes for a second, then turning back to motion out the window. "See the sun?"

"Yes."

"Well, if we are still sailing south, how come it is on our left?"

≈   ≈   ≈

Harvey looked furious when he burst open the main cabin door and stormed out onto the deck, his eyes burning with rage. He marched straight up to Marcus, who was alone at the wheel ever since Grace had gone back to her cabin, and immediately began shouting obscenities right into his face. He was drunk, angry, and spitting as he shouted, yelling about how he had "just about had enough," and insisting Marcus turn them back around toward Saint Thomas again.

Taken by surprise for a moment, Marcus did his best to diffuse the situation and calm Harvey down. He was in the process of explaining his reasons for turning when Jayden and Brianna came out to see what was happening. The exchange became so heated the couple kept their distance, staying back by the cabin door.

"Look, if you will just take a step back and calm down for one minute," Marcus said, not in a shout, but as commanding as he could manage. He placed a hand on Harvey's shoulder in an effort to get him to move out of his face. The British man's breath stank so badly of rum it made Marcus wince. He looked into Harvey's glazed eyes and quickly realized reasoning with him in this condition was not going to be an easy task.

"Take your bloody hand off me," growled Harvey. "And I will be as calm as I damn well want to be."

Marcus lowered his hand and put it back on the wheel. "Okay then, but please, Harvey, if you would just step back—"

"Why the bloody hell have you turned us around?" Harvey roared. "Ay? What gives you the right?"

"Look, the reason I turned is because I saw a flare on the horizon over there." Marcus pointed toward the northern sky ahead, but the British man did not follow his directional gesture.

"You saw a flare?"

"Yes."

"Are you kidding me? You saw a ruddy flare?"

"Listen, Harvey, I am telling you it won't take long, just an hour or so to go back and check it out."

"Without a working radio? You must be the most stupid person I have ever—"

"It doesn't matter whether we have a radio or not," countered Marcus. "If someone is in trouble out there we must go back and see if we can help."

"In trouble, you say?" Harvey moved forward a bit more. "Well, what the bloody hell do you think *we* are in?"

"I mean it, Harvey. I need you to step back from the wheel. I am serious."

"Are you forgetting you still have a dead body down there in one of your cabins? Are you forgetting he was one of your passengers? That's right, mate, *your* responsibility?"

Marcus let out a deep sigh, gritted his teeth, but said nothing for fear of losing his cool any further. He really had just about enough of the British man and knew, if he was not careful, he would say or do something he would regret later. Harvey had been a thorn in his side from the moment he stepped onboard.

"Hey, hey," Jayden said still standing at Brianna's side by the door. "Look, there is no need for this, guys. I think we are all just a little tired and emotional. Harvey, what do you say we calm down a bit and discuss this inside in a more rational manner?"

"Discuss it? Don't make me bloody laugh. A few minutes ago you didn't even want to talk to me."

"That's because you're a drunk," shouted Brianna. "You are a horrible person, Harvey. That is why no one likes you."

The cockpit fell strangely silent for a moment as they all looked toward the young black woman in amazement, an unusual contrast to the noisy shouting and screaming of a few seconds ago.

"Listen, mate, you need to turn this fucking boat around

and get me to Saint Thomas right now," Harvey said through gritted teeth, brushing off Brianna's rebuke and staring venomously once more into Marcus's eyes. "I mean it, pal, because I just want to get off this floating shithole and leave you bunch of losers behind. Oh, and by the way, rest assured, I will be telling the police on Saint Thomas *all* about you. Oh yes, all about how shabby this whole operation is and how one of your passengers died due entirely to your incompetence."

"Okay, that's enough," snapped Marcus. "I mean it. Step away right now and sit down. *I* am the captain on this boat, Harvey, not you. And I am telling you we are going back to check out that flare. Like it or not, you have no say in the matter."

"Oh no?" Harvey shouted angrily, moving in even closer. He grabbed hold of the wheel and tried to shoulder Marcus out of the way. A scuffle broke out when Marcus tried to stand his ground and push Harvey away.

"Hey, hey, that's enough!" Jayden jumped forward and got between them to break them apart. But the British man was in no mood to be placated and too far gone to be stopped. As soon as Jayden drew near, he head butted him and knocked him backwards.

Jayden stumbled for a few feet, then tripped and went sprawling backwards to the deck. Brianna came rushing to his aid with a horrified squeal, kneeling down beside him and cradling him in her arms.

Oblivious to what he had just done and still seeing red, Harvey lunged forward to take the wheel again. But, this time, Marcus was ready for him and grabbed his wrists hard before pushing him back.

Undeterred, he immediately moved forward once more to try and take over the wheel.

Marcus finally had enough. As Harvey made a lunge toward him, he side stepped out of the way and punched him with a left hook. "Now that is enough!" he shouted as Harvey went down. "I am ordering you to go below now and stay in your cabin until we reach Saint Thomas."

"No bloody way." Harvey snarled angrily, kneeling down and holding his right jaw, a trickle of blood running from his nose.

Marcus took a step forward and went to say something to him, but was forced to stop in mid-stride when Harvey grabbed one of the dinghy's small wooden oars, stored beneath the seating, and began swinging. It caught Marcus in the midriff and knocked the wind from his sails. He hunched over holding his stomach, gasping for air when Harvey jumped to his feet and brought the oar down on his head.

"What have you got to say now?" he snarled venomously.

Marcus was curled over on the cockpit floor at this point, dazed and shocked from the blow, holding one hand on his head and the other out to Harvey in a gesture of submission. But Harvey stepped closer with the oar raised above him. Before Marcus could say or do anything, the British man swung it down and caught him hard on the left shoulder. Shrieking from the painful blow, Marcus scrambled backwards to get away from him. Holding his head and shoulder, he moved away as far as he could until he came to rest against the rear seat and could go no farther.

"No!" Brianna screamed at the top of her voice.

Harvey was not listening. With pure hatred in his eyes, he took a step forward and raised the oar above his head again as he prepared to bring it down. That was when Brianna emitted another loud, blood-curdling scream. This time, however, it was not intended to stop the British man, but was, instead, an outburst of pure shock and utter disbelief.

Harvey stopped in mid-swing, turning his gaze down with a look of surprise. His eyes went wide. Glistening in the sunlight, metallic and red, the pointed tip of a silver spear stuck out from the middle of his chest.

≈   ≈   ≈

Brewster called Isabella on the VHF shortly after she returned to the cabin. She was out of breath, having just emptied another two buckets of water over the side. It was exhausting, repetitive work, but as Brophy advised her, each one taken from the flooded bilge bought them another precious few minutes afloat. The hastily repaired pump had packed in again a short time ago, Brophy's valiant effort having been for nothing, and he and she were now in the process of launching the dinghy to abandon ship.

She could see the pain etched on his face when he had told her it was over. With the pump now well and truly broken, beyond repair, they were dead in the water and going down fast. The *Dirty Nellie* was listing more and more to starboard by the minute, her prow starting to lift as the incoming water overfilled the bilge and began flooding the cabins.

When Brophy had climbed into the dinghy and had reached out a hand to help her in, a loud crackle had been heard emanating from the radio and a voice had called out her name.

"Miami Metro calling Detective Garcia. This is Miami Metro calling Detective Garcia. Over."

"Make it quick," Brophy had said when she'd turned to go back inside the cabin. "Damn it. Don't get caught in there when she goes down."

"How are you all doing out there?" Brewster asked when she finally picked up the microphone. "Any luck catching up to the other boat? Over."

Isabella hurriedly explained the situation, telling him she only had a couple of minutes to talk. She also told him that Brophy said they were so close to the Virgin Islands they could probably reach Saint Thomas by dinghy within half an hour.

"Well, in that case, I'll get straight to it," said Brewster. "You will be glad to hear we finally have a lead on Mike's killer. I'm going to play you a quick excerpt from our interview with the infamous Richie Regazzoni. Is that okay? Over."

"Go ahead," she said, wiping a bead of sweat from her brow. "I'm listening. Over."

"All right, here it is," he said, clicking the small silver recorder on and holding it up to the microphone.

To keep her feet out of the rising water, Isabella moved away from the navigation table and sat down on the middle step leading up to the cockpit and listened with bated breath as the voices filtered through the speaker.

"I need to know that what I am about to tell you will be kept strictly between us?" Richie said with an air of concern in his tone. "I mean, I could really lose my job over this."

"Richie, my friend, considering you have already lost your wife, and that this is a murder investigation into her death, I really think you should just tell us what it is you know and forget about how it might look to your employers," said

Brewster.

Silence for a moment.

"Well?" asked Brewster.

"Okay, look, there was someone else. She was a patient at the Broward Facility where I work. I know it is forbidden, but she was one of the more normal patients, as we call them. At least, her chart simply said she had suffered a breakdown and needed a few months to rest and recover. So, that was how it started, really just a bit of innocent fun, that's all. Oh, and for the record, she was the one who began chasing me."

"Go on. We are listening."

"I don't know how it happened. Went bad, I mean. Before I knew it, things just kind of got out of control. Mentally, she seemed stable, at least to begin with. But, when she was suddenly discharged from the facility, she began stalking me at every turn. Heck, I hadn't signed up for that. When I told her we had to stop, that my wife and I were trying to patch up our differences, she refused to accept it. I think she had the rest of our lives planned out together. It was creepy. Shit, she even had a vacation booked for us in the Caribbean."

"On a cruise to the Virgin Islands?" asked Brewster.

"Yes. She said it would be a kind of honeymoon for us. But how did you know that?"

"Go on with your story," Captain Franklin's voice could be heard saying. "Is that when she turned violent?"

"No, not exactly," said Richie. "I mean, not right away. Not until I told her that Gina was pregnant and we had patched everything up. Then she went absolutely crazy, started shouting down the phone at me."

"Shouting? What did she say?" asked Brewster.

"Just things like, I would be 'sorry for betraying her' and it 'wasn't over.'"

"And you didn't think to mention any of this when your wife was murdered?"

"Look, I really didn't think there was any connection. You see, the news was saying that the killer, a guy, had been burned to death in a fire. That being the case, she never even crossed my mind. Heck, now that you are saying the killer is still out there, I still don't really believe she is involved. She may have issues, Detectives, but I don't think

she would ever be capable of doing something like that."

There was a rustling sound from the other end of the line as Brewster switched off the recorder and took a sheet of paper from a folder in front of him.

"Are you still there, Garcia?"

"Yes, but not for much longer," Isabella told him, moving up the steps to the open cabin hatch, stretching the microphones cable to the limit as the *Dirty Nellie* was almost completely flooded below her.

"Well here is a small section from the patient's progress file," Brewster said before quickly continuing to read. "Despite ongoing mental issues, patient five-one-zero was released from the Broward Mental Health Facility by court order on August eleven, two thousand and fourteen. Her release was against the advice of her treating psychiatrist. Following her discharge, she is believed to have stopped taking her medication and has failed to turn up for the last four patient appointments with the service. Attempts by her medical team to reach her with phone calls and visits to her home have gone unanswered."

≈ ≈ ≈

Harvey squinted his eyes and slowly turned around. Grace stood behind him in the cabin doorway. The spear gun was in her hands. She did not say a single word, simply leaned down and began reloading.

"Oh, you stupid, bloody bitch." He groaned in disbelief, dropping the oar to the deck and raising both hands to the spear tip in an insane attempt to push it back through to get it out. He suddenly looked sober, his eyes focused, wide open in shock.

Marcus pulled himself painfully to his feet, just in time to see Grace releasing another spear toward Harvey's stomach. This time, the force of the impact sent the British man stumbling backwards until his knees gave way, and he turned and slumped over the side rail. With his feet still touching the deck, eyes open, his torso and arms were left dangling into space above the foaming water. Grace stood expressionless, still saying nothing. As the other three looked on in horror, she dropped the spear gun to the cockpit floor, reached into the waistband of her jeans, and casually produced a revolver.

As she cocked the hammer back, a strange silence befell the boat. With Harvey lying dead across the hand rail and Brianna still cradling Jayden on the ground, his nose bleeding and clearly broken, Marcus found himself staring mystified into Grace's eyes. Neither of them spoke. They just stood looking at each other in silence. Marcus was left speechless and confused. With his heart pounding in his chest, he put his hands out to Grace and raised them in a non-threatening manner, motioning for her to lower the weapon. He thought he might be able to make her see sense.

"Stop there, Marcus, that is close enough," she said in a calm, detached voice.

"Grace, what are you doing?" he asked in puzzlement. "Please, Grace, just put down that gun, and let's talk about this."

"I'm afraid there is nothing to talk about," she said calmly with a shrug of her shoulders.

"But you killed him."

"Why, you should be grateful. He was about to crack your skull open with that oar."

"Grace, I don't know what to say."

"How about thank you?"

"Girl, you did the right thing," Brianna said, helping Jayden to his feet. "He hurt my man and was about to, like, kill poor Marcus. We all saw it."

"No," exclaimed Jayden. "It's not right, honey. Killing is never right."

"Shut up!" snapped Grace. "That is enough from both of you. I had just about had all I could take of Harvey and his bullshit, so I really do not care whether you two think it is right or not."

Brianna looked confused. "But—"

"Enough, I said! Now, I don't have any more time to waste out here." She turned her attention back to Marcus, but now pointed the gun at the black couple. "I like you, Marcus. I really do. But if you do not turn us back around now, I promise I will shoot these two where they stand."

Marcus knew by her tone she was not bluffing, could see by the cold look in her eyes she would not hesitate to kill again. As Brianna began sobbing uncontrollably, he realized there was something about Grace that was not normal. Her gestures, her calmness, her tone. She was not fazed by what she had just done or by what she was threatening to do. He had not spotted it before, but now he did. Now it was plain for all to see Grace was a killer. She had done this before, he knew with certainty. And she would surely do it again with only the slightest provocation.

Without another word, Marcus placed both hands on the wheel and spun it hard to starboard, ducking his head as the boom came swinging around from the port side. He tightened the sheets until the sails were taut, tied off the lines, and then turned his eyes back to Grace.

"Look, what is going on?" he asked, shaking his head. "Why are you doing this?"

Without speaking, Grace waved the gun at a terrified Jayden and Brianna and motioned them to move back toward the stern. She edged closer to them as they went and pointed the revolver at the dinghy sitting on the bathing platform behind them.

"You have ten seconds to get in it and leave."

"This is madness," said Marcus. "They haven't done anything to you."

Grace ignored him and waved the gun toward the dinghy again. "Nine seconds."

"Grace, please. Tell us why you are doing this." Brianna pleaded with tears in her eyes and a look of horror on her face.

"Eight seconds."

"Can't we talk about it?" asked Jayden.

"You can talk as much as you want when you are in that dinghy," she said coldly. "I mean it. Now, if you want to live, slide it into the water and climb in. I won't say it again."

As soon as they had moved the dinghy into the water, him holding his bloody nose and her sobbing loudly, Jayden climbed in and raised his hands to help Brianna join him. Keeping her finger on the trigger, Grace reached down with her free hand and untied the line. She kept the revolver pointing at them as she kicked the dinghy away with the toe of her shoe. She stood watching from the bathing platform as they immediately started to drift away with the tide.

"Please, Grace. They will die out there." Marcus pleaded

as Jayden wrapped an arm around his wife's shoulders for comfort. "Why are you doing this? It isn't like you."

"How do you know what I am like?" She turned away from the dinghy and pointed the gun in his direction now. "How would any of you know what I am like, or the things I have had to suffer?"

"Look, it is not too late," Marcus quietly said, trying to appear as calm and reassuring as he could. "Please, Grace. Let me turn back for them. Then we can go anywhere you want. Anywhere."

"Just keep heading south," she said.

"You know they won't last more than a couple of hours out there in this heat. The Gulf Stream will take them away from land and push them out into the Atlantic. At least let me turn around and throw them some water."

"South."

"They don't deserve it, Grace. Please, I am begging you. They have been nothing but nice to you from the start."

"*South.*"

When Grace raised the gun and pointed it into his face, cocking the hammer back, Marcus finally realized it was hopeless. He sighed deeply with resignation and turned his attention back to the island of Saint Thomas on the horizon. He remained like that for a few minutes, saying nothing, wondering to himself what exactly was happening. Why had Grace suddenly turned into such a monster?

"I won't hurt you if you don't betray me," she said in a whisper from her nearby position, now on the seating to his right.

"I'm sorry?" As soon as he turned his head to her, a shiver ran down his spine. Grace was not talking to him, but voicing out loud the thoughts in her own head. As he watched her grab Harvey's ankles and flip his lifeless body over the side, he realized then that he may never know what this was all about or why she was behaving in such a cold-hearted manner. He understood at that moment how dangerous and unbalanced she really was. Marcus realized with an aching wrench in his gut that Grace could not be reasoned with because she was insane.

"But then," she continued in a whisper to herself as she turned back to him. "They all betray me eventually."

CHAPTER NINE

THE SAVAGE

She parked the old blue Chevrolet she had stolen at the minimart in the alley behind Richie's house and then climbed the back fence unseen. The darkness was her ally as she made her way across the rear lawn and stepped up onto the patio. She waited for Richie and that bitch wife of his to go upstairs before prying the sliding door open with an old screwdriver she had found in the trunk of the car.

When things went quiet, she took the biggest knife she could find from one of the kitchen drawers and then silently but purposefully made her way up the staircase. Her thoughts were not exactly clear as she reached the upper landing. She had come seeking revenge for Richie's betrayal, but she only had a faint outline in her head of what she was going to do. Her main priority was to make him suffer. Nothing else was more important than that. She did not know how exactly she was going to achieve this, but he had lied when he said he loved her, and she was going to make him pay.

She hovered outside their bedroom door for the longest time, hidden in the shadows, listening to them sleeping. But then a low cooing noise from the nursery next door drew her attention, and she made her way quietly inside. She stood at the end of the large wooden cot for a while, not looking down on the baby lying there, but staring trance-like at the framed photograph she had taken from the wall and carried upstairs with her.

Richie had his arm around the bitch, and they were both smiling, holding their newborn baby like they were the happiest people on the planet. It made Grace want to throw up. That should have been her in the photograph, she thought *angrily. If he had kept his word and not lied to her, the two of them would be setting sail in the morning for the glorious, romantic Virgin Islands. A honeymoon, of sorts. A chance for them to start a new life together, away from the distraction of wives and babies and hospitals and psychiatrists. Maybe even have a child of their own.*

Grace laid the photograph across the tiny baby's feet and raised the knife. She turned the blade slightly until it caught the ray of moonlight creeping in through a gap in the curtains. She stared at her own reflection in the metal for a few seconds. And then she knew what she had to do. Killing Richie's baby would teach him the ultimate lesson for the way he lied to her, and it would also make him suffer as much as she did. He would never forget what he had done, and more importantly, he would finally understand the consequences for having betrayed her.

Grace leaned over with the knife and reached in to place the point directly beneath the baby's chin. But then, she heard a creaking floorboard in the hall outside and stopped suddenly, listening to the approaching footsteps. She retracted the knife and backed up into the shadows behind the door a split-second before Richie's wife came shuffling in. She felt an overwhelming sense of power right then, standing unseen while the bitch who had stolen her man stood with her back to her. She could hear her muttering something to herself, could even smell the soap and shampoo she had showered with. This was a good feeling, she mused with squinted eyes. She was in control of the situation and this whore would live or die by her choosing. But then the woman suddenly leaned up from the cot and stood upright.

Grace knew what she was going to do right there and then. Without the slightest hesitation, she sprang into action. Anticipating the woman's movement, she lunged forward from the shadows and slapped a hand over her mouth from behind, stopping her from turning and forcing her body violently against the edge of the cot. And then a flash, the shaft of moonlight reflecting off metal as Grace raised the long, double-edged kitchen knife. Richie's wife tried desperately to scream for help, but it was no use. Grace would not let her. She pressed her hand so firmly against the whore's mouth that she bit into the corner of her lip and tasted blood.

Richie's wife tried to struggle, to raise her arms and swing away, gasping as Grace wedged her body harder against the cot and brought the razor-edged blade sweeping down across her throat.

When it was done, Grace stepped calmly back from the body with the blood-stained knife still in her hand. There was a faint, satisfied smile on her face as she looked down upon the body. Now that she had taken her revenge, her love for Richie vanished like the mist. As if a hungry belly had just been filled, her heart no longer yearned for him. She had set herself free, and she realized in that moment she no longer even liked or respected him. She would not take him back now even if he came begging on his knees.

Grace turned for the door and left the house the same way she came in, heading off down to the Miami marina to board the boat that would take her off to a new country and a new life. The cruise might be returning to South Florida in a few days, she thought as she climbed the back fence and started the car, but she would not. Pretty much everything she owned in the world, including her passport, was in the canvas bag on the back seat. When she reached the Virgin Islands she intended to stay, to meet her soul mate, perhaps, and settle down to a life of happiness and contentment.

But then, in the darkness, she spotted the low beams of another car following. She made a few twists and turns to be sure it was keeping up with her. When she was certain it was, she swung the Chevrolet into the harbor parking lot in an effort to lose it.

≈   ≈   ≈

Marcus sailed into a small, deserted cove on the northern shore of Saint Thomas, lowering the mainsail and dropping two anchors, one forward and the other aft. All the while, Grace stood behind him with the revolver in her hand, watching his every move. When they were secured to the bottom of the stony bay, she ordered him below to her cabin and made him stand with his back to the door while she placed her canvas bag on the bed and packed her possessions.

"What are you planning to do now?" he asked after a few seconds, a nervousness in his voice that betrayed his suspicions.

"Do?" Grace seemed a little surprised by the question.

"Are you planning to kill me too? Like Harvey?"

"Harvey was a dick," she replied with a smirk. "But you are different, Marcus. I knew it from the moment we met."

Marcus said nothing, just watched in silence as she finished packing and zipped up the bag with one hand, the other still holding the gun that was pointed in his direction.

"Oh, no," she continued as if offended he would even ask such a thing. "You and I have a connection, Marcus. I know you feel it too. I could see it in your eyes when we shared that moment up on deck."

In that very instant, he knew what he had to do. Remaining in her company for much longer would surely result in his death. Grace was dangerous and delusional. Whatever idyllic fantasy world her twisted mind had retreated into, he knew it would only take a simple look or a word out of place to turn it back into a hellish nightmare.

Just then, Grace became distracted and looked down. The zipper had become stuck as she pulled it closed, and for the briefest moment, she turned her attention and the gun away from him and began using both hands in an effort to free it.

Marcus seized the moment. Without hesitating, he lunged across the room and shouldered Grace with such force she fell over the bag and crashed to the floor on the other side of the bed. Knowing she was still holding the gun, he turned toward the door, opened it, and ran down the walkway as fast as he could. A gunshot echoed out as he reached the steps up to the main cabin, a bullet smashing into the wooden panel to the right of his head, sending splinters in every direction.

Ducking low, Marcus grabbed the handrail and sprinted up the steps to make his escape. He reached the top and ran toward the door without stopping. Grace was close behind, he knew, and there was not a second to spare if he wanted to live. But then his heart sank and he emitted a groan of anguish. The main cabin door would not open for him. She had locked it, he realized with a sickening feeling in the pit of his stomach. How could he have been so stupid? In his frightened state, he had not noticed her doing so, but he realized she must have turned the key and taken it when she ordered him down there at gunpoint.

Marcus turned away from the door and sprinted down the other set of steps that led into the port hull. He raced to the end and ducked into the farthest cabin he could find in the desperate hope of escaping on deck through the small Perspex skylight. But once inside, he stopped for a second with his back against the door, looking down at the dead body wrapped in tarpaulin on the bed. He realized then that Grace had murdered Benjamin as well. His death had not been an accident as they had all thought. As this revelation hit home, a bullet smashed through the door panel to his left, narrowly missing his head.

"I know you are in there," Grace said from the walkway on the other side. "Marcus, do you hear me?"

Marcus reached down and turned the key to lock himself in. He knew it was not a strong mechanism and would only serve to keep her out for a couple of seconds. But that was all he needed.

"Marcus, come on out. I am not going to say it again."

"Why did you have to kill Benjamin?" He shouted out to her, moving the body over so he could step up onto the bed. "He was just a mild-mannered guy who never hurt a fly."

"I had no choice. He got in my way," she said from the other side of the door. "I am not a savage, Marcus. Jesus, I am really hurt you would even think such a thing. I only do what I have to do to survive."

"You mean killing people?"

"I have only killed those who deserved it or threatened to hurt me."

"Benjamin did neither, and you *still* murdered him," Marcus said, reaching up to open the skylight. The safety hinge only allowed it to open a few inches, but he began working on it, twisting and pulling it to break it free. If he could do so, he knew he would be able to open it enough to climb through.

"He was putting the radio back together again," she said irritably. "As soon as I arrived on board, I opened it up and took the biggest, most important looking part out. I had only narrowly escaped the police back in Miami and had to be sure they didn't figure it out and radio you to return."

The hinge suddenly gave way beneath Marcus's fingers and there was a sharp *snap* of metal. "So what, you just up and killed him to stop him from fixing it?" He shouted, hoping she had not heard the noise of the breaking hinge and put two and two together. When she kept talking, he emitted a deep sigh of relief, certain he had gotten away with breaking the skylight without her hearing.

"Benjamin cornered me in the storage room and told me he knew I had sabotaged the radio," she said. "He knew as soon as he saw the part was missing that somebody had deliberately taken it."

"But why blame you?" Marcus asked. As soon as the last word left his mouth, he took a deep breath and began pulling himself up through the open skylight. "I thought he accused Harvey of doing it."

"Would you believe that, after they argued, Benjamin went back to examine the radio some more and found one of my red hairs tangled up inside the damn thing? Well, it's true. As soon as he saw that, he knew it was me. But his mistake was coming to me first. He should never have done that. He should have just gone to you."

Marcus managed to get an arm out on deck and then pulled himself up enough so his head and shoulders followed. The sharp sunlight blinded him for a second, but he squinted his eyes and twisted around so his other arm came through the tiny opening. He could almost taste his freedom as he pushed down on the deck with both palms and wriggled his entire upper body out. But then, in one split second, his hopes were dashed, and he knew it had all been in vain.

"Keep going," Grace told him unemotionally. She was standing on the deck behind him, gun in hand. "That's it, you're almost through."

Marcus walked a few paces ahead as Grace directed him back down into Benjamin's cabin. After she made him shoulder in the locked door, she ordered him to sit on the edge of the bed beside the dead body. She then stood in the doorway watching him for what seemed like an age. The heat below deck was intense, oven-like, and Marcus found himself wiping beads of sweat from his brow.

"So, what are you going to do now?" he asked eventually.

Grace sighed. "I think I have come to a conclusion," she

said with a cold sadness in her voice. "I do like you, Marcus. I really do. But I just don't think it is going to work out between us."

"Grace—"

"I gave you every chance, but you just betrayed me like all the others. So now, I have no other choice but—"

"You *do* have a choice," Marcus said, swallowing hard as he watched her hold the revolver out at full stretch. He knew his time was up and, if he was going to save himself, this would be his last chance. "Look, if you lower that gun, I will stay with you when the police come. I swear. You have nothing to worry about, Grace. You and me together. We will tell them how you thought Harvey was going to shoot me with that revolver, and how you killed him with the spear gun instead. You saved my life, Grace. You will be a hero, and the two of us can have that dinner we talked about."

"No, I am sorry," she said with a shake of her head. "You know, I actually thought you could be the one. But, well, I guess it just was not meant to be."

"But why?" he asked again. "Please. At least tell me what this was all about."

"What it's all about is that I have finally had enough," she said with a nonchalant shrug. "I told you how my parents died when I was young, but what I did not tell you was how my father was an alcoholic and a bully. He used to beat my mother black and blue on a daily basis. When he started abusing and beating me in the same way, she finally stood up to him. One night, she stuck a kitchen knife in his back while he was on top of me and sent him straight to hell."

"My God, I am so sorry you had to endure that. I did not know."

"When she went to prison, I was taken in by my aunt and uncle. But she was my father's sister and an animal just like him. She didn't abuse me physically or sexually like he did, but she put me down at every opportunity she could. She used to tell me it was all *my* fault, and she would lock me away for days at a time. It continued almost every day and night for four years until, well, until I finally ran away."

"Shit, Grace, you should have told me. Now, at least I understand."

"You understand nothing! All my life I have been used

and abused by people. My fiancé strung me along for two years, while all the time, he was sleeping with my best friend. Well, I got even with him. Oh yes, I did. I cut the brakes on that rat's car one morning before he drove to work, and I put him in a wheelchair for six months."

"Jesus."

"That was when the court sent me away, you see. The doctors said I had a mental break, but would be fine after an 'indefinite period of rest and therapy.' Can you believe that shit? But I don't think I ever did have a breakdown. I think the truth is I had just had enough of being mistreated. I vowed there and then that I would never be used or abused again, no matter what. Right away, it made me stronger than I had ever been. Powerful, even. Well, anyway, I spent three months in that hospital and was finally getting my life back together when *he* came along."

"Who?"

"Oh, just a guy," she said quietly with venom in her voice. "He was a nurse on my floor. He was kind and good-looking, paid attention to me and told me he loved me. And, when I told him I only wanted a serious relationship, he swore we would be together when I got out. He said it was over between him and his wife, and they were just going through the motions and would be getting a divorce. I really loved him, you know. I gave him my heart and my soul. I gave him everything. Then, I got released unexpectedly, and it all changed so quickly. Suddenly, he told me how he and his wife had decided to make another go of it. He didn't want to see me anymore, just pushed me aside like a discarded plaything. His wife was expecting their child, he eventually told me, and he did not have any room in his life for me anymore. And even though I begged him, pleaded with him, told him how I had booked this vacation for us, he just would not change his mind. I don't know, with hindsight, I must have been stupid. I see that now. I actually thought this trip would be a way for us to get away from all those outside distractions, to let him get to know me better so he would see how much I really cared and how we were meant to be together."

"What did you do?" Marcus asked with a feeling of dread in his heart.

"I got even," she whispered coldly, "like I always do. I

went to his home to kill him for his betrayal."

"Oh shit."

"But I didn't do it. I changed my mind and did something worse. Much, much worse. I made sure he would have to live the rest of his miserable existence with the consequences of his betrayal."

"Grace, what did you do?"

"Enough now," she said, raising the gun higher and clicking back the hammer with her thumb. "I'm afraid, Marcus, it is time to end this and move on."

"Just one more thing?" Marcus asked, desperately trying to buy another couple of seconds.

"Time is up," she said in a whisper.

"But—"

"No more delays, Marcus. Close your eyes. It will all be over soon."

≈ ≈ ≈

Isabella and Brophy pushed off the dinghy and motored away from the *Dirty Nellie* as she listed to port and finally slipped beneath the water. Within seconds of her disappearing, the last bubble of air rose from her hull and she sank deeper into the depths of the Caribbean. Pointing down, she rolled in the water and then flipped over, turning full circle before spiraling downwards on her final, inevitable journey.

As she descended deeper, the sunlight faded. It grew colder and darker about her. The half-light became pitch-blackness until she finally touched bottom amid a cloud of swirling sand and stones. Then silence. With the seabed settling slowly about her keel, she lurched slightly from side to side, eventually coming to rest on her starboard side. She was alone now, surrounded by a myriad of tiny fish and multi-colored organisms swimming in and out of her cracked timber shell.

Brophy and Isabella were in sight of land now, and they didn't look back as they sped frantically toward the island of Saint Thomas. The *Dirty Nellie* had been their home for the past few days and had served them well, against all the odds, getting them within touching distance of the faster and more powerful *Wild Rover* before finally making the ultimate sacrifice. She would be missed, and they would probably mourn her passing at a later date. But, at that moment, there were other, more pressing matters on their minds.

When they eventually reached the beach about twenty minutes later, they followed the shoreline south for another ten, scanning the small bays and inlets as they motored past. Then, when they finally spotted the *Wild Rover* moored in the center of a secluded cove, they turned in past the breakwater and got within twenty feet of her before cutting the engine.

As they brought the dinghy alongside the large catamaran, Brophy jumped on board and tied them to its stern rail before reaching down to help Isabella climb up the wooden steps. Once they were both safely on the bathing platform, she put a hand on his arm to hold him up. She withdrew her revolver and motioned for him to stand aside and follow her.

Isabella moved off, but she had barely taken a step toward the cabin door when she stopped and pointed down with a worried expression. Brophy's heart sank upon seeing the spatters of blood on the lacquered white deck at their feet, an intermittent trail of crimson running from the center of the cockpit toward the nearby starboard side rail.

Isabella took a deep breath and moved on, carefully sliding open the main cabin door and moving cautiously inside. When she and Brophy entered, they stopped for a moment to listen before moving off down the steps into the port hull upon hearing voices. With her leading the way, gun at the ready, they made their way down the walkway toward the cabin at the end. She moved quietly but with purpose in front of Brophy, eyes fixed ahead and finger on the revolver's trigger. When they reached the half-closed door at the end of the narrow corridor, they immediately noticed how the frame had been split and the lock was hanging off. Brophy placed a hand on her shoulder to stop her.

"What is it?" she asked in a whisper.

"That's Marcus's voice," he said.

"And the other one? The woman?"

Brophy just shrugged and shook his head.

Motioning for him to move a few steps away from her, Isabella turned back toward the broken door and took a deep breath to steady herself for what was to come. This was the moment, she realized, the end of the journey that had begun with Gina Regazzoni and Mike Ryan's deaths in Miami a few days earlier. Isabella knew their killer was on the other side of that door. She gripped her revolver tighter in both hands, exhaled loudly, and then nudged open the panel with the sole of her shoe.

"Miami Police!" She screamed, stepping out into the open.

The words had barely left her lips when two sudden shots rang out, forcing her to duck down low as the bullets smashed into the wooden door frame above her head. Brophy leaped forward into the doorway and grabbed her in one movement, pulling her back into the walkway and out of harm's way.

"Grace!" She shouted after a few seconds' silence, still hunched down beside Brophy with her back to the wall and her gun pointing ahead. There were only two women listed as passengers. She took a chance. "Grace Logan, we know it's you in there."

No response.

"It's over," she said after a moment. "We know all about what you did back in Miami. So drop the gun now and come on out with your hands above your head."

"Marcus, are you okay in there?" Brophy called out in desperation.

Another few minutes passed with no reply and without the slightest sound from inside the cabin. Finally, when it became clear they were being ignored, Isabella decided to act. Hunching her shoulders and lowering herself down to offer a harder target, she swung back into the open doorway with her revolver at the ready and her finger on the trigger.

"Goddamnit!"

Brophy peered around the corner to find the cabin empty except for the tarpaulin-covered body lying on the bed and a set of feet sticking out from behind it on the floor. Brophy rushed frantically in past Isabella to find Marcus regaining consciousness, holding the side of his head where Grace must have hit him. He rushed to his son's side, put an arm around his shoulders, and helped him to his feet.

"Marcus, hey, are you okay?"

"I...uh..."

"Sh, son, take it easy," he said reassuringly, the relief

etched on his face. "Don't try to move until you get your breath back."

Marcus squinted his eyes as he stood up. Still nursing his head and looking dazed and confused, he turned from his father to Isabella. "She tried to shoot me before she left," he muttered, sounding pained. "She's mad. Totally insane. She put that gun to my head and pulled the trigger, but it was out of bullets."

"Where did she go?" Isabella cried anxiously from the doorway.

"Back up on deck." Marcus replied, pointing upwards. "Through that skylight."

Isabella moved like lightening upon hearing the news. Without hesitation, she spun around and sprinted back down the walkway toward the main cabin. When she neared the door, however, she stopped for a moment, checking that the cockpit was empty through the small window above the navigation table. Seeing there was no one there, she pushed open the door and moved through it with caution. She eased herself out into the cockpit and the blinding sunlight with her gun still at the ready. That was when Grace hit her over the back of the head with an oar, splitting the wood down the middle and knocking her to the deck. Having been hidden from sight on the cabin's roof, she now lowered herself down into the cockpit to stand over Isabella.

"You stupid fucking bitch." She spat venomously as she reached over Isabella's collapsed body and pried the gun from her grasp. She took a step back and pointed it down. "Christ, you're the one from the boathouse back in Miami. Who the hell are you anyway?"

Isabella barely managed to sit up, holding the back of her head, which was now bleeding. Blood ran down her left shoulder, staining her blouse. Grace watched her through squinted eyes, as if sizing her up like a cat waiting to pounce on an injured mouse.

"Miami Metro." Isabella groaned as she painfully pulled herself up onto the leather seating. "Grace Logan, you are under arrest for the murders of Gina Regazzoni and Detective Mike Ryan."

Grace laughed. "Is that so?"

Isabella went to stand up but heard the revolver's hammer click back. Squinting in the sunlight, her eyes met Grace's for the first time, and she saw how deranged the woman really was. She suddenly understood it all now. The eyes staring back at her were those of a psychopath, cold and calculating, without a trace of feeling or empathy.

"Well, you know what?" Grace said with a cold-hearted smile, raising the gun and slowly beginning to squeeze back the trigger. "You can add your own name to that list of the dead."

"Hey!" Brophy shouted from the cabin doorway, a small handheld flare in his hand.

Grace spun her head toward him. Brophy clutched the flare tightly in his right hand, the fingers of his left gripping the bright yellow ignition string that hung from its base. "You drop that gun or so help me God, I will set this thing off."

Grace eyed him for a moment before raising her free hand in a gesture of capitulation.

"No, Brophy, look out!" Isabella screamed, realizing instinctively that Grace would not surrender under any circumstance, and noticing how she was now turning the gun around toward him.

Before he could respond to her warning, Grace swung around and fired a shot at him. But Brophy was faster, ducking to his left as she did and pulling back on the string in the same lightning fast movement. The flare ignited in his hand, sending forth a ball of fiery luminous sparks that exploded about Grace's stomach and immediately set her alight. Brophy rolled out of the way as she began lashing out at him. He quickly moved around her toward Isabella.

Screaming in agony and engulfed by the orange flames, Grace dropped the gun to the deck and scrambled toward the handrail, immediately throwing herself off the side of the *Wild Rover*. There was a loud explosion of fire and steam when she hit the water below, her black, charred body visible for only the briefest moment before it slowly sank and disappeared into the bubbling white foam. Isabella sprang to her feet, grabbed the revolver, and ran to the side just as she went under. She stood watching for a couple of minutes with her hands on the side rail.

"She's finished," Brophy said quietly, joining her at the rail.

Isabella sighed. "Thank you for saving me," she whispered after a few seconds, keeping her eyes fixed on the water below and nursing the wound on the back of her head.

Brophy put an arm around her. "Hey, I think we should get you inside and put some ice on that."

"Oh shit, how is your son?" Isabella suddenly asked, turning her attention back to him as her senses returned.

"A bump on the head, same as you," he replied with a little nod. "But he will live, thank God. And he has you to thank for it. We both do."

Before she could respond, an intermittent siren sounded in the distance. They both turned to see a small police launch coming alongside at speed, a couple of armed police officers standing on its prow. Jayden and Brianna Kingston were both sitting huddled together behind them on deck with blankets around their shoulders. They waved as Marcus emerged from the *Wild Rover's* main cabin.

Still holding the side of his own head, he joined his father and Isabella and enthusiastically waved back to them with a smile. As he did, the young captain emitted a deep sigh.

Brophy released his arm from Isabella and moved toward his son, shook his hand vigorously, and then pulled him in close for a hug.

"You couldn't have timed it any better," Marcus said when his father finally released his grip. "That woman was a lunatic. One minute she was normal and cheerful, the next, I don't know, she just flipped out. Totally and utterly insane."

The police began to board from the *Wild Rover's* stern, and Isabella stepped forward to show them her badge and explain what had happened. As soon as her identity was revealed, however, the officers told her they knew what was going on. A phone call from her captain back in Miami had alerted them to the situation. Isabella sighed with a mixture of exhilaration and relief as they went on to explain how they had been motoring the northern coastline for the past few hours on the lookout for the two sailing yachts' arrivals.

"Marcus, this is Detective Garcia," Brophy told his son a few minutes later when a couple of the officers went below to inspect the *Wild Rover,* and Isabella joined them on the starboard side. "She is the one who talked me into coming after you."

She took Marcus's outstretched hand and shook it. "Call me Isabella."

"It's very nice to meet you." He smiled. "And thank you so much for everything you have done."

Isabella's eyes met Brophy's for a split-second and they shared a glance, both realizing their journey had ended. Without each other's help, they would never have made it this far. No words were spoken between them as the captain of the police launch called for them to come on board. They smiled silently to each other, Isabella feeling a sense of inner satisfaction.

CHAPTER TEN

CHARLOTTE AMALIE

Isabella sat alone at the bar of the George Hotel in the bustling town of Charlotte Amalie on Saint Thomas. Talking to Captain Franklin on the phone, she looked down at the glass of Kentucky bourbon on the counter before her. She was exhausted, having spent the entire previous day and night in police headquarters. The morning was taken up giving her own statement to the local detectives, the afternoon and evening spent aiding them in their interviews of Jayden and Brianna Kingston as well as young Marcus Brophy. They had all told the same harrowing story, one of tragedy and murder at the hands of a woman who had suffered some sort of mental break with reality. Grace Logan had presented herself as a friendly, outgoing individual. Everyone had liked her from the start, not for one moment suspecting there was a vicious, cold-blooded killer among them, nor realizing that a savage insanity lurked behind her mask of normality.

Detective Brewster had emailed his report from Miami Metro, confirming Grace had indeed recently been released from the Broward Psychiatric Health Facility. There would, of course, be some serious questions asked as to why she had been signed out so early, especially as her own psychiatrist was not in favor. But Isabella knew that was for another day, something to be addressed after she returned to South Florida.

"So, what now?" Captain Franklin asked on the phone from his office back in Miami. "You *do* know you don't have to come back right away? You are due some time off, Garcia. So why not take a few days and do a bit of sightseeing while you're there?"

"Maybe. Look, I'll let you know what I decide in the morning," she replied, knocking back the remains of her bourbon. "Right now, I really just need to get something to eat other than the candy and chips they have been feeding me from the machine down here in police headquarters."

"They treating you all right?" he asked, sounding concerned.

"Sure, they run a pretty professional department down here."

"And after you eat?" he asked. "What then?"

Isabella sighed wearily. "Then, Captain, I think I am going to get drunk and maybe catch up on some sleep."

"Well all right, that does sound like a plan. Have one for me and Brewster while you're at it."

"Is he there with you now?" she asked. "I would like to thank him for everything he did."

"He's on leave."

"Oh? That doesn't sound like Brewster."

"He and Tish are taking the girls to Disneyland for the weekend. She said she was willing to give it another go if he promised not to spend so much time at the office. So I told him to take some time off, and when he comes back, I will make sure his caseload does not get too much for him."

Isabella was taken aback for a second, genuinely pleased at the news. "You are a good boss, Captain," she said quietly.

"Hey, got to keep the troops happy, right?"

"Sure. I guess."

"Look, I will leave you to it then. Call me tomorrow and let me know what you are going to do. If you *are* taking some time off, though, I will need to know so I can reassign some of your workload."

"Uh-huh."

"By the way, Doctor Walker and Sergeant McGregor send their best."

"Tell them both I said thanks for everything," she replied. "I owe them a few beers when I get back."

"Oh, and before I forget, Mike Ryan's funeral is scheduled for next Wednesday."

"Yeah, I know. Brewster emailed me the details," she said with a sigh. The pain had not gone away. "One way or another," she continued. "I will be there."

"Goodnight then," said the captain. "Oh, and once again, Garcia, thanks for everything. I will admit I was mad at you for disobeying my orders, but now I am glad you did. Just don't you go making a habit of it, okay?"

"Night," she said quietly, hanging up and motioning for the young hotel barman to remove the bar phone and get her another drink.

As he did, she slowly swung her chair around and cast her gaze across the darkened lounge. It was a large room, full of tourists in brightly colored shirts and dresses, sitting in small groups, drinking cocktails and deep in their own conversations. There was a pianist playing soft blues and jazz in the far corner while a young waitress hurried about carrying exotic-looking drinks back and forth to the tables on a large silver tray.

"Hey, I hope you are not drinking on duty," a voice said cheerfully from behind.

Isabella turned to see Patrick Brophy and his son, Marcus, standing beside her at the bar. They looked as if they were dressed for a night out, wearing proper shoes and freshly pressed shirts and trousers. It was a bit of a strange sight for Isabella, one she was not expecting. Brophy, in particular, caught her attention. He was finally clean-shaven and fully dressed. He was still ruggedly handsome, of course, but now with that windswept hair combed and all gelled down.

"You two certainly scrub up well." She smiled, raising a hand for the barman to return. "What would you like to drink?"

"I think we should be the ones buying you a drink," Marcus said from his position at the bar beside his father.

"Hey, this is on Miami Metro's tab," she replied with a mischievous smile. "If I were you, I would order a double. I know I certainly have."

"Well, in that case," Brophy said, turning cheerfully to the barman. "I will have a cold beer and an Irish whiskey chaser."

"Make that two," Marcus said with a wink.

They waited for the drinks to arrive and then sipped at the ice cold beers as if they were the first ones they had ever drunk.

"So, how are you two doing now that everything has died down?" asked Isabella. "What is happening with your boat?"

"Things couldn't be better," Brophy said. "The police are going to release the *Wild Rover* back to us tomorrow morning, and thanks to that phone call your captain made back in Miami, the insurance is already going through on the *Dirty Nellie*. And you? I see they finally let you leave the station. I swear, at one point, I thought they were holding you captive in there."

Isabella smiled and nodded. "Yeah, well, you know how it is, lots of reports to complete and loose ends to be tied. I had to act as liaison between Miami and Saint Thomas. Bit of a bureaucratic mess, to be honest. But it is all sorted now."

"Any luck finding the body yet?" Brophy asked.

The mood turned a little more somber as Isabella shook her head, knocked back her second bourbon, and then simply shrugged. "No, not yet."

"You know, I have been sailing these waters for a few years," said Marcus. "The rip tide around the northern part of the island is notorious."

"Yeah?"

"He's right," said Brophy. "The truth is it may have taken her body out to sea already. You do know there is a chance it will never be found."

"I really hope that is not the case," Isabella said with a shake of her head. "I would really like to see a body. You know, to get final closure on this case."

"So anyway," Brophy said after a few seconds silence, "how long are you planning on staying here?"

Isabella shrugged. "The night, the week? I haven't made up my mind yet. Who knows? Maybe I will get myself a job with the Saint Thomas police and stay here for good."

Smiling at the thought, Brophy excused himself and went out to use the restroom. When he was gone, Marcus sat himself down on the stool next to Isabella and placed his elbows on the bar. They sipped at their drinks in silence, not speaking for a while, a comfortable pause between two people who had just been through a tough few days and now deserved a little quiet time.

"He really likes you, you know." Marcus eventually said quietly.

Isabella turned her gaze to find him looking back with a mischievous grin.

"Oh yeah?"

"I think his words were you are 'his type of woman.'"

"So what type is that?" she asked with raised eyebrows, motioning for the barman to bring another round.

"Shit." Marcus laughed. "I should not have said anything. He would kill me if he knew. Please, Detective, forget I opened my mouth."

"Not so fast," she replied with a playful smile, not letting him off the hook so easily. The truth was she was not just flattered, but genuinely pleased with the news. She felt a little bit like a teenager again, gossiping about boys at the back of the bus. "If you don't want me to say anything, then spill. Before he gets back, tell me exactly what kind of woman is his type?"

"Oh, you know. I guess the strong, independent sort."

"Really? Is that how he sees me?"

"He actually said you kept your head really well when things got rough out there. You didn't panic or get hysterical."

"Hysterical? Hmm. Nice of him to say that."

"He said you're not afraid to get your hands dirty. You were a quick learner when it came to sailing and navigation. He was very impressed. And believe me, it takes a lot to impress my old man."

"Well, he is a good teacher," she said as the drinks arrived.

"He also said he finds you very attractive, Detective, and you're good company to have around."

Just then, Brophy returned and retook his place at the bar, raised his freshly-filled whiskey glass, and knocked it back in one gulp. He put it back down and beckoned the barman to return, waving a hand to indicate he should pour them all another round. Then, noticing the awkward silence, he turned his gaze to Isabella and Marcus, catching a look of amusement in their eyes.

"Wait. What is going on here?" he asked. "What the hell did I miss?"

"Well, that's me done for the night," Marcus exclaimed, standing up from the stool, stretching his arms, yawning, and then turning to shake Isabella's hand. "I hope to see you again tomorrow, Detective," he said with a wink. "Enjoy the rest of your evening."

"What has he been saying?" Brophy asked suspiciously when Marcus was gone.

"Nothing much." Isabella smiled.

"Look, Detective, don't bullshit a bullshitter."

"If you *must* know," she replied. "He said that you find me attractive."

"Is that right?" Brophy asked, looking slightly embarrassed.

"Oh, yes. And he also said you think I am your 'type of woman.'"

"I will frigging kill him," he muttered with a deep sigh.

"Well?" asked Isabella.

"Well what?"

"Well, do you find me attractive or not?"

Brophy shrugged nonchalantly and then stared deeply into her hazel brown eyes. "Let's just say that you, Detective Garcia, do not scrub up too bad yourself."

Isabella laughed out loud, placed a hand on his arm, and shook him a little. Their next round of drinks arrived and they knocked them back within seconds.

"Hey, you want to get some dinner?" he asked after a short pause, motioning his head back toward the archway leading into the dining room.

"Yeah, that sounds nice," she said with a warm smile. "Our first date."

≈ ≈ ≈

Marcus slipped his plastic key card into the narrow slot and withdrew it, waiting for the light to flash green, before pushing down on the handle and opening the door to his hotel room. The side light came on the moment he placed the card in the power slot on the inner wall, revealing a small, but tastefully decorated room. There were two single beds in the center with wooden nightstands on either side, a flat screen television fixed to the far wall above a long wooden dresser with a mirror attached. The metal sliding door was open to the narrow balcony, the full-length net curtains blowing inward on the warm sea breeze.

Marcus slid the glass door closed and dropped his wallet and phone onto one of the beds. Kicking off his shoes, he turned and made straight for the shower. The water took a few seconds to get hot, but when it did, he stood beneath it for a long time, letting it run over his bruised body in a soothing fashion.

When he eventually finished showering, he turned off the water and emerged from the bathroom wearing nothing but a large white bath towel around his waist. He stopped at the foot of the bed for a moment, noticing the sliding door had not fully closed. Checking there were no missed calls on his phone, he walked over to give it a final push, but then changed his mind and decided to open it fully again and step out onto the balcony for a breath of fresh air.

The night was calm and still outside, the view from the fifth floor over the town of Charlotte Amalie clear and unbroken. He could see right down to the harbor where the lights of the various cruise ships glistened in the darkness. There was loud music and laughter coming from somewhere nearby, and the smell of fish and steaks being barbequed in one of the surrounding restaurants. Tourism was the life blood of the island. It was what drove the economy, and without it, the local population would not be so affluent. Marcus had always loved the atmosphere of the Virgins, and although it was not too far from his home in South Florida, each time he sailed into port it felt to him like he had been transported to another world.

He suddenly noticed a slight movement behind him through the corner of his eye. Grace sprang from the shadows on the balcony without uttering a sound, plunging her knife down into Marcus's back with such force it sent him staggering forward onto the handrail. He felt a surge of pain shoot through his body as his knees went weak and his legs buckled beneath him. He tried to turn to face her, but barely managed to swing his torso around before she hunched down and head butted him in the abdomen. The blow knocked him off his feet and sent him careening backwards over the rail, the knife still in his back.

Screaming at the top of his voice, he flayed his arms out as he fell, only just managing to grasp hold of the rail to stop himself from falling to his death. But it was a painful reprieve for Marcus, for as soon as he grabbed the lower metal bar, his upper body jerked backwards and his torso smashed against the side of the concrete balcony. With the wind knocked from his lungs, he looked up to find his left arm hooked around one of the rails. He reached out and grabbed hold of another with his right hand. It was a miracle he was not lying dead on the pavement below, but he was now left dangling precariously in space, totally helpless and at her mercy.

Grace leaned over the edge of the balcony to look down into his eyes, her snarling teeth glistening in the moonlight. Her long red hair was singed and almost gone, her throat and chin blackened from the fireball that had sent her over the side of the *Wild Rover* the previous day. She did not speak a word as she stared at him, but her hate-filled gaze said it all. There was pure, unadulterated evil in her eyes as she looked down upon him, a glint of insanity and a look of vengeance directed solely toward him.

"Please," Marcus pleaded.

Grace did not answer. In a calm, unhurried manner, she simply lowered herself to her knees and began prying the fingers of his right hand loose. He tried to resist but it was impossible. She bent them back one by one, breaking each in turn until he released his grip and swung away, held only by his left arm now, which was still hooked around the metal balustrade.

"Please, Grace," he repeated to no avail.

Grace leaned forward with teeth showing and bit down deep into his upper arm, drawing blood and making him scream in agony. She put her left foot through the gap in the railings and kicked violently out at his face.

Marcus swung his body away to evade the first blow, but then as he helplessly swung back in, shrieked in pain as her heel caught him on the bridge of the nose. He felt his grip loosening, knowing then it was only a matter of seconds before he would surely let go and fall to his death. That was when a shot rang out from back inside the room, forcing Grace to gasp and turn around in surprise.

≈ ≈ ≈

Isabella and Brophy rushed onto the balcony as she made her escape, leaping over the rail to her right and jumping across the narrow gap onto the balcony next door. While

Brophy reached over to pull his son back up, Isabella holstered her revolver and took off in hot pursuit. But Grace was fast. She moved from one balcony to the next like a cat, leaping and then running and then leaping again until she reached the last balcony and finally swung herself down onto the fourth floor below. Once there, she disappeared from Isabella's sight.

Before following her down, though, the detective quickly glanced back to see Brophy holding Marcus in his arms, his cell phone to his ear, calling desperately for help.

"Is he okay?" she shouted across the divide. "Do you need me?"

"Go!" roared Brophy. "I've called an ambulance. Just go!"

She climbed over the end rail, took a deep breath, and then swung her own body down into the darkness as Grace had done. Isabella's feet hit the edge of the larger balcony below on the fourth floor, and she fell forward to land heavily on her knees. She sprang up uninjured, and withdrawing her gun once more, looked carefully through the open glass door into the dark, unoccupied hotel room before her. Through the net curtains, she could just make out a faint glimmer of light ahead, and after a few seconds, realized it was coming through the half-open door into the hallway on the other side. Without hesitating, Isabella entered through the patio sliding door and moved quickly across the room until she reached the other end, looking left and right for an ambush as she went. Grace was not to be trusted, she knew. She had set a trap for her before, back in the boathouse, but this time, Isabella had no intention of walking into it unprepared. When she reached the main door a few seconds later, she peered suspiciously around the frame, fully prepared for her adversary to be waiting. But there was no one there. The hall outside was empty.

For a moment or two Isabella feared she might have lost Grace due to her cautiousness, but then she spotted something at her feet just outside the door, a dark stain in the light blue woolen carpet that drew her attention. With her revolver at the ready, she lowered herself to her hunkers and picked at it with her thumb and forefinger. Blood, she decided, and still fresh. Standing back up, she followed the dotted trail as it led down the hall toward the emergency exit at the far end. Isabella's spirits were raised as she went. The sight of the blood instilled a sense of satisfaction in her. She was pleased she now had a trail to follow and hoped it would not be long before she caught up to her prey. But that was not the only thing that gratified her as she reached the fire door at the end of the hall. Isabella knew now that her gunshot back on the balcony had not missed its target. That *did* please her. She could not deny it. That pleased her more than anything.

Moving without hesitation, she burst through the emergency fire door and made her way down the narrow, dimly-lit stairwell to the parking lot out back. The air was warm, the crickets chirping in a loud chorus as she made her way outside and began searching around each and every vehicle she passed. It was even darker out here, barely lit by a single yellow street light, and not nearly bright enough to pick up the blood trail again. But when a vehicle's engine revved loudly on the other side of the lot, Isabella turned in that direction as its tires screeched rubber onto the cracked asphalt. She jumped up onto a low concrete bollard just in time to see a small silver car speeding out through the main gate, its back wheels spinning furiously as they hit the curb and sent a hubcap rolling off into the grassy verge.

Gun in hand, Isabella sprinted around to the front of the building. Pushing past groups of noisy tourists converging around the hotel lobby, she immediately spotted and jumped into a rented green Nissan waiting to be valet parked at the entrance. The hotel employee in the red waistcoat shouted angrily after her, but she did not look back or acknowledge him. She simply rammed the car into gear and took off at breakneck speed through the main gate.

She caught up with Grace on Dronningen's Gade just after she turned off onto Veteran's Drive, which fronted the harbor on the way down to the sea. Grace had obviously spotted her as they approached Frenchtown and immediately tried to ram her off the road at a sharp bend, but Isabella forced her car back with an equally violent maneuver. Their side mirrors clipped each other and disintegrated in a mass of plastic and glass, their front fenders becoming entangled for a few seconds until Grace's fell off and was mangled beneath her back wheels.

Then disaster struck for Isabella. Just as she was about

to ram into Grace's car in a final effort to get her off the road, she lost control of the Nissan, and it went into a spin. It eventually came to a stop in a cloud of dust, back wheels in the grassy verge, facing in the opposite direction. Isabella cursed as she restarted the engine and managed to take off again, but the damage was done. The delay had allowed the silver car enough time to get out of sight.

≈ ≈ ≈

Minutes later, when she reached the harbor entrance, Grace swerved off the road and sped through the busy parking lot toward one of the massive cruise ships nearby. She knew the detective would not be far behind. She needed to disappear until things died down. A number of coaches had parked by the gangway steps with the passengers in the process of boarding their floating hotel after a busy day's sightseeing around the island. Grace abandoned the small silver car and joined the throng, keeping her head bowed low as they filed noisily up the gangway and made for the open ship's door at the top. The chaos only intensified when the vacationers reached the security desks and x-ray machines inside the opening. Within seconds of reaching security, an angry exchange broke out with one of the elderly passengers who had lost his boarding card and was demanding access. Grace used the distraction to sneak unseen past the two weary security guards at the gate, who were momentarily preoccupied by his loud protestations.

As soon as she passed them and was safely inside, she made straight for one of the large glass elevators down the plush, carpeted hallway. She managed to get one to herself and immediately headed up toward the main deck. Her intention was to shake off her pursuer, but also to use the elevated position to keep a lookout for the troublesome detective whom she knew would probably be along at any second. But that had to take a back seat to her immediate condition, she suddenly realized, only now noticing how a steady trickle of blood was running down her arm. As she emerged from the elevator a few minutes later, back into the warm night air of the pool deck, she headed off toward the women's bathroom and began tending to the bullet wound in her shoulder.

She wrapped a towel around her hand and punched one of the wall mirrors above the row of shiny ceramic sinks, then used a sliver of broken glass to dig the bullet out of the wound. Grace clenched her teeth and groaned as she did so, but her anger served as a distraction to the pain, her thirst for revenge as an anesthetic.

The female detective had foiled her for the very last time, she resolved bitterly as the mangled bullet eventually came out and fell into the blood-stained sink below. Mentally, she placed her at the top of her list for retribution, looking at the burnt and blackened flesh of her neck and chin in the mirror, deciding she would be dealt with when the time was right. But now was not that time, Grace decided as she cut off a tiny strip of towel and stuffed it deep into the wound. She then wrapped the rest of the towel around her shoulder and slipped her blouse back on over it before washing herself and wiping down the sink and worktop.

≈   ≈   ≈

Isabella flashed her badge to the two waiting ship's officers at the top of the gangway stairs and then followed one of them off in the direction of the main security office. She had followed the narrow winding road Grace was on when she last saw her, until she eventually hit a dead end. She then slowly retraced her way back and, seeing nowhere else where the car could have gone, finally turned off into the harbor car lot. She thought her prey had eluded her once more after driving around fruitlessly for about ten minutes, looking up and down the rows of parked cars. But just as she was about to leave, one of the tourist coaches fired up its diesel engine and pulled away, revealing the small silver car sitting empty behind.

Five minutes later, Isabella and the ship's senior head of security stood side by side in a small dark CCTV room behind the bridge. There was a young officer sitting with his back to them, surrounded by computers and flat screen monitors, showing them footage from the various cameras on the starboard side that evening.

"There!" Isabella shouted after a few minutes. "Go back.

Go back."

The young man pressed rewind until the detective slapped a hand down on his shoulder. "There. Play it from there."

As she and the older security officer watched the playback on the main screen, they saw a female figure with head bowed approaching the busy entrance door to the ship. Seconds later, while the guards were preoccupied with another passenger, the figure slipped past unnoticed. It was a grainy shot, and they could not make out the woman's lowered face, but Isabella knew instinctively it was Grace. After issuing instructions to the young man at the computer, she was soon watching the footage from another camera angle that showed the woman making her way down the hall and disappearing into one of the elevators.

"Can you pause and zoom in to the floor display above the elevator door?" she asked excitedly. "To let us know which deck she got off on?"

The young man shook his head. "I'm sorry, Detective, the playback does not have that capability."

"Damn it." Then, turning to the man beside her, she asked, "Can you organize a deck-by-deck search then? This woman is a deranged killer. Believe me. You don't want her wandering around your ship for too long."

The older security officer nodded his head in agreement. "Okay, Detective, follow me. I will have some of my men join us on the bridge. We'll spread out from there and take it deck by deck until we find her."

But as Isabella turned to leave with him, a message crackled over his radio. Excusing himself, he stepped away to one side for a second, turning his back as he conversed over the walkie-talkie in a low voice.

"What was that all about?" she asked when he was done. Her suspicions were raised after overhearing him issue orders to "have maintenance and a cleaner put on it immediately."

"Oh, nothing that would concern you," he said nonchalantly. "Just routine stuff onboard a ship of our size."

"Someone hurt?"

"No, no, nothing like that. Simply a broken mirror in one of the women's bathrooms and some bloody towels stuffed behind the toilet in one of the cubicles. Now, Detective, first we will probably need to organize a sweep of the lower—"

Isabella was on that news like a light. "That's her!" she exclaimed. "That's my perp."

The security officer looked surprised, raising his eyebrows and staring back at her without speaking.

"Where is this bathroom?" she asked excitedly.

"Huh? I don't think—"

"Where is it?"

"It's up on the bathing deck," he said as she ran past him. "Level seven."

Minutes later, Isabella walked hurriedly around the outer edge of the bathing deck with eyes peeled, her revolver tucked into her waistband, hidden by her jacket so as not to alarm the surrounding passengers, but easy to reach at a seconds notice. A rock band was playing classics on a small stage above the brightly-lit pool, while about them, the deck was crammed to capacity with vacationers, some heading for the main dining areas and others toward the nearby theater for the ten o'clock show.

She made her way through the bustling crowd until she entered a set of automatic glass doors and found herself in a noisy buffet restaurant. The area was large and open, filled wall to wall with wooden tables and chairs around a circular food counter containing various displays of ice sculptures. There was a long line for the buffet, and Isabella stopped to the left of it, turning full circle among the throng of people coming and going with trays, searching and inspecting each and every one of them. And then, something out of the ordinary caught her attention.

"There, there, ma'am," one of the attendants was saying to a distressed passenger on the other side of the dining room, a middle-aged woman who was standing by the wall with her two children, tears in her eyes. "Are you sure you left them here?"

Isabella made her way over to hear the woman's reply.

"Of course I'm sure," she said in a deep southern accent. "I left them right here while we went up to get our food."

Isabella flashed her badge. "What seems to be the trouble?"

The woman turned to her with a look of relief that at

least her complaint was being taken seriously.

"My purse and shawl are gone," she told Isabella with a tear in her eye. "I left them here on the table but someone has taken them."

"Ma'am, what color is the shawl?" asked Isabella.

"It's red," said one of her children, a boy of about nine or ten whose eyes were wide with excitement as if a bank robbery had just taken place.

Before Isabella could reply, another of the passengers stepped forward from a nearby table. "Hey, ma'am, I saw a young lady pick them up about three minutes ago."

"Where did she go?" Isabella asked excitedly.

The man was elderly and not too good on his feet. Turning to point the way, he had to lean on the back of one of the chairs for support. But as soon as he steadied himself, he motioned toward a nearby exit.

Isabella was gone before they could say anything else, rushing off at speed through the glass door and out into a busy walkway lined with gift shops and various bars filled with piano music and noisy patrons. She spotted a young ships officer dressed in white standing nearby and approached him with her badge in hand.

"Red shawl?" the man repeated after she had explained who she was and who she was looking for.

"Yes," she said anxiously. "Did you see her come this way?"

"Actually," he muttered thoughtfully.

"Yes?"

He raised a hand and motioned to his right. "I do remember seeing a woman fitting that description go into that elevator a few minutes ago."

Isabella raced over to find the floor display above the elevator door had counted down through the different levels of the ship until it eventually stopped on number two.

"Hey!" She shouted back to the officer who was still watching her with interest. "What's on deck two?"

"Storage," he said with hands behind his back and a shrug of his shoulders. "Mainly food and beverage. But it is off limits to—"

Isabella was gone before he finished speaking, bursting through the adjacent double doors and out onto the metal stairwell that ran from top to bottom. She jumped the steps three at a time as she descended into the bowels of the ship, only withdrawing her revolver when she reached deck two and stood panting at the heavy metal fire door in front of her. As soon as she pushed it open, she knew her prey was inside. It was like a sixth sense to her, an instinct she had come to trust over the years as a homicide detective.

"Grace Logan, I know you're in here!" She shouted at the top of her voice, scanning the huge storage room for any sign of movement. The surrounding area was well lit by rows of fluorescents hanging from the ceiling, but packed to capacity with pallets of canned goods and cardboard boxes balanced on top of each other like pyramids. "It's over, Grace. Finished."

"You are done!" Isabella shouted as she picked up the trail of tiny blood droplets on the white painted floor and began following carefully, cocking her revolver as she inched slowly forward. "Come on out, and I will make sure you get medical attention for that bullet wound."

When she received no reply, Isabella continued on. She eventually came to a dead end, her path blocked by a wall of large metal cooking oil containers. The blood trail had definitely turned that way, she mused in puzzlement. Perhaps her prey had hit the same dead end and turned back without dripping any more blood along the way?

Isabella turned to retrace her steps, to exit the cul-de-sac and try once more to pick up the trail. That was when Grace pounced from the top of the wooden crates. Screaming like a woman possessed, she knocked the wind from Isabella's lungs and sent her sprawling face down to the ground. The gun fell from her grasp as she landed, and they both scrambled for it as they fought.

Grace's strength was fuelled by her madness. She clawed at Isabella's face, tearing at her clothes and pulling her by the hair in an effort to bring her down and finish her off. But Isabella fought back with equal venom. This, after all, was the murderer who had cut the throat of a young mother back in Miami and who had cold-heartedly stabbed Mike Ryan to death. She was not about to let her get control of the situation, or allow her to escape to kill again. This was the moment when justice would finally be served, she resolved as she fought back with every ounce of strength she had. One way or another, it ended here.

Grace gasped when Isabella punched her square in the face, breaking her nose and sending blood spattering into her eyes and down her throat. In retaliation, she lashed out viciously with her right fist, then brought her elbow up and caught Isabella on the side of the head.

With her enemy stunned for a second, Grace seized the moment and grabbed the gun from the ground. Before she could turn, Isabella kicked her heel into Grace's lower back, then jumped on top of her when she fell forward, holding her down, pressing hard into the wound in her shoulder until she was able to pry the weapon from her grasp. She then stood up, panting and exhausted. She took a step back and pointed the weapon down at Grace's chest.

"Grace Logan, you have the right to remain silent," she grunted, trying to catch her breath, wiping a smear of blood from her cheek with her free hand. "Anything you say may be used in evidence against you."

Grace reached out and grabbed a rusted metal hook lodged in one of the wooden food crates beside her. She spat a mouthful of blood to the ground, keeping her gaze fixed coldly on the detective as she slowly rose to her feet in defiance.

"You have the right to an attorney." Isabella went on upon seeing what Grace was doing, holding the revolver tighter in both hands and cocking back its hammer. She knew instinctively what was about to happen. "If you cannot afford one, an attorney will be—"

Grace opened her mouth and emitted a frenzied, blood-curdling scream. She raised the hook above her head and made a violent lunge forward. A shot rang out from Isabella's gun in the same moment she did so, echoing through the confines of the metallic room like a thunderclap, fading as it went, dying out somewhere in the distance.

With a strange look of surprise upon her face, Grace dropped the hook and fell to her knees, keeping her eyes on Isabella as the pain obviously spread. She glanced down for a moment to see a widening crimson stain above her breasts, opened her mouth to say something to the detective, but then rolled her eyes and fell helplessly forward to the ground. Isabella waited for a moment to ensure she was not getting up, then carefully kicked the hook away with her foot and stepped back. It was over, she told herself with a sense of satisfaction. Mike's killer was finally lying at her feet. Grace Logan had left a trail of death and destruction in her wake over the past few days, but Isabella had ultimately sent her to the hell she deserved. Yes, it was finally over. She had gotten justice.

≈ ≈ ≈

"He's just came out of surgery," Brophy said when Isabella joined him at the Charlotte Amalie hospital later that night.

She had been forced to wait around the harbor while the Saint Thomas police inspected the scene of the shooting and recorded her statement. They spent hours talking to the ship's crew and examining CCTV footage, as well as taking photographs of Grace's corpse, before finally zipping her up in a body bag and transporting her off the cruise ship and down to the local morgue.

Isabella had spoken to Brophy on the phone to find out how Marcus was doing and was given a complete update on his injuries and what was happening. But now, when she finally managed to get away and join him at the hospital some time later, there was a worried look on his face, a father's anguish written across his brow.

"What did they say?" she asked anxiously, sitting down on the bench beside him and taking his hand in hers.

"They said it was a miracle the blade did not pierce anything vital," he said. "He's been through the mill, but they said he should make a full recovery."

"Thank God."

"He does have a nasty bump on his head mind you, as well as a couple of broken fingers and a two-inch bite out of his arm. But they have stitched him up and put him on an antibiotic drip for the night."

"He's a strong young guy. He'll be fine," she said with an encouraging smile. "It could have been a lot worse. If you hadn't gone back to the room to get your wallet—"

"Shit, I don't even want to think about that," he said.

"And what about you?" she asked after a brief pause. "How are you holding up?"

"Me? Apart from getting the fright of my life, I suppose I'm doing fine. A bit shaken is all. And you?" he asked quietly, putting an arm around her shoulders. "Did you really get her?"

Isabella nodded an affirmative.

"So, it's definitely over then?"

"Yes," she said. "It's definitely over."

After a few minutes contemplation, Brophy emitted a long, weary sigh of relief. "You know what, Detective, I was wondering something."

"Yeah? What's that?" she asked with a look of curiosity.

"I don't know. I was thinking that maybe you could help me sail the *Wild Rover* back to Miami in a couple of days. It would probably save you buying an airline ticket."

"Is that right?"

"It wouldn't be a free ride, mind. Oh no. You *would* have to help me sail."

Isabella thought about it for a moment, before leaning up and kissing him on the cheek. "I can think of nothing I would like more," she said with a smile.

The End

ABOUT THE AUTHOR

Frank Sullivan lives in Ireland. A Graphic Designer and Illustrator by profession, he is a keen writer, artist and sailor who has lived and worked in various locations, traveling extensively to places like Hawaii, French Polynesia, Europe and South Florida.

Over the years he has edited a trade magazine and written many articles and short stories, as well as illustrating for various magazines and newspapers. His first novel, Deadly Shore, was well received with excellent reviews. Savage Crossing is his second book.

www.ingramcontent.com/pod-product-compliance
Lightning Source LLC
Chambersburg PA
CBHW031507210626
46807CB00026B/2468